I0525841

# THE TOWERS OF METROPOLIS

AIRSHIP 27 PRODUCTIONS

AN AIRSHIP 27 PRODUCTION

The Towers of Metropolis Volume One
collection ©2016 Airship 27 Productions

Metropolis: A Literary Appreciation © 2016 Fred Adams Jr.
What Right Law? © 2016 William Patrick Maynard & Michael Richard Maynard
The Metropolis Murders © 2016 Michael Panush
Servo Surrugate © 2016 Kevin Noel Olson
The Man from Air Tower 12 © 2016 Erik Franklin

Published by Airship 27 Productions
www.airship27.com
www.airship27hangar.com

Interior illustrations © 2016 Pedro Cruz
Cover illustration © 2016 Michael Kaluta

Editor: Ron Fortier
Associate Editor: Fred Adams Jr.
Marketing and Promotions Manager: Michael Vance
Production and design by Rob Davis.

ISBN-13: 978-0692735381 (Airship 27)
ISBN-10: 0692735380

Printed in the United States of America

10 9 8 7 6 5 4 3 2 1

# THE TOWERS OF METROPOLIS
## VOLUME ONE
## TABLE OF CONTENTS

# METROPOLIS: A LITERARY APPRECIATION

## Fred Adams, Jr.

For thirty years, I taught college level courses in Science Fiction and routinely began each semester with a screening of Fritz Lang's *Metropolis*. Most of my students had never seen the film before, but many were familiar with specific images, particularly those used on record album covers and posters.

The students were, in the main, amazed at the visual effects in a film made without the benefit of modern film technology, and while their opinions varied regarding the quality of the story, general agreement existed as to the unique quality of the film-making.

As an English professor, I delved into the themes, literary motifs, and allusions Lang incorporated into *Metropolis*, as well as the "firsts" in Science Fiction film it presented, including the creation of a robot that passed for a human, and the character of Rotwang, the prototypical mad scientist. It arguably also presents a forerunner of Steampunk fiction with its steam driven mechanisms.

At the age of nearly ninety years, Lang's *Metropolis* remains a marvel to all who see the film. Its rich visual imagery and its groundbreaking technique dazzle the viewer to the point of eclipsing the literary underpinnings of the story.

Granted, Von Harbou's novel, on which the film is based, is at times a ponderous work, yet it provides a set of images and scenarios in prose that Lang translates into the visuals that entrance the viewer and in a second aesthetic layer, actualize the themes that define the story.

Von Harbou uses allusions and allegories based upon myths, legends, and works of literature to strike responsive chords in the reader. Included are: Pygmalion, The Bible, H. G. Wells' *The Time Machine*, and particularly, Samuel Taylor Coleridge's poem "Kubla Khan."

Rotwang's creation of the mechanical woman he calls "Parody" and "Futura" is a recreation of his lost love Hel, who left him to marry Joh Fredersen, and who died giving birth to his son Freder, Futura has every outward aspect of humanity, but she is painfully cold to the touch, as Joh Fredersen learns.

Rotwang's Parody is a perversion of the Pygmalion myth; rather than becoming a warm, loving woman, she becomes a destructive force, usurping Maria's position as a trusted spiritual advisor and betraying the workers of Metropolis, inciting them to riot as part of Fredersen's sinister plan to justify bringing a harder hand of control upon them.

Biblical motifs abound. Freder is an obvious Christ figure, come down from above and descending into Hell (the underground city) and re-emerging to act as the "Mediator" (the term used in 1 Corinthians) between the head and the hands, between the powers that rule and the workers, making a Holy Trinity of the Olympian Father Joh Fredersen, the Son, Freder, and the Holy Spirit embodied in Maria, the inspiration of the workers.

Rotwang is Satanic and represents the close link between science and sorcery as well as technology's displacement of religious faith in the modern world. In both the novel and the movie a pentagram shines on Rotwang's door and in an often reprinted production still, behind the Maria-robot in his laboratory. In the film, on the set of doors in the subcellars of Rotwang's house, the pentagrams are inverted.

As for the theme that religion has become a societal appendix, Von Harbou discusses the Gothic cathedral, a structure as out of place in the steel-edged world of Metropolis as Rotwang's sinister Hansel and Gretel witch's hut of a house:

The Master of Metropolis had already considered, more than once, having the cathedral pulled down, as being pointless and an obstruction to the traffic in the town of fifty million inhabitants. But the small, eager sect of Gothics, whose leader was Desertus, half monk, half one enraptured had sworn the solemn oath: if one hand from the wicked city of Metropolis were to dare to touch just one stone of the cathedral, then they would neither repose nor rest until the wicked city of Metropolis should lie, a heap of ruins, at the foot of her cathedral.

Fredersen tolerates the existence of the cathedral, as he tolerates the existence of a religion that is, as Marx wrote, "the opiate of the people." Likewise, he tolerates the existence of Rotwang's incongruous house as a necessary evil. Of Rotwang's house, Von Harbou writes:

It was said that a magician, who came from the East (and in the track of whom the plague wandered) had built the house in seven nights. But the masons and carpenters of the town did not know who mortared the bricks, nor who had erected the roof. . . .Set in all the doors stood, copper-red, mysterious, the seal of Solomon, the pentagram.

When popular sentiment to remove antiquities arose,

Then the words were spoken: the house must die. But the house was stronger than the words, as it was stronger than the centuries. With suddenly falling stones it slew those who laid hands on its walls. It opened the floor under their feet, dragging them down into a shaft, of which no man had previously had any knowledge. It was as though the plague, which had formerly wandered in the wake of the red shoes of the magician [a nod to the ruby slippers of the Wicked Witch in Oz?] still crouched in the corners of the narrow house, springing out at men from behind, to seize them by the neck.

It is in this house that Rotwang works his sorcery *cum* science and perpetuates the evil of its architect.

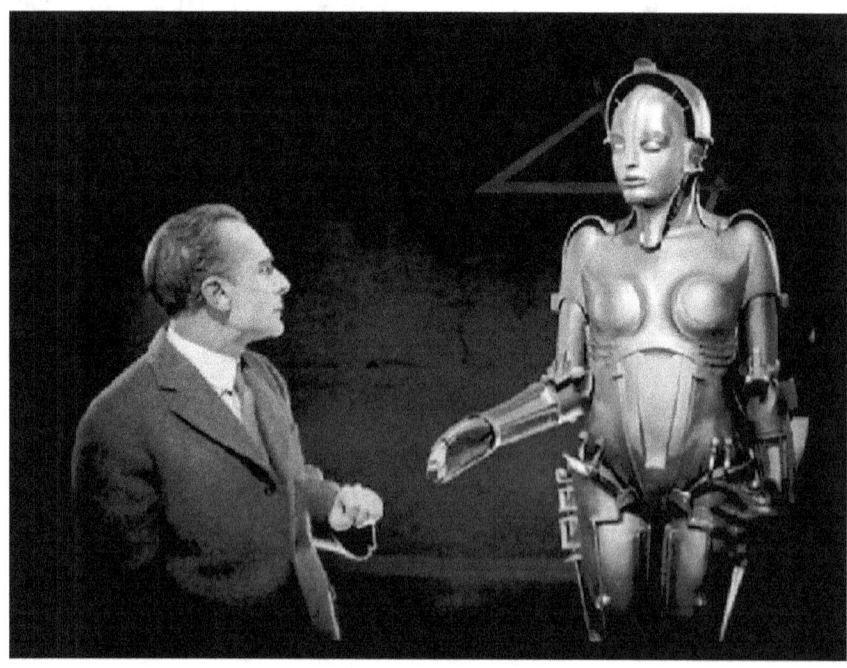

Maria's telling of the Tower of Babel parable puts a Marxist spin on the story with a touch of Thomas Carlyle thrown in. Workers toil ceaselessly like cogs in a machine, never seeing a direct result of their divided labor and never sharing in the goal of the elite who have commissioned the tower, nor will the workers share in the rewards of its completion. Thus the enterprise breaks down. The new Babel is the result of a more refined process, but without the "mediator between head and hands"; it too is doomed to failure.

Maria is called "The Virgin" by Freder, making her an obvious Virgin Mary whose preaching gives hope to the laborers. The robot Maria's provocative dance, which incites a riot, is performed atop a seven-headed dragon right out of the Book of Revelation, casting her as the Whore of Babylon, riding the apocalyptic "Wild Beast."

The most prominent debt the novel and the film owe to *The Time Machine* is the forcing of the workers underground, along with all of the practical functions and operations that maintain the leisurely ornamental surface world. This displacement begins the process of turning the working class into Wells' Morlocks in 800,000 years.

The first Morlock Wells' Time Traveler sees in the far future is a "bleached, obscene, nocturnal Thing," and like its fellows, it has "flaxen hair on its head and down its back, evolved from eons of underground dwelling. The Time Traveler says: "But gradually, the truth dawned on me: that Man had not remained one species, but had differentiated into two distinct animals, . . .this . . . thing which had flashed before me, was also heir to all the ages."

The workers' children whom Freder sees at the start of the novel are described as having "dwarves faces, grey and ancient. They were little ghost-like skeletons, covered with faded rags and smocks. They had colorless hair and colorless eyes. They walked on emaciated bare feet." The sunless world of the workers makes each new generation Morlocks in training.

Wells published a scathing review of *Metropolis* in the April 17, 1927 *New York Times*. Terms such as "silliness" and "malignant stupidity" characterized his attitude toward the film and its creator. In his greatest diatribe, Wells refers to *Metropolis* as an "unimaginative, incoherent, sentimentalizing, and make believe film."

Though he never mentions *The Time Machine,* Wells accuses Lang of plagiarizing his 1897 work "When The Sleeper Awakes" with its ranks of blue-clad laborers living in subterranean warrens below the cities, and the use of the word "robot," (Czech for "worker") Karel Capek used for his mechanical men in the 1920 play *R.U.R.* Von Harbou never uses the word in her novel, although it appears in the dialogue cards of the film, and arguably, by 1927, the word "robot" referring to a mechanical man (or woman) had entered the speculative fantasy lexicon, if not the mainstream language.

Wells attacks the film on many more fronts, enough to require a separate essay to address them all. But this carping about the film is less than fair because as a film maker, Lang was limited by a production budget (*Metropolis* nearly bankrupted UFA), and as an author, Wells was limited only by his imagination.

Wells' review seems to be a case of the cold, appraising eye of a historian applied to the actualized vision of an arch Romantic. At the beginning of *Metropolis*, a statement from Von Harbou appears on the screen:

> This film is not of today or of the future.
> It tells of no place.
> It serves no tendency, party or class.
> It has a moral that grows on the pillar of understanding"
> 'The mediator between brain and muscle must be the heart.'

*Metropolis*, novel and film, is meant to be taken as a parable, a moral fable, not as an absolute prediction, and the same could be said of *The Time Machine*.

And it is Von Harbou's and Lang's romanticism that draws upon one of the most poignant sources for the imagery and themes of *Metropolis*, novel and film, Samuel Taylor Coleridge's poem "Kubla Khan," particularly in portraying the link between science and sorcery personified in Rotwang.

Coleridge's poem begins:

> In Xanadu did Kubla Khan
> A stately pleasure-dome decree:
> Where Alph, the sacred river, ran

Through caverns measureless to man
Down to a sunless sea.

We may apply the identity of Kubla Khan to Joh Frdedersen, the Master of Metropolis, and the pleasure dome well describes the Club of the Sons, the palace of delight at the top of the city where Freder sports with his young friends at the beginning of the film. The poem's reference to the river and sunless sea plays out in the subterranean waters that erupt below the cave-like workers' quarters and threaten to drown the workers' children:

And from this chasm, with ceaseless turmoil seething,
As if this earth in fast thick pants were breathing,
A mighty fountain momently was forced;

The poem's strongest correspondence lies in Rotwang the evil scientist:

And all should cry, Beware! Beware!
His flashing eyes, his floating hair!
Weave a circle round him thrice,
And close your eyes with holy dread,

Von Harbou describes Rotwang as having "dense, disordered hair over the wonderful brow of the inventor . . . and in the eyes under this brow the smoldering of a hatred which was very closely related to madness." Lang translates this image to the screen in what has become the model for science fiction's mad scientist, holding his mechanical right hand higher than his left, symbolizing the ascendance of technology over humanity.

The weaving of a triple circle points to the supernatural power of Coleridge's character, and in the film, Fredersen tells Rotwang that when his advisors fail him, he turns to Rotwang and his sinister mix of science and sorcery for solutions.

As science fiction, *Metropolis* has become dated, as is the fate of any science fiction film when technology overtakes it, yet it has endured as an entertaining and intriguing film for nearly ninety years because of Lang's translation of Von Harbou's novel from the page to the screen, providing us with unforgettable images: the balletic movement of the workers tending the Moloch machine, the transformation of the robot to Maria's likeness in Rotwang's laboratory, the crucifixion clock, the Seven Deadly sins coming to life in a grotesque *danse macabre*, and the immolation of the Maria robot as if she were a medieval witch.

A story that is of no place and of no time, like a fable, is of all place and time. Following Thea Von Harbou's literary work, Lang evokes a stunning cinematic presentation, credited in great measure to the innovative work of Karl Freund, who, with a hand-cranked camera and a few lights created absolute magic on the screens of a fledgling art form.

The fact that *Metropolis* has endured for ninety years as a staple of the science fiction genre is reinforced by its inspiration of the stories in this volume, *Towers of Metropolis*. This anthology represents a closing of the circle, fiction that is based on a film, that is based on fiction.

# WHAT RIGHT LAW?
## WILLIAM PATRICK MAYNARD &
## MICHAEL RICHARD MAYNARD

## PART [1]

Sitting in the pilot seat, the grizzled Frenchman with the neatly-trimmed white moustache set his jaw firmly in anticipation of the onrushing gravity. He pulled back on the controls and allowed the biplane to finish its final aerial somersault before beginning its descent to the waiting airstrip below. Many miles beneath them, a sleek black sedan had pulled up at the airstrip with a small convoy of police escorts in tow.

Joh Fredersen, the renowned industrialist emerged from the brightly polished vehicle once the biplane banked and came in for a smooth landing on the runway. He was escorted by the uniformed officers to the biplane that brought a visitor from the South American colonies. A lean, dark-skinned man with a pencil-thin black moustache pulled off his goggles and descended the rope ladder down from the biplane's passenger seat.

"Jorge Rosas?" Fredersen inquired of him in a voice loud enough to be heard over the dying propellers.

"I am," the famous architect beamed. Fredersen noted the peculiar twitch at the left corner of his mouth as the newcomer smiled. "It is an honor to meet you, Señor Fredersen."

"Good, Good! I wished to personally be on hand to welcome the man who shall restore my country's capitol to its former glory," Fredersen replied with a seemingly sincere smile.

"I shall do my best to ensure your dream metropolis shall be the new Babylon!" Rosas boasted as he landed on the ground with the practiced bounce of one who is accustomed to travel by biplane.

The industrialist beckoned the Latino towards the waiting sedan. As they climbed into the back seat, Fredersen muttered, "Metropolis, I rather like the sound of that."

He was still pondering all that vision might entail as the driver set off toward the waiting city.

14

Rosas looked out the window as they drove past a crumbling hotel and clicked his tongue in distaste. Fredersen again noted that peculiar twitch at the corner of the man's mouth.

"Such squalor in these streets, surely this shall not exist in your new capitol."

"One would certainly hope not," Fredersen yawned as he drearily looked out his window at the grey empty buildings and the grey hollow faces on the people who lived in them.

✝✝✝

The black sedan pulled up a winding cobblestone driveway leading up to Fredersen's impressive estate. As the car pulled to a stop and the warm purr of its motor fell silent; a small, cheery, blonde-haired toddler came running from the house towards the car.

"Papa, Papa!" the little boy shouted.

Upon seeing Rosas climb out of the back seat of the vehicle, the child backed away in alarm.

"It's alright, Freder, this is one of Papa's friends. Señor Rosas will be rebuilding our great city," Fredersen explained to his son.

"All by yourself?" the boy asked excitedly.

Both men chuckled amiably at the remark.

"Not quite," Rosas told the little boy. "I will be designing the city so that others may build it."

"Oh, okay," the boy nodded his head in response. A butterfly fluttered by close at hand and with that unexpected distraction, young Freder scurried off in pursuit of a brightly-colored dream that lay just within reach.

✝✝✝

A short while later in Joh Frederesen's well-furnished study, Rosas was downing his second glass of Scotch.

"... And we shall have a beautiful garden at the top of the city where all can relax in the evenings," explained Rosas as he tilted the empty glass toward the waiting decanter. "Thank you," he nodded to his host as the glass was filled for the third time.

"It all sounds quite lovely. I willingly give my full approval to all you have proposed," Fredersen replied, returning to the comfort of his armchair.

Rosas shifted in the seat opposite him.

"Coincidently, your son did bring to mind a question that has been puzzling me for some time. By what means shall this dream city of yours be constructed? The decline in population made me question whether you have the necessary labor force for the truncated schedule you have committed to in order to realize this project before the next general elections. The original Babylon was able to use slaves, but surely that is not an option for you."

"You need not worry about the construction. It is being handled by Professor Rotwang," Fredersen replied, standing up. He beckoned Rosas to the door. "You will find your studio and bedroom on the second floor at the very end of the hall to the left. If you'll excuse me, I think I should like to retire now. Good evening."

Rosas drained his glass and set it on the coffee table between him and the industrialist.

"Good evening, Señor Fredersen," he nodded and standing, made his way to the stairwell.

✝✝✝

Months passed and Rosas worked diligently on the plans for Metropolis. One day, as the architect was drawing out the final plans for the Pleasure Gardens, he was interrupted by an incessant stream of knocks upon his office door. Sighing as he got up from his desk, Rosas opened the door. A queer-looking man with strangely waxen features stood in the doorway, panting.

"Quick! Hide me! They will surely kill me if you don't," the man gasped.

Rosas' first impulse was to hurriedly shut and lock the stranger out, but he was struck by the queer-looking man's eyes. There was something about them…as if they were somehow familiar.

"Come inside," he said as, on impulse, he motioned him forward and quickly shut and locked the door behind him. "Now, who are you?"

"My designation is Alpha-3752," responded the strange man with the waxen features.

"Why should anyone want to kill you?"

"I am the prototype for the synthetic workforce to be used in the construction of Metropolis. I escaped Professor Rotwang's care when he brought me here for a demonstration to Mr. Fredersen. They are searching the grounds for me now. Please don't let them know I am with you whatever you do. It is not safe for me anywhere. If the public learns of my existence, there will be chaos."

"Chaos? Why should there be chaos?"

"Mr. Fredersen told my creator if the populace was to learn private industry is creating a synthetic workforce to augment their numbers, there would be revolution in the streets. Think how many in the old city already live in squalor. Think how they would behave if they were to learn the jobs they might hold were given away to manufactured workers."

"But why would Fredersen and his cronies even want a synthetic workforce?"

"An army of such workers will keep the project on task or ahead of schedule. We are more efficient and more reliable and easier to control or discard as need be."

"That is terrible."

"It is truth. Man sometimes makes the truth terrible."

Rosas stared into that strangely waxen face. His brow furrowed as he searched those familiar eyes.

"I can't put my finger on it, but I feel as though I somehow know you. Have no fear. I will give you shelter as you wish."

"I am in your debt," replied the waxen-featured man with a stiff nod.

Rosas barely heard his response, for his mind was turning over the lengths his employer was willing to go to realize the dream of Metropolis.

✝✝✝

The next morning when Rosas left the guestroom where he slept and unlocked his studio, he made an unexpected discovery. Alpha was seated at the side of the table, but his face had now changed.

"A moustache," Rosas exclaimed, "why do you now have a moustache identical to mine?"

"What do you mean?" Alpha replied, quizzically. "Is there any other kind?"

"Well, yes. There are many styles, but that is not the issue."

He stared at those waxen features that somehow seemed less inhuman with the addition of the moustache.

"Well, never mind that now. I have decided to have a word with Fredersen this morning about what you told me regarding his plans for a synthetic workforce. Have no fear that I will give you up. I gave you my word I would protect you. I have no intention of going back on it now."

"That is very noble of you, but I fear if you confront him about his plans, you will be worthlessly throwing you life away."

"Nonsense," Rosas smiled as the left corner of his mouth began to twitch spasmodically. "I am much too important to the success of this project for Fredersen to cast me aside now."

Alpha-3752 stared at the door curiously long after it had shut behind his savior.

✝✝✝

Rosas found his host in the kitchen sipping his morning coffee.

"Ah, good morning señor," Fredersen smiled at him. "I am enjoying the fruits of your countrymen's labor."

"Yes," Rosas smiled bitterly. "So you like to tell me. As it happens I would like to speak to you about your own countrymen's labor."

"Oh?" The smile instantly vanished from Fredersen's face. "And how does that concern you?"

"I am an architect, señor. As you are well aware. Always I am concerned with the creative side of the equation, but what of your side, my friend? What of the operations? How will you ever bring Metropolis to life in time to win the public support and therefore the presidency, eh? We both know this is why resurrecting the capitol is so important to you, yes?"

"It is one way," Fredersen shrugged, "but there are other paths to power. If not this term, then next. I am a patient man."

Rosas watched the industrialist stare into his eyes for some sign of doubt. He forced himself to smile amiably and then felt the painful nervous spasm that caused his mouth to twitch uncontrollably when he smiled.

"Surely, my friend," Rosas continued, "you have a sense of how the project is progressing. Do you think you will finish on schedule? Do you have sufficient manpower to even come close?"

Fredersen laughed and stood up from the table and approached the architect.

"I think I understand what is wrong."

"Do you?"

"Yes, my friend," Fredersen's parroting of the phrase seemed to hold a menacing quality. "You are concerned you have fallen behind schedule with your designs. Do not worry. We have sufficient work in front of us for many months. Just keep at the schedule as best you can. As I have told you, I am a patient man. I would rather see Metropolis in its full glory than accept its vision compromised. Why should anyone enjoy a lesser Metropolis that is cheaper, eh? It would be like settling for one of my friend Giorgio's jamborees with those talentless youngsters banging away on their crude instruments when one could enjoy a symphony instead. Go, my friend. Back to your studio. Create! Dream! And let me worry about making your dreams a reality."

✠✠✠

When Rosas returned to his studio and locked the door behind him, he found Alpha seated exactly where he had left him as if the synthetic man had not moved once during the interim. What to make of this peculiar specimen? He was certainly real enough and yet Fredersen had said nothing that would allow him to pursue a line of inquiry regarding his augmenting the workforce constructing Metropolis.

"You are an enigma," he told the waxen-featured man at his table. "I need proof of what you say. Not that I disbelieve you, but I cannot make an accusation without facts to back them up. Perhaps I might find something at Professor Rotwang's laboratory."

✝✝✝

The oddly shaped stone house that stood in the shadow of the deconsecrated Gothic cathedral where C. A. Rotwang made his home was an imposing sight. It appeared constructed on an angle as if it were about to fall in on itself. Portions of the foundation were in ruins. Little wonder there were rumors of murders and black masses having been held here while the nearby cathedral was still a place of worship. Briefly, Rosas considered the fact that he may have made a mistake in pursuing the matter. Still, nothing ventured, nothing gained, he told himself as he reached for the heavy iron knocker and announced his arrival.

Silence was his only answer so he repeated the resounding boom on those massive steel doors that appeared constructed so that a herd of giraffe might gain entryway. Rosas wondered if this decidedly European vogue of design were created specifically to enrage an architect schooled in the master masons of the past. His reverie was interrupted when the great doors suddenly swung inwards as if of their own accord.

He stood there for a moment, pondering what he should do. Gradually, he found the courage to step inside. The interior of the house had been gutted and transformed into something more akin to a baroque castle. A grand staircase wound its way upward as if built to resemble a giant corkscrew. Rosas paused at the first step, his hand upon the wrought iron rail, and listened for some sign of movement, but the entire house was silent.

Moving away from the steps, he investigated the first floor and came upon a trap indicating a cellar. Kneeling down, he touched the trap and felt a hum of energy course through his arm. Fascinated, he lifted the trap and as he did so, the room flooded with light so brilliant, he was forced to shield his eyes with his free arm.

Moving inexorably like a moth to a flame, he began to slowly descend the rope ladder that was attached to the wall just inside the crawlspace. His descent was perilous, but the electronic hum and the blinding light somehow made him feel protected. He continued to move shakily downwards one rung at a time. After what seemed like hours, he reached the last rung and, trusting blindly to fate, let go and dropped a few feet to the stone pavement below.

His heart was still racing furiously as he steadied himself with one hand resting against the stone wall. He was aware he was panting for breath. Rosas forced his eyes shut long enough to concentrate until his heartbeat was under control again.

Turning, he beheld the contents of the wondrous laboratory once his eyes adjusted to the brilliance of the light. All throughout the room were large glass containers filled with what appeared to be water. Inside each container, floating upright, was a nude man. All of them had the same waxen features as Alpha. He watched their chests rise and fall and wondered how it was possible for them to breathe underwater.

Regaining control of his senses, he unzipped his breast pocket and removed a small camera. Stepping back a few paces, he began snapping pictures furiously. He captured as many as possible from every conceivable angle.

"Industrial espionage is a punishable offense."

Rosas spun at the voice and saw a squat little toad of a man whose head was crowned with a wild shock of prematurely white hair that stood out in great points as if no brush had ever attempted to tame it.

"Dios mío!" Rosas swore and was aware of the involuntary twitch at the side of his mouth.

"A foreigner as well! This is an even more serious situation than I feared."

"Wait! Please! Hear me out! I am no spy," Rosas stammered nervously. "I am Jorge Rosas. I am the architect designing Metropolis for Joh Fredersen. Please, you will ask him. He will tell you. I came here to meet with Professor Rotwang. I knocked upon the door. One, two, three times and then it open…like magic. I came down here because the trap upstairs, it hummed with electricity and the bright light, it made me want to see. That is all."

"I am Professor Rotwang," the repulsive toad of a man smiled simply at him. "Why are you taking pictures of my synthetic men?"

"Who would not do the same in my shoes, Professor?" Rosas appeared at a loss for words. Nervously, he felt his mouth begin to twitch spasmodically. "Men who can breathe underwater? It is too marvelous for words. One must have proof that the eyes are not playing tricks on the mind."

"Give me your camera," Rotwang held out his right hand. Rosas obeyed the command without a second's hesitation. Rotwang flipped open the back of the camera, exposing the film to light. "You did wise to obey me. My word here is law. There is no greater authority than me in this laboratory."

"What…what are these synthetic men of yours?"

"Do you know something, Señor Rosas?" Rotwang asked, his eyes narrowing suspiciously. "You ask a great deal of inconvenient questions. I don't think I like you very much."

Rosas' eyes widened in apprehension.

Rotwang threw back his head and laughed, "Do not look so frightened, señor. I don't like anyone very much. Come. We shall pay a visit to your 'good friend' Joh Fredersen and see what he has to say about your snooping around my laboratory."

✛✛✛

"Hello, Rosas," said Fredersen with a smile when the guards brought him into his office. Then the industrialist picked up the heavy glass paperweight of his dream city that rested upon his desk and swung it hard into Rosas' jaw. The architect felt his head snap to the right as teeth broke and blood filled his mouth until he gagged.

"Now that I have your attention," Fredersen continued calmly, "might I ask you what business it is of an architect to stick his nose into my workforce? After all, it is not as if they were your countrymen, yes? Why the bleeding heart, señor? Why does your conscience trouble you so that you are reduced to snooping and spying on matters that cannot possibly concern you? Could it be that you have made a friend?"

Rosas' head lolled against the back of the chair, but for the guards who held him upright, he would have slipped into unconsciousness.

"No, no…." he stammered, "I have met no one. There is no one else."

"Really?" Frederesen's voice was barely a whisper. "That interests me greatly because you were put to a test, my friend. This is a critical time for me. As you know, I intend to be the next president, but also, and more importantly, the Master of Metropolis. I cannot afford any weak stones in my foundation. Surely as an architect, you appreciate that concept, yes? So I put your loyalty to the test and you were found lacking. Most disappointing, señor, most disappointing. The man with the vision to build Metropolis must be loyal to its Master. The head must be loyal to the heart."

"You have no heart!" Rosas spat a bloody tooth from his mouth as he

*"Could it be you have made a friend?"*

spoke. The front of his shirt was wet with crimson stains. "That little boy of yours, he could teach you what it is to have a heart. You lost yours when you sold your soul."

"Freder?" The industrialist pondered his young and innocent son for a moment. "He is but a boy. He will learn what it is to be a man. I will show him the way. Today, he dreams of chasing butterflies in the Pleasure Gardens you have promised him. Tomorrow, it will be maidens he pursues. The day after tomorrow, I will initiate him into the true pleasures of Metropolis and he will learn that it is man's destiny to dominate...to conquer."

"You're sick," Rosas sneered at his employer. "Your darkness will corrupt that innocent boy. You'll pervert him into following your path."

"What do you know of my path?" Fredersen bellowed. "My path is the presidency. My path is becoming the Master of the greatest city this world has ever seen...a city you shall build for me."

"I will build you nothing," Rosas' voice fell so that Fredersen had to strain to hear him speak. "I would undo all I have done."

"You speak treason," Fredersen waved his hand dismissively. "It seems I have need of a new architect." Leaning forward over his desk, his hand depressed the intercom button. "Send in Señor Rosas, please."

The door opened and Rosas watched as his identical twin entered the room.

"What madness is this?" the baffled architect questioned.

"Not madness, my friend," Fredersen replied, "science. I believe you have met Alpha-3752 before."

Rosas stared dumbfounded as the truth dawned upon him. The waxen-featured man with the pencil-thin moustache so like his own was standing before him now and his own mother would have been unable to tell them apart.

"He was your test, señor," Fredersen's voice seemed to take on a melancholy twinge. "If only you had displayed integrity and come to me right away and told me you had discovered the runaway synthetic worker; then I would have known you were a man of honor, a man I could trust to build my Metropolis, a man I would be proud to call my friend. Instead, what did you do? You lied to me. You deceived me. You went behind my back and intended to expose me, to ruin me. This is not loyalty. This is not what I demanded of you. Those who are loyal to me are shown loyalty in return. Those who betray me shall be shown justice."

"You need me," Rosas lifted his head until his eyes met Fredersen's.

"Without me, your dreams will vanish. There is much that is in my head alone."

"Oh no, there you are mistaken, my friend," Fredersen shook his head. "Alpha-3752 has the same memories, the same intelligence, even the same fingerprints as you. He is, for all intents and purposes, Jorge Rosas perfected. My friend Rotwang is a genius. He understands what it is to be loyal."

Rosas turned wondrous eyes unto those of his identical twin, but found no mercy there, only a cold, unemotional gaze that held his unquestioningly.

"What of the people? What did you say to Rotwang? Once they discover you are giving their jobs away to these synthetic men of his, there will be revolution in the streets."

"There will be no revolution," Fredersen shook his head again. "You were so gullible to believe all you hear. There are two dozen synthetic men, no more. Each is growing the features of the men whose genetic blueprint is imprinted in their synthetic soul. They will replace my most trusted collaborators one by one. Except for Rotwang whose genius could never be replicated and whose loyalty is beyond reproach. The others will be perfected. Never sick, never tired, always obedient; they shall serve me better than ever before. They will know me as their Master.'

"Rosas!"

The architect lifted his head again only to realize Fredersen was addressing the synthetic man.

"Remove this imperfect copy of you. I have need of only one architect with the vision to realize my dream Metropolis."

Alpha-3752 nodded his head and turned toward the man who had unknowingly given him his identity. Dispassionately, the synthetic man's hands went round the architect's throat and with a quick jerk, he snapped his neck as if it were a twig. Releasing his throat, he watched the man's head slump forward.

The guards released their hold on the dead man and he tumbled out of his seat and fell to the floor. Alpha-3752 turned towards Fredersen and smiled. "It is finished," he intoned lifelessly. Fredersen noted with approval that a faint flicker of a twitch appeared at the corner of the synthetic man's mouth as it smiled. Rotwang had never failed him yet. Two dozen such perfect companions would guarantee none would dare question his right to rule over first Metropolis and then the entire nation. History would never recall the name of that great architect, Jorge Rosas, but it would never forget the name of Joh Fredersen, for he would write the history books himself.

# PART (2)

The day everything changed was the day the police motorcade drove down our street. I had no desire to join the ever-growing throng of neighbors crowding their tree lawns to watch the dull grey armored cars and marching blue and black-uniformed soldiers as they passed by in oppressive silence. Some were angry, some were in awe, most were simply curious.

"I didn't marry a man, I married a coward!"

Anastasia's stinging indictment had left me numb. No man wants to hear his wife berate him as a coward, least of all in front of their children. Was I a coward for seeing little point in purchasing a handgun to protect my family from Fredersen's government? They controlled technology so great and so powerful that we could never hope to challenge it and persevere. We had argued many times over the years whether guns belonged in a home with little children, but never before had she belittled me as less than a man for holding fast to my position on the issue.

I watched her tear out the front door in a burst of adrenalin and rage. She stomped off angrily toward the tree lawn hollering invective at the motorcade. Within hours, the media were referring to the events of that day as "the bloodless coup." You can't trust the press any more than you can the history books. They all lie. "The bloodless coup" only meant there were fewer casualties than predicted.

I still can't hear the phrase without feeling the anxiety rise up from the pit in my stomach until I was certain I would retch. The only memory it conjures in my mind is seeing my Anastasia lying there crumpled on our front lawn, her insides ripped apart by bullets from an overzealous keeper of the peace during a manly show of force following the Fredersen government's declaration that we now lived under a state of martial law.

Even then, the irony was not lost upon me that my wife was killed by just the sort of man she berated me for not being. There was no sense of vindication in this knowledge, only a gnawing numbness that deadened my emotions.

✠✠✠

I pressed stop on the archaic memory device and watched the analogue tape spin from one spool to the next. It was my treasure, the means of preserving my memories in a permanent record. No one keeps their memories any more...not in these days of the Last Four. That is how we are differentiated; our Last Four replaced the names given to us at birth by our parents. Even the last names we used to holler to one another from the shop floor were discarded in the upgrade to our Last Four.

My treasure is so important to me for without it, I fear I would not be able to keep my memories of Anastasia and our children. I recall vividly the feeling of despair the first morning I awoke in my cot in the work camp not knowing what had become of my son and daughter. It was the same feeling that greeted me upon waking every morning. It was the one constant in a world where identity was becoming extinct.

It wasn't just my memories that were disappearing, of course. Everyone was losing their memories and with them, their every thought of independence. It was the water. There was something in the water. There had to be. It didn't taste the same. They told us it was purified, but I knew it was the water that was making us forget. It was dulling our minds as well. We could not think as we once did. We had no fight in us anymore.

They came for 4471 this morning in the mess hall. He was not following dietary restrictions to stave off obesity and was captured on the security camera taking more than his allotment of red meat. All workers are allowed one slice. The rules are simple: everyone takes their fair share; know your Last Four; and always obey the Law.

✙✙✙

I awoke this morning to a terrifying sense of loss. There was only the work camp. I could not remember ever having been a child or anything of life before the work camp. There had to be something else.

Frantically, I searched through the drawers of the cold metal desk that was bolted to the wall of my cell. There was an archaic memory device inside one drawer. After fidgeting with it for a few seconds, I found it was possible to play back the analogue recording held on the spool.

I was shocked to hear my own voice speaking to me…spinning fanciful yarns of a world that did not exist. Tears streaked my cheeks as I listened to my own familiar voice telling unfamiliar tales. Why should these stories of a wife and children I never had affect me so?

Perhaps they were real, but it seemed impossible. How could I have a wife and children and not recall such important details? No, it had to be propaganda…a clever forgery put forth by enemies of the state to deceive me. There was only the work camp. There was nothing else but work. All that mattered was feeding fuel to the Great City.

✙✙✙

I finished my shift and felt more tired than ever before. It was the stories of having a family that the man who sounded so uncannily like me told. What if they were true? What had become of them? Why couldn't I recall my past before the work camp?

I gathered up the memory device and stepped out of my cell. We were only permitted outside our cells when it was time to work or at the designated meal times. I waited calmly for the guard to notice the aberration in my behavior and take me in for questioning. I didn't have long to wait.

"What the hell are you doing outside your cell? What's your Last Four?" he barked at me.

I heard myself mutter a response in that cowed voice we all used when the guards spoke to us. I have always hated authority, but I've never had the strength to kick it in the teeth the way I dreamt of doing. I despise myself for not having the courage to do so.

I stopped and tried to remember how I could have always felt that way and why. Where did the anger come from? I stopped thinking as we reached the Boss' office and the guard pushed me hard right up against the thick iron door while he held his hand against the sensor to read his identi-chip. The heavy iron door slid soundlessly into the slot in the doorway and the guard roughly pushed me forward.

"What are your last four?" the unpleasant man seated behind the desk asked in a disinterested tone.

I mumbled my response.

"Loud and clear!" the guard snarled as he placed my memory device on the Boss' desk.

I repeated the digits as requested.

The Boss was preoccupied with my memory device. "What is this?" he asked the guard, his tone only slightly less interested than before.

The guard shrugged, "I haven't a clue. I found him outside of his cell holding it. He said he wants to ask you a question."

Finally, the Boss looked up at me. He set my memory device down before him on the desk and raised his hands in supplication, "Ask. What is your question?"

I stared into those sunken eyes and knew he would not have the answer.

"You heard the Boss, ask your question!" the guard pushed me forward.

"What was there before the work camp?" I asked in a quiet voice.

The Boss' face turned purple and he began to shake. "Beat him," he told the guard. The man did as he was requested and, from what I could see through my swollen eyes, he enjoyed his work.

✝✝✝

When I awoke I was back in my cell, lying on the concrete floor. Every part of my body ached as I struggled to sit up and support my weight against my cot. Happily, I saw my memory device lying there on the sheet, seemingly undamaged. Nervously I pressed the playback button and listened to my voice tell me fairy tales of a time when I was happy and free and not alone.

✝✝✝

"You're outside of your cell again?" The guard's patience was clearly lacking today. "Didn't get enough of a lesson yesterday?" He raised his fist to strike me once more.

"Please," I begged him, "I need to see the Boss and ask him another question."

✝✝✝

"Let's hear it," the Boss said with the same disinterested tone of voice.

"Why did they take our names from us?" I asked softly.

The Boss smiled slightly at my question. "Beat him," he told the guard. "Do it harder this time."

The guard did not disappoint. This time I slept longer, but the pain was worse when I awoke.

✝✝✝

"I don't bloody well believe it," the guard swore when he next saw me outside my cell. "You just don't learn, do you?"

I looked up at him for a moment and tried to find something human in his eyes. I read only hatred there.

"I need to ask the Boss another question," I said quietly.

✝✝✝

"It seems you're quite the joker," the Boss said when he saw me. He didn't smile when he spoke.

"I think he's mental," the guard added.

The Boss shot him a quick glance to let him know he was not to speak unless spoken to. He turned his attention back to me. "What's your question, bright boy?" he asked.

"How many beatings will it take before I see the Master of Metropolis?" I said in a quiet voice.

The Boss laughed hard and his face finally showed genuine emotion as if he was enjoying himself. "More beatings than you'll survive, my friend," he nodded toward the guard who did the only job he was likely ever good at.

✝✝✝

He was wrong, of course. I had the constitution of an ox someone had told me long ago. I wasn't sure what an ox was, but it was obviously strong enough to survive twelve beatings. I had three broken bones that were healing badly by the time I was finally taken under police escort to the home of Joh Fredersen, the Master of Metropolis.

Just seeing the upper world was a treat. There was sunlight, real sunlight. It was so much brighter than I imagined. I wondered if I had ever seen it before, felt its warmth on my arms and face. I couldn't now as I looked through the window of the speeding car.

The Master of Metropolis' home was a palace. That was only fitting. He was our Master, after all. A Master deserves a palace because he is Master. It was the Law. I didn't know that for sure, but it was always safer to believe in the Law than to question it.

I tried not to look around as they brought me through the servants' entrance. The kitchen smelled delicious. What I wouldn't give for even a minute in that pantry without a guard. Then I was taken into the dining room and allowed to sit at the end of a table so wide, twenty people could have dined there.

Only one other person was seated there for at the opposite end of the table, slowly eating a sumptuous meal that made my mouth water, was a fierce-looking man whose jaw shook while he ate. I had never seen him before, but a man knows when he has met his Master. I watched him spear his meat with a fork and listened to the sound it made while he bit into it with his sharp little teeth. He was a god.

"I understand you wanted to see me," he grunted between bites of meat. "You've achieved your life's ambition it seems. Though the privilege may yet cost you your life. Well? Come, come…I haven't got all day. I don't need you spoiling my dessert."

"I want the truth, Master," I said.

"What is Truth?" he replied.

"You are Master of this world. You would know the truth."

"Your logic is simple," he lifted a towel to his lips to wipe away the grease as he spoke, "but flawed. I am the Master of this city, not the world. Not yet anyway. Although some might argue that it is the same. I prefer not to get ahead of myself. Hubris is the downfall of the mighty. What truth do you seek that I might sate your appetite for knowledge so that I can get on with my dessert?"

"I know there was more to this life than feeding fuel to the furnace that powers the city. I know once I lived above ground. I had a wife. We had a family…children. I don't know what happened to them. I know we forget everything, even the names we were born with, because of what you put in the water. Why do you do these things, Master? Is life in Metropolis not supposed to be good?"

The old man dabbed at the corners of his mouth and shifted in his chair as he passed gas audibly. Setting the towel down on the table, he folded it into thirds and then looked up at me and replied, "Life in Metropolis is good because I tell you it is. You forget everything because life before Metropolis was a life of pain and torment and misery. Now you are provided for. Now you have no wants, no cares."

"Now we have no love," I replied.

"Don't ever speak that word to me again!" his voice was like thunder as he struck the table with his fist. "What do you know of love…or loss? How is it you remember these things?"

"I have a memory device. It talks to me and tells me what I have forgotten," I replied.

The anger faded from the Master's face as his mouth hung agape for a moment. "How extraordinary!" he sighed. "I want it. Now."

He held his left hand out for it as the guard brought my memory device forward. He turned it over in his hand and hit the playback button. He listened to my voice for a moment and then hit stop/eject twice. Pulling the cartridge from the device, he smashed it on the floor beneath his boot until the tape was destroyed.

"There are your precious memories," he spoke the words calmly to me. "Be happy I have set you free. Take him away."

The guard came and lifted me up from my chair as the Master returned to his soup.

"I am not free."

The Master dropped his spoon with a loud clang that made the soup splash from the bowl.

"What did you just say?"

"I am not free," I repeated the words. "I am immune to the water."

His hand shook as he waved a finger in my direction.

"Leave him. It seems Rotwang has found himself a new lab rat."

✝✝✝

I can honestly say I didn't much care for Professor Rotwang. It seems sometimes that people who look and act the least human will treat others the most inhumanly. Professor Rotwang personified this axiom. For what seemed like days, he had me strapped down in his laboratory in various positions while he probed and prodded and poked. My body was still battered from the beatings and broken bones I had endured. His medical investigations took an already sore body and subjected it to sadistic violations. Not once did his face betray anything approaching emotion. I had no reason to think he enjoyed hurting me. I had no reason to think he enjoyed anything in this life ever. He just was.

"There is no medical explanation for his resistance to the drug," Rotwang told Fredersen as they both pretended I couldn't hear or understand them while I lay strapped down on the table between them as they spoke. "Sometimes, there is a phenomenon related to very strong levels of belief that allow a specimen to withstand physical, chemical, or psychological change because of the strength of said beliefs. A question of mind over matter, if you will. This appears to be one such case. The specimen was reacting normally by his own admission until the memory device convinced him to believe in something he could no longer recall. That belief, as unrealistic and inexplicable as it is, gave him hope and made him question reality. There is nothing anyone can do or say to convince him otherwise. Such people, gratefully few in number, are the exception. My recommendation is we destroy him. He is useless to the program."

Fredersen thought this over somewhat and then replied, "No, we keep him alive for now. I find this mind over matter business fascinating. I may yet find a use for him. Have him cleaned up and brought to me. I will speak to him and decide his fate at that time."

"As you wish," Rotwang replied. If he felt any resentment at having his recommendation overruled, he did not disclose it by word or manner.

✝✝✝

The second time I met with the Master of Metropolis in his dining room, I knew him for a man and not the god I had at first thought. This recollection was my first true understanding of what they were discussing about me. I could not only remember, but I could reach conclusions based

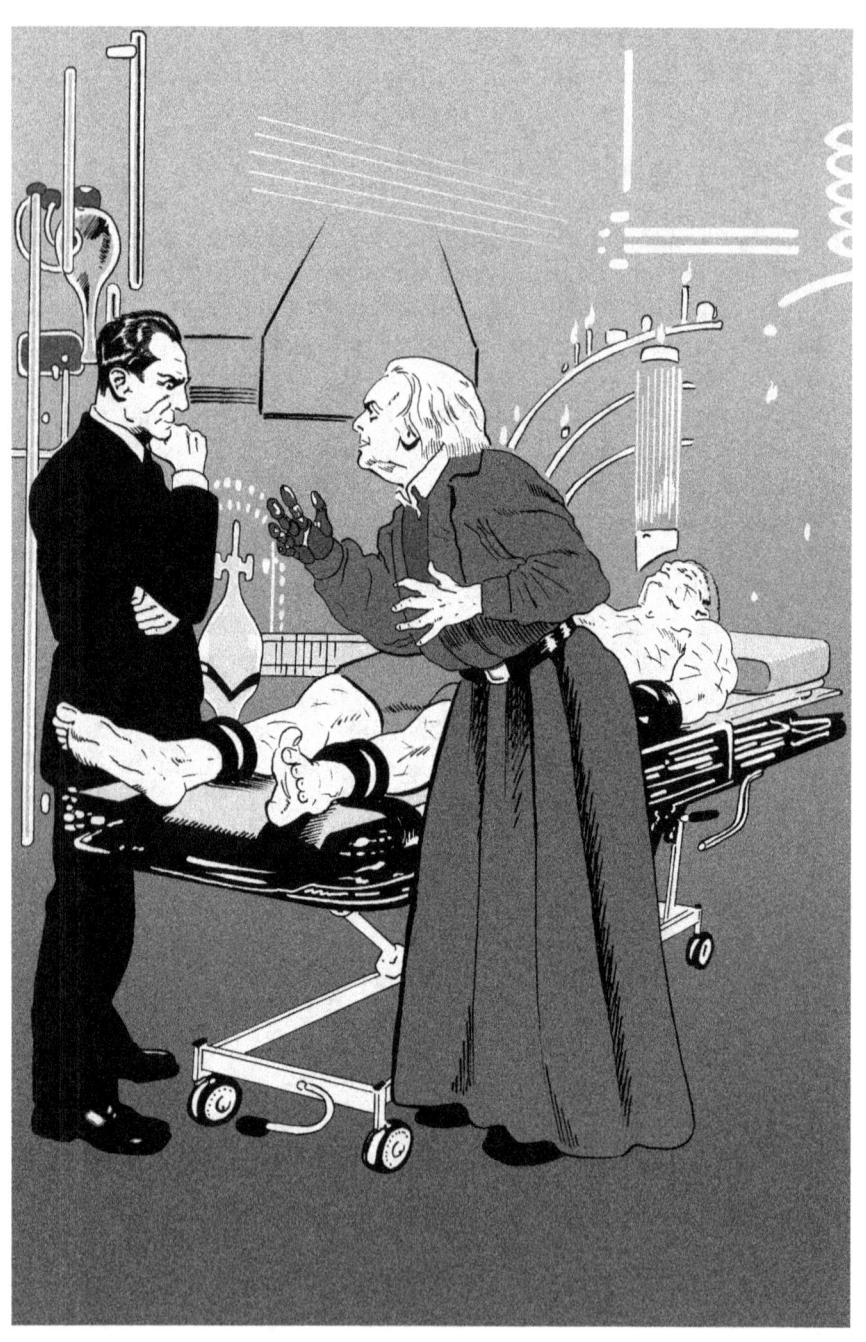

*"No, we keep him alive for now."*

on what I had learned in the past. I knew this made me dangerous. It should have made me cautious perhaps, but it only emboldened me to speak the truth as I understood it. There is no shame in an honest man being put to death in a world of liars.

"You mentioned you might have a use for me," I said to my host. "I am curious what that might be."

Fredersen looked at me in stunned silence. Clearly, he was a man unaccustomed to having others speak before he spoke to them. Perhaps he was also startled by the difference in my behavior. He chose not to reveal anything; he merely cleared his throat and answered me in his fashion.

"There are two classes in Metropolis, my friend. Those who live underground and work all day and are provided for in all of their needs by the government and those who live above ground and rule as the elite. Which would you rather be, hmm?"

If he was expecting an answer to his question, he was disappointed. If disappointed he was, he did not show it, he simply resumed speaking.

"How would you like to eat meals such as you have seen me eat here? How would you like to dress in as many different combinations of clothes as one could imagine?" He leaned forward on the table with his palms resting on it and stared hard into my eyes, "How would you like to possess what no one else has in your world, a family of your own?"

He whispered the word "family" as if it was the mere concept that made me cling to my belief and not the fact that I once had a wife of my choosing and children as the product of our union.

"Think of it, my friend, a family!" Again he hissed the word as if it were forbidden, "Metropolis has very nearly zero population growth thanks to the birth control in our water supply. Pregnancies are allowed at a rate of replacement only and that rate is adjusted only once every three months as the statistics become available. We have the perfect sustainable society, but sustainability comes at a cost. How would you like to not have to pay the cost, hmm? Consider that as one of the elite, you can have any woman in the underworld you wish and taker her, by force if you like, in full knowledge no one can do anything to make you pay. No child, no rape, no avenging honor. All the things that used to be held sacred in the Old City are gone, fallen away in our new Metropolis."

He paused for a long while and I noticed that he had started to salivate while he spoke.

"I think," I said at last, "that I should prefer death than to be a man such as you."

I failed to take in account when I said those words that death might not be the immediate result of having insulted the Master of Metropolis.

✝✝✝

Transcript of Presentation to Joh Fredersen by C. A. Rotwang
Subject: 3631
Date: 31122021
Conducted a full battery of psychological deconstruction on subject with televisual monitor simulating thought images as detected by brain wave analysis and voice to text visualization. Purpose of psychological deconstruction to analyze root of subject's ability to resist external stimulus of chemical, psychological, and physical nature. Subject was confined to a table and placed under sedation while brain and heart monitors were attached. Psychological stimulus was applied in the form of text and voice command to "always obey the law" transmitted at 90 second intervals throughout the process. Voice tone and text design were altered to combat emotional complacency on the part of the subject.

The earliest images to form on the screen were of recent occurrences involving a guard beating subject outside his cell or inside the Boss' office, if you'll pardon the use of that vulgar title for what we would term a warden. First significant breakthrough occurred 27:30 into process as image of a middle-aged female corpse lying in the grass near the street appeared. Cause of death would appear to be bullets fired from an automatic weapon. Partial exposure of intestines. Subject flashed back to this image multiple times throughout process suggesting emotional attachment to same. Suggest corpse was subject's wife as recalled by memory device, now destroyed. Pity that. Might have made our task a bit simpler.

Visualizations of subject's children from opening presents to reading stories together to taking walks in the park to multiple visits to the zoo... all the way back to their births comprised most of the next hour. Subject seemed to fixate on mundane aspects of domestic life placing heightened value on children and subject's interaction with them. This likely accounts for subject's failure to rise beyond menial labor tasks throughout his working life as his mind was fixated on providing his children with the attention denied him at the same age as we shall shortly see.

If you'll pardon our moving out of sequence, I would refer us to event first recalled 1:33:45 into process as image of a middle-aged female corpse, apparently subject's mother, our records indicate subject's mother expired of cardiac arrest when subject was approximately 11 years old. Note will be made to event recalled just following this recollecting what appears to be an argument with subject's mother just hours before she expired. I'll refer your attention back to first significant breakthrough occurring at 27:30 and note similar sequence recollecting what appears to be an argument with subject's wife just prior to her death. Recurrence of these sequences suggests traumatic association formed in youth towards losing loved one following argument. Suggest this trauma played a significant role in subject's pathological resistance to defending himself when beaten as subject associates conflict with loss and suffers paralysis of emotions.

Next, we will focus upon subject's rather extraordinary tolerance to abuse in all manifestations. Now this one, we must move near the end of the process at 7:45:13 before we find what we shall term Event One. As a toddler, subject was sexually abused in presence of father by other adult males, identities indeterminate. Hardly matters anyway, they're all surely dead by now. Pay close attention to subject's face at the time of abuse and note the change from intense concentration and pain endurance to psychological dissociation. You will note all outward signs of pain have vanished and subject appears, for all intents and purposes, to no longer be present in the moment. Event One suggests advanced coping mechanism employed at time of abuse allowed subject to subsequently endure tremendous amounts of physical and emotional suffering without taking on predatory nature of abuser later in life as is common in most cases of this nature. One should also note that subject's resistance to inflicting physical violence himself is also highly abnormal and likewise relates back to aforementioned psychological dissociation at the time of Event One.

There, sir, we have the root, as it were, of subject's uncanny ability to resist all external stimuli. Now, identifying what the coping mechanism precisely was that later triggered his highly sedated and, it should be noted, addicted physiognomy to respond to the aural memory response of the playback of recordings he could no longer recall having made, much less lived through, is of primary importance. However, you will be pleased to know that I do believe we have done just that. I refer to a periodic recurrence of a seemingly benign nature of an image of a white tablecloth covering what appears to be a small table. This recurs periodically throughout subject's life. Unsurprisingly, I missed the significance of it the first few passes through the tape. Here is one right now at 6:12:03 into the process. See?

Now, let me replay that, but this time we shall zoom in on the small table and you will notice upon the white table cloth is a small gold dish. This rather fascinates me for if we replay those last two seconds again and zoom in still closer and pause, you will detect the presence of small circular white objects inside the gold dish. These are, I am quite sure now, pieces of bread. Bear with me a moment as we zoom out and play once more. Did you catch that? I'll replay it this time reducing the frames per second eight-fold. There! Do you see it now? I nearly missed it the first few times through.

"I see nothing, Rotwang. I see a wall. Nothing more."

Yes, sir, but upon the wall. Watch. I will replay it this time reducing the frames per second sixteen-fold. There! I've paused at just the right moment. There is your coping mechanism that the aural stimulation of loss of wife and children triggered after all this time.

"It's a crucifix. So the subject was a Roman Catholic at one point. Why would this concern us?"

Ah, that's what you're missing, sir. Subject was not simply Roman Catholic in his younger years, he was a Believer. It was real to him.

"What was real to him?"

Transubstantiation. Subject believed in real presence at Holy Mass. That was the significance of the bread in the dish recurring and then his mind flashing to the crucifix. He believed his God walked the earth as a flesh and blood man and died in expiation for his sins. As a toddler, this is quite remarkable when you think of it, as a toddler, he made a primal association with the crucifix and his own suffering at the hands of his abuser and allowed his belief in his God to literally transport him out of his body and away from his pain. He subconsciously returned to this coping mechanism again and again throughout his life. This allowed him to avoid repeating the pathological behavior one associates with most victims of childhood sexual trauma. This allowed him to withstand the chemical, physical, and psychological conditioning he had received since laboring in the furnaces below ground these past few years. This is a fascinating case study of what we may be able to harness were we to replicate these same sets of circumstances with other subjects of the same formative ages. Think of the military value that might be gained…

"Enough, Rotwang! I don't wish to hear another word about this coping mechanism of yours. The subject expired upon conclusion of the process. Let it die with him. One man destroyed his world and another man saved him. It's a charming story where I play the villain's part. Metropolis has no place for humble-born saviors. We have our head, we have our hands. We have no need for a mediator. Metropolis is now and ever shall be a world without end. I do not wish to be reminded of the pointless superstitions we outlawed. They are part of the Old City. They have no place in a modern Metropolis. This interview is terminated."

# PART (3)

It was dark when Rotwang returned to his abode. He felt that familiar shiver of revulsion as he passed the deconsecrated cathedral and reached the oddly-shaped stone building he called home. The jagged tower of stone was so much more than just his refuge from the outside world; it was his gateway to the past. It was the key to the truth about this world that so few others understood.

Moloch was the answer. It was because of Moloch that Metropolis thrived. Few could accept that truth, certainly not Fredersen. They would learn soon enough. Moloch would not be content to remain a graven image forever.

He glanced round furtively as he reached the doorway. Pausing before putting his key in the lock, he took a step back as a shambolic figure moved forward from the shadows and hobbled toward him carrying a bundle in its arms. Rotwang watched the shifting movement of the figure as it dragged a twisted leg behind as it approached. His eyes focused on the bundle carefully held in its arms. Whatever was swaddled within the blanket moved slightly as if struggling to escape. Rotwang gasped with excitement in spite of himself at the mere thought of the treasure contained within.

The ragged figure was near enough for him to make out the wrinkled face wreathed in stringy white hair. That twisted mouth split into a mockery of a smile revealing a few missing teeth and a swollen tongue. It held the bundle out for him to observe closely as if a street vendor proffering freshly baked goods. Rotwang lifted a corner of the blanket and peered at the contents of the bundle.

"I see you had sense enough to ensure it stayed alive this time," he sighed.

The ragged figure nodded its head eagerly and held out a quivering hand.

Rotwang reached into his pocket and passed a handful of marks to the decrepit figure before him.

"So little?" the creature asked, disappointed.

"Yes," Rotwang replied, lifting the bundle slightly in his arms, "it is little. Scarcely worth what I've paid you for it. Be gone from my sight, you wretched little worm."

The sexless old creature's ghastly smile collapsed and it withdrew slowly, scarcely willing to turn its back to Rotwang. It needn't have worried for once out of sight; the crone's hideous visage was gone from Rotwang's mind as he busied himself unlocking the great door whilst carefully balancing the bundle in his arms.

Just inside the door and out of the elements at last, one had an immediate sense of the dimly lit surroundings with the cold draft from those great windows that whistled mournfully when the wind blew. Wrapped tightly within the swaddling blanket, the infant stirred and let out a bleating cry. Rotwang scarcely paid it any mind as he climbed the twisting corkscrew staircase two steps at a time. At last, he reached the top and stepped out into a vast open room dominated by that same terrible iron-wrought gaping-mouthed image of Moloch that adorned the furnace room beneath the city.

The infant let out a wail as if it sensed the fate in store for it as Rotwang moved forward cautiously, one deliberate step at a time. Truth be told, he feared waking his god too soon, for Moloch was not a mere image to Rotwang, but something terrible and alive and hungry for sustenance. Moloch craved the blood of innocents as he had for untold centuries. The lives of the workers beneath the city were unsatisfying. He must have blood not yet corrupted by the wanton needs of weak flesh.

Rotwang set the child down upon the floor in front of that terrible visage whose eyes burned to possess its tender flesh. Moving to the iron grating to the right of the idol, he lifted the heavy iron pincers and locked their grip around a pair of burning hot embers. Carefully, he bore the glowing red embers over to the idol and positioned the pincers just behind the tongue in that gaping iron mouth. Releasing them, he heard them drop and sizzle as steam rose out of the mouth. He stood there for a moment, pondering the sight before him as flames danced in the back of the mouth and licked the air just out of reach of his clothing. Returning the pincers to the iron grating, Rotwang turned for the child.

The child...the child was the reason for all of this. No, not this child, but the loss of the woman he loved. The only woman who had ever made him feel complete, made him feel alive...the only woman he would have given the world to make happy, but the world was not what she chose. She chose Fredersen.

Hel, born to be my happiness, a blessing to all men, lost to Joh Fredersen, dying in giving life to his son, Freder.

The words echoed round his mind until he thought he would be lost to madness forevermore. How could she? He, who had understood her and satisfied her like no lover before him had…or so she told him in the quiet moments afterwards when he held her close and her face danced in the light of the fireplace. Perhaps her words were only lies. Perhaps she was merely accustomed to propping up men with their fragile egos so they could find the confidence to achieve greatness.

Did he say men? There were no men before her with her incomparable beauty and her fierce intelligence, there were only boys. She craved love and attention. Not from one man alone, for Rotwang tried with all his heart and soul to give her all the care she required, but from as many men as she could successfully juggle. Despite his devotion, Rotwang's work demanded he could not always be at her side and she was not a woman willing to be alone.

"The loneliness is nigh on impossible for me to bear," she would cry and for many months, he believed her and did all he could to make her feel protected and cared for and loved. She assured him he did just that like no other man she ever knew, but always in the back of his mind there was the needling doubt that she was rarely alone. Always, in the back of his mind, Rotwang knew he was not the only one to hear those same sweet words of love. Always, in spite of her anger and tears and pleas that he must believe what she said, he knew she would always deceive him. Behind that beguiling smile and those soulful eyes, there lurked a fatally wounded scorpion determined to take as many victims with her as possible before she finally succumbed.

Now that he knew the truth at last, Rotwang understood that it wasn't loneliness that drove her; it was a gluttonous lust for as many hearts as possible. No, that still wasn't it, for it was not love she craved, not really. She wanted the devotion of as many men as possible. All of them had to place her above all others. All of them had to believe they were her special one. She would moan that she longed for a true partner, an equal, but in truth she had no intention of ever giving her heart to any one man. What use is a single devoted partner when one can have so very many hearts to toy with?

He loved her. He loved her with a jealous passion and yet his heart made him forgive her when he caught her in her lies. He loved her with a jealous passion and yet his heart made him believe her when he knew he could taste another on her lips. He loved her with a jealous passion and yet his heart made him believe one ridiculous fabrication after another of where she had been and whom she had seen and how innocent it was in actuality.

Eventually, she came to be so sure of his blind love that she had the audacity to lie to him and demand he believe her words even when the truth was right before his very eyes. She was so sure of his love that reality itself could be denied if she demanded it. Truth was nothing, a mere trifle to be dispensed with at will. All that was required were for those eyes to hold his gaze and make him repeat her lies and then a soft and tender lingering kiss and he would be ashamed he ever questioned her love.

Rotwang began to hate himself for his weakness. It was the first step in hating her for not letting his love overcome her weaknesses and heal her damaged heart. He gave her everything she asked, but she wanted more than she would ever request. So it came that he mustered the courage to break her down and admit the truth at last. She struggled as he knew she would. After all this time, she was sure she had him under her spell, but ultimately, she broke and he left her in her misery to wither and die or accept his love.

Faced with only two choices, she did what he should have anticipated; she rejected both options and gave her love to Joh Fredersen instead. He knew Fredersen was both his friend and rival. He wasn't the only rival Rotwang had for her affections. At the time, he didn't even blame him. Who could not fall in love with her? Was she not the Grail every man sought to win? Was she not the fatherless child every man longed to care for? Was she not the loving wife every man longed to embrace? She was all that and more. She was soft and intelligent and so very perceptive. She made Rotwang, with his dark and cynical soul, laugh and love life and feel like a boy again. Who could not fall in love with such a woman?

He could not blame Fredersen or any of the others for surely he would be the one to persevere. Who else gave her more time and affection? Who else was more generous? Why, of all her lovers, surely Fredersen had the least time for her. Naturally, if she wanted to crush Rotwang forever, selecting Fredersen to give herself to was the perfect final blow to ruin him for daring to hold a mirror up to her inexcusable, heartless behavior and demand her love as the price.

Hel, born to be my happiness, a blessing to all men, lost to Joh Fredersen, dying in giving life to his son, Freder.

Part of him wanted to be glad that she was dead...that she should die giving birth to that bastard child of his traitorous friend. Yet, the only ones he wanted to see dead were Fredersen and that accursed child of his who looked so like his mother. A son...why did it have to be a son? The cruelty was unending. When would the pain end? It had been years and

"Who could not fall in love with such a woman?"

the pain only worsened with each passing season. What had she called him the last time they spoke? A tormented soul…he had hated her for that because it was true…because she had the intelligence to recognize it and the uncaring heart to multiply that torment a thousand times with her callous disregard for his love.

What would it take before he had quenched the fires of that dull, aching pain that would not cease to burn in his soul? He turned to Moloch for the answer. Moloch asked for the blood of innocents and as much as he wanted to give him the infant Freder as a sacrifice, he could not take the risk. So it was that Rotwang dealt with the dregs of Metropolis to sate Moloch's unending hunger. He sometimes considered that Moloch was just like Hel herself in that insatiable desire for more. Hel did not want hearts for love, either. She used them, drained them, broke them, and felt some temporary pleasure from having hurt others the way she had been hurt as a child, but it was never enough. There had to be more and more. She was fatal to him and all men. She belonged dead and yet, he would give his very soul to have her back.

That was the promise Moloch had made him. Very quietly one night, he heard the voice in his head, "If you give me the blood of innocent newborns, you shall have Hel for all eternity."

He hadn't understood how such a thing was possible at the time. He didn't need to understand for Moloch only demanded Rotwang demonstrate his faith and trust in his newfound god. Rotwang was accustomed to believing he could find honor among the most terrible of monstrosities for not only had he loved Hel with all his heart, he loved her still, even now, after all her betrayals, after her terrible death.

Rotwang bent down and grasped the infant in his arms. Only now had he realized how uncontrollably the child was wailing. The poor helpless infant, hungry and cold and scared knew nothing but a rending pain and a mercifully quick death as Rotwang plunged the dagger through its tiny chest. He held the infant's body out into the gaping iron mouth of his god and let the blood pour out over that lascivious tongue eager to lap at the life-juices of the sinless. Hel was so like Moloch, so terrible…and yet, if Moloch would give him the means of restoring her to life and giving her heart to him, it was well worth committing such unspeakable crimes to sate the demon he dared call a god.

Tears streaked Rotwang's cheeks as the flames consumed the infant's bloodied body. The stench was unbearable. The first few times, he had actually been sick, but now he only wept in silence for it was the only time he could release the pain from his tormented soul. Another innocent life destroyed while Moloch laughed and Rotwang wept. The man who loved Hel more than all others had found Hell as his reward.

# PART (4)

"Papa, you're home!" Freder yelled excitedly as he saw the black sedan pull into the driveway.

The days were long with his tutor and the boy longed for play and fresh air and the sunlight that crept through the blinds upon the windows of his study. Freder lived in the most beautiful home in all of Metropolis, but the boy was so very lonely, like his mother before him, but none had yet corrupted him and so his heart was still pure and untouched by evil. Soon, that would all change, for his father had promised to ensure his son grew up to be a man.

"Would you like to play a game, Papa? Would you like to play Chess, perhaps?"

Joh Fredersen sighed. The boy could not understand what it was to be Master of Metropolis. No one worked harder than he, though he did not sweat and slave underground to fuel the furnaces that powered the city. Joh Fredersen gave his very life; his very soul to Metropolis for it was Metropolis that made him feel loved. It was Metropolis that made him feel important and needed and intelligent and powerful. It was Metropolis that fed him the lie that no one was more intelligent than he and no one wielded more power than he. He had built Metropolis. It had been his vision from the start. It was his path to greatness. Metropolis was his city… his new Tower of Babel that would reach the clouds and allow him to unseat God Himself from His throne. All that was demanded in return was that Joh Fredersen willingly gave his entire life to his work. He had no wife, there was just the boy. Fredersen was a man; he had no time for childish games.

"Tomorrow, I swear to you, Freder," he told the disappointed child just as he had every night, except for those when the boy was already asleep when he returned home from his office. His office…his gateway to rule over his dominion…his portal to look out over all of Metropolis and see that it was good. Joh Fredersen was a slave to his dream city, but he could not see it for it had convinced him he was its master. Like so many great men, Joh Fredersen chose to believe the lies.

"Would you read me a story, Papa?" Freder asked. The timbre of the boy's voice betrayed his loneliness and desperation for some connection with the father who did not love him and chose to abandon him without ever leaving.

"Freder, I'm surprised at you! I've told you before you are too old for me to read stories to you. If you must have stories at your age, you must read them yourself."

"I...I only wanted you to read a short one so that I could show you the story I wrote today..."

"A man does not need to dream up stories, Freder. A man lives his life. Put away your toys and stop daydreaming. Make something of yourself, Freder. Make me proud. Be a man."

Freder felt himself sink lower than ever before. He would never be like his father. He would never give up his dreams, his hope of escaping to a better world. He could not know that his father had felt the same when he made Metropolis his prison world.

The boy retreated to his room and flung himself upon his bed. He twisted his pillow sideways so that it rested beneath his chest. He hugged it as if it were the father he dreamed of having. His tears were warm, but the pillow was soft as he rubbed his eyes dry.

This could not be his real home. This could not have been his real family. He must have been stolen from his real family. They would not have a great house, but there would be a mother and father who loved one another. They would be good people and Freder would have a brother and sister. There was a hole in their life now for they had lost their son just as there was a hole in his life for he had lost his true family. Freder's real father would love art and music and read stories and dream up new ones when all the old ones had been exhausted. He would never discourage his son from dreaming, he would never deny him his company...he would never betray his trust. His real father would love him. His real father would be someone he could love.

Freder used to feel guilty for rejecting his father, but now he felt nothing for him and that made him feel even worse. The boy shut his eyes tight, hoping to cry, but no tears would come. The pain in his heart ached, but his heart would release no more tears that day. It was then the idea came to him. He knew how he would win his father's affections. He should have thought of it sooner.

Joh Fredersen was working in his study when there was a knock upon his door. "What is it?" he snapped. "Freder!" he gasped in surprise since it was long after the boy's bedtime.

"I've brought you a present, Papa."

"You've brought me a present?" Fredersen laughed, but for a moment he actually felt touched at the gesture. "Freder, you know better. I have all a man could want. I have no time for presents."

He looked closely at the boy's face, so like his mother's. He looked at the tears that were welling in the corner of his eyes. Slowly, the boy approached his desk and withdrawing his arm from behind his back set a paperweight down upon it.

Joh Fredersen reached forward, mystified, and lifted the glass likeness of his dream city up from the desk.

"Where did you get this, boy?"

Freder smiled at the way his father's voice shook with emotion.

"I found it in the trash can in your office the day Señor Rosas changed."

"What do you mean the day he changed?" Fredersen set the paperweight down and stared hard at the boy.

"He used to scare me, but that day he was different and I've liked him ever since."

Fredersen felt relief in spite of the perspiration that had unexpectedly dotted his forehead in response to his son's remark. Rotwang really had succeeded in perfecting Rosas and all the others that he had replaced with synthetic upgrades one by one. The boy had noted the difference, but preferred the synthetic man to the flesh and blood original. This was truly proof of their victory.

The boy pointed to the paperweight on the desk as he spoke, "The city was sticky to touch from that dark red syrup that was all over it, but Señor Rosas washed it off for me. He told me you could always wash away a stain no matter how deep it ran. He said that a man could always be saved if he would just wash away the stain. He's a nice man. I like him lots."

"Yes," Joh Fredersen said, but the words of the synthetic man disturbed him and he wondered if it was indicative of a flaw in his design.

# PART (5)

Moloch burned. He had watched these imitative chimps build their pointless monuments to their fame everlasting through the centuries. He had watched those same monuments crumble and be forgotten to antiquity after first being covered in moss and abandoned by the descendants of those that built them. And to think they believed they had evolved. The truth was it was Moloch who spurred them on to greatness for it was through their hubris he would claim their souls.

Moloch hungered. These imitative chimps had first caught his attention when they were barely out of the caves. They were nomadic tribesmen wandering desert lands in search of meaning, eager to believe any explanation for how their world came to be, eager to bow down and worship whatever they could not understand. It had not been difficult to impress them. Sometimes they knew his true name, other times they called him Baal or Apis or the Horned God. He was Legion. All it took was but a whisper and the word spread like fire. The innocent children were cast in the flames far and wide. First their enemies' children, then the children of their servants, and finally their own children were offered up. Nothing was too good for their god.

Moloch laughed. So much blood and so many tears...the women gnashed their teeth and beat their breasts and tore their garments to see the fate of their children. So it was that he whispered to them a second time and it was done. Drums were beat throughout the sacrifices to drown out their lamentations. Laws were passed that penalized the women for any public display of grief. The laws became more draconian, in keeping with his will, and the women were required to smile while their children burned. These imitative chimps had so much potential. He loved moving among their numbers in search of more souls to damn.

Moloch waited. There was a limit to the intelligence of these desert people. They were the first to embrace him as a god, it was true, but he required much more. He required a conquering spirit that would spread his name throughout the world. He required far more than these scattered tribes of merchants and fishermen, he required an empire. He required a proud people who knew the shame of their recent barbarian past. A conquering people who would absorb the culture and beliefs of all they vanquished for always they were conscious they had no legacy of their own worth preserving. Oh these Romans were so easy to manipulate. They promised so much more than the Levantines with their wailing misery and petty grievances. Moloch was happy to promise the Romans so much more in return provided their empire spread across this miserable planet.

Moloch schemed. He was patient despite the unending conflict with the so-called God of Abraham. There had been an unending contest between the two over which would be worshipped by the nomadic tribes that claimed kinship to that revered patriarch who was barely more than a savage by contemporary reckoning. Now it had taken a turn for the worse when that fool of a Roman Emperor decided to embrace the same God. All of Moloch's careful planning seemed to have been for naught, but he soon had a contingency plan in place. If he would not be worshipped by an empire, then he would infiltrate their numbers from all levels and corrupt from within.

Moloch whispered. It was said that where two or three gathered in the name of the God of Abraham, He was there. So it was that Moloch strove to add a third to every couple to form a romantic triangle. He could wreak untold havoc for generations by exploiting the weakness for the pleasures of the flesh in these imitative chimps. Once he destroyed their families, he could have access to their children. Once he corrupted their children, he would have their world.

Moloch would be patient a while longer. He turned his gaze to Metropolis. He loved that city with its priapic spires threatening to violate the heavens. He hadn't been so proud of his influence on those imitative chimps since Babylon. And he owed it all to one woman. Hel was her name. He had been with her since childhood. Twisting her, tormenting her, taking her natural beauty and goodness and distorting it into something terrible with an insatiable need for devotion.

Every Babylon must have its whore. Hel grew into an alluring, fiercely intelligent creature who was the perfect snare for the hearts of so many men. She learned to be everything they wanted her to be and could never find a moment's peace to know what she wanted for herself. Thanks to his tinkering with her when she was young, she would never know. Her path took her from one man to the next.

She was the perfect trap. She would always appear to be the prize these men had dreamed of all their lives. When he had first set upon her, he could never have imagined how useful she would prove. He knew she would be a destructive force who would inflict damage on others before destroying herself, but he could never have foreseen the repercussions that would follow in her wake. He swelled with pride as if she had been his creation and not just a child he had corrupted.

Thanks to her, Metropolis stood today as a testament to man's vanity and the two men responsible for the most amazing city in the world were both lost because of her interference in their lives. Thanks to them, the souls of everyone in this great city were lost. And thanks to her, Rotwang was on the verge of creating a parody of her that would do even more damage and usher in a new artificial race of beings to spread over the world.

Moloch laughed for it was with Parody that he would have his greatest triumph. For it was with a parody of the human race that he would sow the seeds to destroy this world once and for all. For now, there was just the machine-man with which Rotwang sought to realize his dream of restoring Hel to life.

Rotwang felt his eyelids flutter. There were times when he felt as if Moloch lived inside his mind and he knew the demon's thoughts. Such hatred…such burning hatred for the human race from the dawn of time. Usually Rotwang told himself it was his own bitter cynicism giving rise to such thoughts, but other times he believed he had a psychic bond to the demon and that it shared its memories with him.

The machine-man was the next step up from his synthetic men. A fully functional machine-man would truly be artificial life as complex and as varied as any born from the womb. He was so close. It was just a matter of days before he could bring Parody to life. Yes, he did envision making Parody be Hel reborn, but he feared she would callously crush his heart a second time. No, it was better if he found a different face for Parody…a face that would ensnare the heart of young Freder. He had watched the boy grow to manhood. The best way to destroy your enemy was to destroy that which mattered most to him. Letting Parody lead young Freder to ruination until he could not bear to live with the pain any longer would be the sweetest revenge he could inflict on Joh Fredersen.

His mind turned back to Hel, the only woman he had ever loved. He knew he was not a handsome man. The opposite sex had never paid him any mind and he, likewise, was untroubled by their presence in the world. They tolerated one another only. He had been dedicated to his studies as a schoolboy and to his research as a man. He had no time for petty affairs of the heart…until he first set eyes upon Hel.

She was like no other woman. The sun seemed to shine from her face when she smiled. Her beauty was beyond compare. She gave him a confidence he had always lacked. She made him feel special. She promised him he was special to her. Later, he would learn she said these same words to others before him and during their time together. She understood that so many men were driven by insecurities. She knew how to reach them and build them up. The words she deployed were carefully chosen to convince the recipient the sentiments expressed were unique to him.

As much as he loved Hel, Rotwang understood that she was, at heart, a cruel and faithless woman and would never be anything else. That same pain was what he wanted to share with Freder, Hel's son. Parody would be his means of initiating the young man into the world of a pain that never ends, a broken heart that never heals. Parody would corrupt him or destroy him. It mattered little which outcome was the final result so long as Joh Fredersen's son suffered. It was the best revenge he could have on the friend who had stolen the woman he loved from his side.

It had been torture continuing to work with Fredersen and seeing the two of them together. Rotwang was reliant upon Fredersen for not only his job, but his very identity. A consequence of that dependence was seeing Fredersen as the man Hel chose as her husband. It was more than Rotwang could bear and so it drove him to desperation…it drove him to Moloch. It took a devil to understand the suffering Rotwang endured at the hands of that woman. It took a devil to understand he both loved and hated her. It took a devil to appreciate that everything about Metropolis reflected that duality. Hel drove Rotwang to reach greater heights, but ultimately he wanted to hurl her from the city's tallest precipice. Parody was his means of having her back once having seen her dead and buried.

Oddly, Hel's own death had left him numb. He did not cry. He knew only emptiness. He did not pity Fredersen. Although his old friend took the loss of his wife hard, Rotwang felt no compassion. Whatever hurt Fredersen suffered, it was not enough to compensate for the betrayal he knew. The tap of his burning rage had opened. There was no going back. It would consume him and then…Moloch take his soul.

Rotwang glanced down at the shrouded female form beneath the white sheet on the table before him. He ran a quivering hand lovingly over its every curve. He started with the feet and worked his way up to the head. Cold metal every inch of her. He needed warmth. He needed to make Parody fan the flames of ardor in the hearts of all who beheld her. A moving statue was not the answer. He needed more than another achievement of the technical superiority of Metropolis. He needed more than the semblance of life. He needed a woman…a warm, willing seductress who would tempt man with more than forbidden fruit. Original sin was not enough, Rotwang needed Parody to lead man to damnation. Moloch demanded it and Rotwang would obey his god.

He pulled the sheet back and beheld that still and lifeless metallic form. It was feminine, yes, there was no denying it, but it was a machine more than a woman. Angrily, he tore the sheet off the table and cast it to the floor. He climbed, awkwardly, onto the top of Parody's unmoving body and lifted himself over her so that his face was inches from the immobile metal features of the woman he created. He bent his head to hers and, shutting his eyes, pretended it was Hel beneath him once more. His lips parted and touched hers. They were cold to touch. He felt his saliva spread upon the shiny metal surface and found himself sobbing uncontrollably.

She was hideous. She was a monster. He could not make a woman. He could not bring Hel back to Life. Moloch had cheated him. Moloch had led him to his greatest height only to let him fall to the lowest point. He could not bear this. The pain was too great. No man with his intelligence should work so hard and fail. There was no justice. Who was to blame for this? God was the only answer. Rotwang hated God with every fiber of his being.

Biting down hard, his teeth sunk into his own forearm savagely. It was a foolish gesture, certainly, but the part of him that still believed he was created by God saw it as the only means of spiting his Creator. The pain was not what he anticipated. The blood was warm and smooth as it spread quickly across his forearm and dripped onto his chin. It was not yet sticky, but more akin to the sweetest syrup he had ever tasted. It felt strange in his mouth. Soft upon his tongue and yet heavy as it collected in the back of his throat. He fought back a wave of revulsion as he forced himself to swallow it down.

Releasing his hold on his arm at last, he turned it and let the blood drip down onto the face of Parody beneath him. He watched the crimson stain bring color to her lips and cheeks. Somehow, his blood made this woman of shiny reflective surfaces appear alive for the first time. He lowered himself almost reverently with no thought of his self-inflicted injury. Shutting his eyes once more, he believed it was Hel beneath him and he kissed those blood-smeared lips with all the passion he could muster.

Her lips felt warm!

It must be an illusion, he told himself. He was merely tasting the warmth of his own blood. He looked down upon that face with its marvelous cheekbones and proud nose and watched the blood cascade down either side of the face. He kissed her again, even more passionately this time until he was convinced communion was achieved and they were one flesh.

He was not mistaken, his blood had warmed her cold metal lips. Not only the lips, but gradually he felt the warmth spread beneath him. It was as if Parody was thawing from some deep freeze and letting passion claim her body once more. He had done it. He had achieved his dream. Hel was alive. She just needed blood. Just like Moloch. The blood was the life. The blood held the key.

His blood. His blood. His blood. He repeated the phrase like a mantra as he rose and fell on that hard metal body and basked in the warmth that started to envelop it. Hel would live. No, he was mistaken. Parody would live. Parody was alive. She slept yet, but soon she would awaken and take her place among the gods.

It had been worth the lives of the infants that Moloch had demanded for centuries. After all, had Hel not paid with her life for the infant Freder to be born? Rotwang bit into his forearm again and again. A starving man handed the fleshy leg of a steer would have behaved no differently.

More blood, he heard Moloch cry out, I must have more blood.

More blood, he heard Parody plead with him, I must have more blood.

There would be more blood, Rotwang swore it. First Freder, then the boy's father. It would not end there. The workers and their children. Those despicable starving beggars that lived underground. Their blood would flow through the streets of Metropolis as if a Great Deluge offered to appease the wrath of Moloch.

Fools, Rotwang laughed, Moloch was insatiable in his bloodlust just as Hel was insatiable in her sexual lust…just as Rotwang was insatiable in his burning need for revenge. Somewhere, Moloch stirred inside the dark corners of Rotwang's minds and intoned, "I will be satisfied."

# THE END

# METROPOLIS: BEHIND EVERY GREAT MAN

It started with a dream. I woke up one morning nearly two years ago with a clear idea of Part Two of this story and with the present title in my head. I wrote it down and thought of it as my *THX-1138*...in other words, yet another dystopian offspring of *Metropolis*. Fritz Lang's German films have always been special to me, particularly his three *Dr. Mabuse* films and *Metropolis*. The latter already worked its influence on a Sherlock Holmes story I wrote about six years ago. I filed my story idea and title away for future use and really thought no more about it until Ron Fortier announced that Airship 27 was preparing this anthology. I immediately signed on unaware of what was waiting for me in my private life.

Work generally gives us our identity. I found myself managing a crew of 160 in a 24/7/365 operation in the oil sands of rural Alberta. I lived in a work camp, worked punishing hours, and generally fell apart as a human being in terms of mental and physical health. While I was unraveling in the wilderness and learning my own lesson about heart needing to unite head and hand in labor, my fifteen-year-old son had discovered *Metropolis* for himself and felt compelled to write a story.

Over the phone one night, he shared with me his idea for what became Part One of this story. Together we brain-stormed and found a way to make his idea dovetail with mine. The idea of collaborating with my son was obviously attractive to me. The finished version of Part One is only slightly modified from the draft Michael emailed me just before Christmas 2014.

Since we had already filled in much of the backstory to the film with the first two parts of the story, I went back to Thea Von Harbou's original novel for inspiration. I was struck by how strong a role the occult and religious symbolism played in her formation of the story. I knew then that I wanted to do something with the pagan god Moloch and Parody the *maschinen-mensch* to highlight their connection to Rotwang.

The latter was of such interest to me because the character was played by Rudolf Klein-Rogge, an actor who was a staple of Lang's German work. The interesting personal connection that existed between Lang and Klein-Rogge was that both men had been married to Thea Von Harbou. She was Klein-Rogge's wife first until her affair with Lang ended their

52

marriage. Klein-Rogge subsequently acted for Fritz Lang during the time Von Harbou was now Lang's wife and screenwriter. The complexity of this romantic triangle immediately suggested the triangle between Rotwang, Joh Fredersen, and Hel that forms the backstory of *Metropolis*. This seemed the obvious parallel from life to art at work behind this seminal film.

Armed with this knowledge, I threw myself into Rotwang's world and imagined the sort of man he was, what his boyhood had been like, how he had failed to fit into society before finding his way with his intellect. I considered what Hel must have been like to have loved two such different men as Rotwang and Joh Fredersen. I considered that Hel must have been the key to Rotwang's madness. She would drive him between extremes of love and hate and would lead him to take a pagan deity from antiquity and give voice to it as a separate persona within his own fevered brain.

The fact that so much of my story was driven by madness and voices from the grave or the preternatural seemed just the right mix. After all, there's always something behind every great man to drive him to reaching greater heights. Whether that something is a demon or a woman, all artists require a muse to remain inspired. For Fritz Lang and Rudolf Klein-Rogge; that muse was Thea Von Harbou. I dedicate this story to that unholy union that inspired such great art.

✠✠✠

**William Patrick Maynard** is the authorized continuation writer for the new *Fu Manchu* thrillers published by Black Coat Press. His short fiction has appeared in various anthologies including *The Ruby Files*, published by Airship 27. After 12 years of property management work all over the continent, he finds himself back home with his family in Northeast Ohio hoping to recover his health and his sanity.

**Michael Richard Maynard** will have celebrated his sixteenth birthday by the time of this story's publication. He is a passionate student of the works of J. R. R. Tolkien and George Lucas' *Star Wars* and *Indiana Jones* franchises. This is his first published story.

# THE METROPOLIS MURDERS

## MICHAEL PANUSH

Wide windows formed the walls of Boss Moroder's sumptuously furnished penthouse apartment. Eisenstein stood before the window, staring down at grandeur of Metropolis's bustling skyline through his round, mirrored spectacles. He put his hands in his trench coat as his eyes drifted over the city. Endless skyscrapers, the crisscrossing causeways bristling with automated trains and roaring traffic, and swarms of buzzing biplanes and hulking zeppelins sprawled out before him; an infinite city, with no beginning and no end. The New Tower of Babel, bulbous and massive, loomed over it all. Eisenstein removed his fedora, clutching the hat in his thick hands. For a private detective, Metropolis was a true city of opportunity.

Boss Moroder sat behind him on a Morris chair, his bulk clad in a velvet smoking jacket. A cigar puffed in the corner of his mouth, the smoke obscuring his red face and thinning hair. "Admiring the view, Eisenstein?" Boss Moroder flipped through the day's copy of the *Metropolis Courier*. "It's a good one, I'll admit. But lately, the city's turning sour on me."

Eisenstein turned slowly. His eyes settled on Boss Moroder, the biggest crime lord in Metropolis. Boss Moroder ruled a vast network of gambling halls, narcotics smuggling, and other rackets, stretching from the spires of the main city to the Depths where the workers dwelled. "And why exactly is that?" Eisenstein spoke in a clipped, brisk manner, like the conversation annoyed him.

In answer, Boss Moroder tossed down the copy of the *Courier* on the geometric glass coffee table. Eisenstein could read the headline; the Laughing Man had taken another victim. For the past three months, the Laughing Man had been killing in Metropolis. This latest victim meant he had killed seven people. They were mostly from the Depths, poor workers who mattered only to their families. A chorus girl from the Yoshiwara Pleasure District had been the fourth to die, which drew a decent amount of attention. But it was the way the Laughing Man left the bodies that had earned him his fame and his moniker. He carved smiles into the faces of the bodies, piercing their lips and slicing open their cheeks to put a garish, fleshy grin on each corpse. The police searched everywhere for the Laughing Man, but had little success. Eisenstein didn't expect them to.

The two men looked at the newspaper. "What does it matter to you?" Eisenstein asked. "The Laughing Man hasn't got to any of your people. Apart from the chorus girl, the victims have all been from the Depths. Worker's blood spills daily in this city."

"It ain't the blood," Boss Moroder explained. He leaned over and stubbed his cigar into a glass ash tray. White smoke trickled up as he mashed the cigar. "It's what the blood brings. The police have been searching everywhere for the Laughing Man, and some bright spark figured that the freak is a criminal and that means that he must be in one of my establishments. Ever since the second murder, my establishments have been raided, my men have been pulled off the street for questioning, and my operations have screeched to a halt." He reclined in his seat, staring angrily at the ceiling. "I've had heists that I bankrolled and had to call off. Shipments have been delayed to stop the cops from seizing them." He pointed to the paper. "I'm telling you, Eisenstein, this Laughing Man freak has caused me all kinds of grief."

"Less grief than his victims, I'd say."

"Hmmm." Boss Moroder snorted. "Come on, Eisenstein. He's got this whole city terrified. All of Metropolis is afraid that the knock at the door will be the Laughing Man, coming to carve his smiles. He's targeted the old, the young; men and women. He needs to be stopped, before he kills again. You know it as well as I do."

Eisenstein shrugged. "I never took you for the kind concerned with the public good."

"He needs to be stopped so my businesses can continue. How about that?" Boss Moroder popped open the rosewood case on the corner of his coffee table. He produced another cigar. "The police are saps. You know that as well as I do. Joh Fredersen himself could be barking down their backs and they still couldn't think smart enough to catch the Laughing Man. That's why they're raiding my dives, I think, just so they can say they're doing something. They'll never catch him." Boss Moroder pointed at Eisenstein. "But you can."

"You think so?" Eisenstein turned his fedora over in his hand.

"Sure." Boss Moroder used a cutter to snip off the tip of his cigar. He jabbed it between his teeth and snapped a lighter to life. "You arrived in Metropolis just a few years ago, and your little detective agency has been booming. You cracked the case about the Modern Golem terrorizing the catacombs a few years back. You captured that Vep woman, that Bat-Winged Murderess, as well. And I'm gonna give you an even better reason for catching the Laughing Man."

"I'm not sure I want to get involved with monsters, Mr. Moroder." Eisenstein glanced at his boots. "For any reason."

Boss Moroder torched his cigar. He sucked in smoke and expelled it as he leaned back in his chair like some contented devil. "You've got a vice, Eisenstein. You gamble. You go to the tables in Yoshiwara and all the money you make seems to drift away. It's like you don't want to keep it. Like you're afraid of not living hand to mouth. But right now, your luck has been fading. You're in deep. But I'll make you this deal." He pointed at Eisenstein with his cigar. "Find the Laughing Man and your debts will be forgiven. I know the casinos where you gamble. I know their owners. I can clear all your debts. Once again, you'll be a free man."

"A free man," Eisenstein repeated. He set his fedora on his head. He didn't have much choice about taking the case now. Besides, Boss Moroder was right. The cops didn't stand a chance of catching the Laughing Man. Maybe he could do the job. "Do I need to kill this fellow?" he asked. "Or just find him?"

"You find him," Boss Moroder explained. "Then you contact me. My boys will handle the rest."

"No trial?" Eisenstein asked. "No chance for him to defend himself?"

"He's a sick murderer...a deranged freak." Boss Moroder shrugged. "He belongs in Hell. I'm more than happy to send him there." The cigar swiveled in his mouth. "Rondo! Give Mr. Eisenstein money for expenses."

Rondo, Boss Moroder's broad-shouldered bodyguard and butler, crossed the room. Rondo was a giant in a black velvet tuxedo with a stiff arrow collar and dark tie, his misshapen head, with its square chin and drooping nose, wedged between his broad shoulders. He handed Eisenstein an envelope thick with cash. Rondo bowed politely and stepped back to loom beside Boss Moroder's chair like some overgrown hunting hound. He might very well be the one to kill the Laughing Man after Eisenstein found him.

"You'll take the case?" Boss Moroder asked.

"I'll take the case," Eisenstein agreed. He pocketed the cash. "I've got my girl Hildy on the landing dock on the roof. She'll whisk me away and I'll begin my investigation." He tipped his fedora to Boss Moroder and Rondo. "I'll contact you shortly and let you know how things are progressing."

Boss Moroder nodded. "That's what I like about you, Eisenstein, you're a professional." He waved to the open cigar case. "You want a cigar?"

"I don't smoke." Eisenstein walked past him, heading for the door in the corner.

"Always the professional!" Boss Moroder called after him as Eisenstein brushed his way through the doors. Eisenstein left Boss Moroder to his cigars as he crossed the hallway and went to the gilded elevator, with its shimmering walls. He told the elevator boy to take him to the roof. Eisenstein leaned against the far wall of the elevator as it hummed upwards. He had to get airborne. Metropolis housed an immense population, with towering heights, drooping slums, and not much in between. The search for a single killer wouldn't be easy. Eisenstein didn't want to waste time before going to work. Boss Moroder didn't strike him as the patient sort.

The elevator reached the rooftop landing dock. Eisenstein tossed a coin to the elevator boy as he stepped onto the rooftop. A wind rustled past him, stirring his trench coat as he strode across the gray cement. A heavy zeppelin sailed above the sky, its silver gasbag catching the sun. Biplanes and monoplanes rested in neat rows on the roof, waiting to roll down a small runway and zoom into the sky. Eisenstein walked toward the boxy biplane at the end of the row, a swallow-blue machine with a yellow propeller and a colorful constellation of planets painted along the sleek sides.

A young woman leaned against the plane, reading a pulp magazine. She glanced up as Eisenstein approached. "Hello, boss." She tucked the magazine into the pocket of her sheepskin-lined flying jacket, a smile crossing her face. "How'd the meeting go?"

"We've got a case, Hildy." Eisenstein patted the envelope in his pocket. "A big one."

Hildy Kovacs wore a pair of goggles, dangling down over the slim tie she wore under her flight jacket. She pulled up the goggles and smoothed back her short auburn hair. She had started work as Eisenstein's secretary, but he quickly realized that Hildy was far more useful as a pilot. She was a master behind the wheel of any aircraft, and loved soaring through the crowded skyline of Metropolis. Now, she served as Eisenstein's personal pilot, as well as his assistant and his friend.

She gave the propeller a push now, sending it into a spinning blur, and motioned for Eisenstein to join her in the cockpit. "So it's time to fly?" she asked. They walked to the side of the plane. Hildy took the foremost seat, scrambling behind the throttle and controls, while Eisenstein settled into the back. He didn't enjoy flying nearly as much as Hildy.

"You do love piloting, don't you?" Eisenstein asked. "You could be the first woman on the moon, Hildy."

"I'd love that." Hildy twisted the throttle. The biplane rumbled out of its space and neared the runway. "Where do I sign up for the rocket that'll take me there?"

Eisenstein leaned back in the seat. At least Hildy knew exactly what she wanted. The plane rattled under his seat and he reached for the safety belt. The biplane shot down the runway, tremors creaking through the metal, and then it reached the small ramp at the end. The biplane flew nimbly into the air, caught the wind, and soared. Hildy swung to the side and they zoomed past the hulk of the apartment building, then soared past the skyscrapers as they sped through Metropolis. They sped over causeways and elevated trains, flying free in the gray sky.

Hildy glanced back from the cockpit. "So what's the case, boss?" A speaking tube connected to the back, so Eisenstein could hear her perfectly. "What is it this time? Thieves stealing Baghdad antiques from the Metropolis Museum? Another Andalusian dog-fighting ring in the catacombs?"

"The Laughing Man," Eisenstein replied.

That made Hildy fall silent for a few moments. "You sure about that, boss?"

"All I've got to do is find him," Eisenstein explained. "Boss Moroder will do the rest."

"But the Laughing Man…he's a monster." Hildy gripped the throttle tightly, guiding their biplane down through the buzzing traffic to a less crowded section of the sky. "I've read about what he did in the papers. He's killed seven people, boss. The police can't find him, though they've been trying. Do you think we can really do better?"

"Sure," Eisenstein agreed. "Because the cops aren't looking in the right places."

They zoomed under a causeway. An advertising boy perched on the bridge, tossing down fliers for the latest nightclubs in the Yoshiwara district. Hildy turned the plane, shaking Eisenstein in his seat as they avoided the rain of multi-colored handbills. "So where are we gonna look?" Hildy asked. They zoomed past the causeway and buzzed upwards.

"All, but one, of the Laughing Man's victims have come from the Worker City in the Depths," Eisenstein explained. "Police rarely venture down there. That's what I want you to do. Land the biplane somewhere safe and take the tunnels down to the Depths. Ask around, see if there's anything that connect the victims. Most killers have a certain type of victim that they want, but the Laughing Man's killed all sorts. There must be some pattern that nobody can see." He leaned a little closer, clutching the speaking trumpet tightly. "Is that all right with you?"

"I can handle it, boss," Hildy agreed. "Don't worry."

"Be careful, Hildy. No risks. If you feel that you're danger, get out of the Depths, get into your plane, and fly away." He pushed up his mirrored spectacles. "Sometimes, the surface of the moon can be a safer place than Metropolis."

"What about you, boss?" Hildy asked. "What are gonna do?"

The biplane buzzed past a large neon sign advertising the *Metropolis Courier*. It glowed a brilliant green, even in the daytime. "Take me to the Yoshiwara District. Drop me off the nearest landing dock. I can get where I need to on foot."

"The Yoshiwara District?" Hildy asked with a grin. "What are you going to do in all those nightclubs and casinos?" She twisted the plane, turning around a skyscraper on the way to the Yoshiwara District.

"I'm going to talk with an angel," Eisenstein replied.

The biplane buzzed through the city, speeding him to his destination.

✠✠✠

The Yoshiwara Pleasure District extended for miles, a neon wonderland of stacked nightclubs, crisscrossing walkways, and all manner of vice offered for sale on every corner. The more Bohemian residents of Metropolis frequented Yoshiwara, along with the wealthy heirs of the City Fathers, who spent their families' fortunes in the countless casinos and clubs. Hildy dropped Eisenstein off on one of the upper landing docks and he descended into the neon underworld of the Pleasure District. He walked down a coiling, wide spiral staircase. A few dancing girls on their break relaxed on the platform before their nightclub, smoking cigarettes in their elaborate sequined and feathered gowns. They nodded to Eisenstein as he walked past them. He glanced at a well-dressed drunk in cutaway coat and tails, a monocle poised in his eye. The poor fellow lay on his knees, puking off the railing and sending his vomit rushing down into oblivion. Eisenstein offered him some cash and told him to go find some coffee. Then he came to the bottom of the stairwell, the lower section of Yoshiwara.

An enclosed pathway led to a shadowy establishment. The neon sign showed an azure female angel, her wings flapping in sequence as her impassive, beautiful face watched every customer. The sign below the angel explained that this was the Blue Angel Cabaret. Eisenstein had visited the Blue Angel Cabaret many times; drawn there by the shining lights and the promise of the dancers. He knew the owner and she knew him. They weren't exactly friends, but they would help each other out now and then. Maybe that was the best Eisenstein could hope for in Metropolis.

He pushed past the doors. A hulking bouncer in a dark blue, checkered suit looked him over and nodded, and then he stepped into the main room. The audience, the well-dressed young sons of the rich and a few middle executives and office workers, crowded before the stage while a trio of cabaret dancers in short, spangled costumes weaved their way through a high-kicking routine. A jazz band careened their way through a tune in the corner, making the whole cabaret rock with a pounding beat. Eisenstein walked past the audience and went to the bar at the back. A pudgy bartender poured drinks from cool blue bottles, all set in neat rows. Eisenstein settled down on a stool, turned around, and watched the show. Soon enough, he would be noticed.

"Mr. Eisenstein." The voice, low and husky, came from the end of the bar. Madam Dussel, the owner of the Blue Angel, approached him with a smile. She wore a black suit and bowtie, her shining blonde hair in neat waves beneath her top hat. A cigarette smoldered in the ivory holder between her fingers. "Would you care for a drink, darling?"

"Thank you for the offer, but I'd rather not," Eisenstein explained.

Madam Dussel settled on the stool next to him. "You never drink." She puffed on her cigarette as she hooked a thumb into her cummerbund. "What brings you to the Blue Angel Cabaret, Mr. Eisenstein? Have you come for the atmosphere?"

"It's the best in Metropolis," Eisenstein replied.

"Flattery." Madam Dussel wiggled her cigarette holder at him. "What do you want, Eisenstein?"

"I'm on a case." He lowered his voice. "I'm hunting someone. The Laughing Man."

Madam Dussel's smile vanished. "The girl who died...the chorus girl. She did not work in the Blue Angel. I do not know why you have come here. Or even why you are searching for a monster like the Laughing Man. Isn't that the job of the police?"

"They know the tune," Eisenstein explained. "But they don't know the steps." He turned to face the dancers, his eyes following their rhythmic kicks. Their high-heeled shoes glowed slightly, leaving curling trails through the smoky air. "And you're right. The chorus girl worked in another club. But the killer has a taste for women, I think, or maybe just a taste for flesh. He'll want to go somewhere flesh is on display, so he can sit back and watch." He gestured to the audience. "The police would never raid this place. They might find the sons of the some of the City Fathers attending the shows. Cause far too much embarrassment for everyone.

The Laughing Man knows that. If he wants somewhere he can sit back and watch, he'll go to a cabaret and there is none better than the Blue Angel."

"Not exactly a compliment I can appreciate," Madam Dussel replied. "But you know how it is. We get all sorts coming in, watching the girls. We do our best to protect them. Acts of violence are thankfully rare, but they do occasionally occur." She glanced at Eisenstein. "I think we can protect ourselves."

"Not from the Laughing Man," Eisenstein replied. "Not from someone like him."

"So what do you want from me, then?" Madam Dussel asked. "Shall I talk to the guests? Ask if they've carved smiles into any faces recently?"

Eisenstein shook his head. "No need. The Laughing Man will mostly likely have a strange appearance. Perhaps that is why he disfigures his victims; he wishes for them to look like him. He will be isolated and alone. A stranger to all around him." He scanned the cabaret, examining the secluded booths. "He will be quiet and polite, but very reserved and private. Do you know anyone like that? With a strange appearance?"

"That could be said about yourself, darling. You do never seem to remove your spectacles."

"I'm not the Laughing Man," Eisenstein replied. "I know that at least."

"Well, there is someone who comes to mind." Madam Dussel pointed to the booth at the far end of the cabaret. The shadowed booth rested near the swinging doors to the kitchen, where automated stoves prepared food. Darkness shrouded the booth and it took Eisenstein a few moments to realize that someone occupied it. A single figure sat on the black leather seat, his face hidden in shadow. He looked at the dancers, watching their movements. "He started arriving at the cabaret last month. Since then, he has arrived every day in the early afternoon without fail. He sits down, watches for a few hours, pays for a drink he does not touch, and departs. I have scarcely heard him say more than a dozen words." Madam Dussel lowered her voice. "Tell me, Eisenstein, do you think it is the Laughing Man? Here, in my place?"

"I will have to see." Eisenstein removed his fedora and set it on the bar, then gave the brim a quick flick. The hat spun and landed on the polished, tile floor. Eisenstein stood and walked to his hat. He bent down to pick it up, then stared into the booth.

The single occupant looked back at him. For just a moment, their eyes met. The stranger certainly had an odd appearance. He wore a long, ragged, dark coat with two rows of black buttons and a high collar. His head had no hair at all, with large, slightly elfin ears framing a grotesque face which could have belonged to a malnourished rat. A pointed nose protruded over a mouth full of needle-like teeth, which shone in the low light of the Blue Angel. He looked at Eisenstein and, just for a second, smiled. The grin seemed to extend too far, as if the lips had been dragged back to reveal the teeth. They shone silver. He had metal teeth, pointed like needles. His gloved hands rested on the table, the fingers impossibly thin inside their sheaths of black leather. Eisenstein turned away quickly, taking his fedora back to his stool.

He sat down next to Madam Dussel. "Well?" she asked.

"Go back to your business," Eisenstein said. "I'll wait for him to leave and tail him."

"Is it the Laughing Man?"

Eisenstein glared at her. "Keep your voice down and leave." He turned away from Madam Dussel and faced the dancers. She stared at him for a few more seconds, puffed her cigarette a final time, and then left. Eisenstein sat alone at the bar. He watched the dancers with all the others as the seconds ticked by. The fellow in the booth watched as well. Neither of them said anything or made a move. They just sat and waited.

After forty minutes or so, the man in the booth stood up. He shaded his face with a bowler hat and walked to the doors, his hands in the pockets of his coat. Eisenstein let him reach the door, then stood and followed. He walked past the bar. Madam Dussel leaned at the end of the bar, watching him with wary eyes. Eisenstein touched the brim of his fedora to her in thanks. It was the least he could do. Then he walked out through the door, following the grinning, rat-faced cabaret patron who might be the Laughing Man. He stepped into the cold air, stirred by Metropolis's winds, and walked down the geometric archways. A scrap of black turned the corner, moving down a walkway leading away from Yoshiwara. Eisenstein hustled slightly and caught up with him.

The rat-faced man crossed the walkway, which led to a wide bridge stretching between skyscrapers. Streetlights tipped with diamond-shaped lanterns glowed pale blue, adding pools of light to the walkway. Elevated trains rumbled on their tracks below, making the causeway shake slightly. Aerial traffic buzzed up above. A few people walked back and forth, mostly well-dressed couples heading for the dance halls of Yoshiwara. The rat-faced man brushed past them, his hands still jammed in his pockets. Eisenstein continued his tail.

They reached the center of the bridge. The rat-faced man turned, his dark eyes flicking back over the causeway. Eisenstein gripped the brass railing of the causeway and turned into the distance, pretending to watch a brightly-colored biplane as it rattled past. The roar of the airplane's motor faded and Eisenstein turned back to his target. The rat-faced fellow had continued heading down the causeway. Eisenstein had done enough tailing. He needed to confront the Laughing Man, if that's who he was, and find out the truth. For some reason, he didn't think the Laughing Man would deny the accusations. He was a monster, after all. Maybe he would revel in his guilt. Whatever the case, Eisenstein needed to find out the truth.

He faced the suspect and moved at a faster clip. The rat-faced man continued strolling along. He didn't notice Eisenstein until the detective bumped his shoulder into the fellow's back. The stranger slipped and stumbled but did not fall. He spun around, his dark eyes flashing. He stared into Eisenstein's mirrored spectacles, looking at the reflection of himself. He hissed slightly, not liking what he saw. The silver needle-like teeth flashed again.

Quickly, Eisenstein straightened up. "I'm very sorry, sir." He offered a quick smile. "I can be so clumsy sometimes."

"No trouble." The rat-faced man returned his gloved hands to his pockets. He had a thin, reedy voice; strangely morose.

This time, Eisenstein moved next to him matching his pace. "I saw you in the Cabaret," he explained. "The Blue Angel. In Yoshiwara." The rat-faced man said nothing. He walked ahead, his eyes focused down toward his boots. "Those dames they got dancing, they're something else. But they always look so glum." Eisenstein would have to choose his words carefully. "I wonder why they don't smile. I would like to see them grin, now and then. Let me know that they're enjoying their work. So few do, in this city."

"Yes." The rat-faced fellow stared ahead. "I certainly don't."

Eisenstein walked alongside him as they continued down the bridge. "Do you try to make people happy?" he asked. "Try to transform them? Improve them?"

The strange man curled back his lips, revealing his silver teeth again. "I do what I must."

Now it was time to spring the trap. "How do you make them smile?" Eisenstein asked it casually.

The suspect stopped. He turned around and faced Eisenstein. At that moment, Eisenstein realized that they were alone on the causeway. The

*"The rat-faced man crossed the walkway…"*

other pedestrians had finished crossing and he and a potential serial killer stood alone about two-thirds of the way across the causeway. There were no witnesses around. The rat-faced fellow held up one hand. He pulled away one glove and then the other. His hands, from the wrist on, had been replaced with mechanical claws. Eisenstein had seen mechanical hands before. One scientist that he knew very well had a metal copy of his previous hand, destroyed in his experiments. But the hands on the rat-faced fellow looked completely different. The metal fingers seemed spindly and thin. They ended in lethally curved edges; claws designed to tear and rend flesh. They were weapons. Someone had given this fellow sharp, steel claws, along with his teeth, specifically to be used as weapons.

Eisenstein looked at the claws. "How did you get those?"

"They were given to me."

"You are the Laughing Man?" Eisenstein asked it suddenly though he already knew the answer.

"I'm not laughing." The metal teeth returned, in a cold grimace. "I don't have a choice. I don't want to hurt people. I don't want to make smiles." He drew closer, his voice drifting to a squeak. "I must. I am forced. The doctor; he makes me. He speaks and I must listen." He waved his clawed hands. "You don't understand. I have no choice."

"You're a demon," Eisenstein replied. "A monster."

"I have no choice!" The Laughing Man swung a clawed hand at Eisenstein. The bladed edges of his hand cut through the air, humming as they neared Eisenstein's face. Eisenstein leaned back. The claws whistled just past his cheek. They could have slashed his face apart. He stepped away from the Laughing Man and reached into his coat. He would have to end this fast.

But the Laughing Man simply turned and ran. He pounded straight down the causeway, his metal hands flailing during his gawky run. Eisenstein withdrew his pistol, a compact automatic, and followed. Boss Moroder had promised that his goons would take care of the Laughing Man, but Eisenstein had no chance to contact him. He had to capture the Laughing Man first, or at least chase him and see where he went. Then he could call Boss Moroder and get this case over with. Otherwise, he might end up with a smile carved into his own face.

They hurried down the causeway, running together. The Laughing Man raced toward the end of the causeway and stopped, placing his back to the railing. Eisenstein stopped as well and leveled his automatic. The Laughing Man moved close to the railing. His clawed hands stretched out, playing on the brass. The two men stared at each other.

Eisenstein tried to keep his voice calm. "You don't need to do this," he explained. "Come with me. I can get you help."

"There's no helping me," the Laughing Man said. "I already have a doctor. He doesn't help." He gripped the railing tightly. Suddenly, he lifted himself up and nimbly leapt over the railing. His arms moved with mechanical swiftness. Eisenstein figured he had other implants under his skin, giving him increased strength and agility. The Laughing Man made no noise as he tumbled down. Eisenstein ran to the railing, his hand outstretched.

He reached the edge of the causeway and stared down. The Laughing Man dropped, plummeting downwards through the misty Metropolis air. For a few seconds, Eisenstein imagined him falling down, spiraling into oblivion as he fell past the skyscrapers. Instead, the Laughing Man landed on the roof of a passing elevated train. He slammed onto the roof of the cabin, his claws digging into the metal and holding on. He rose from his crouch and gazed up at Eisenstein, his dark eyes gleaming as his needle-teeth grinned. Eisenstein glared back as he replaced his pistol in his shoulder-holster. He gripped the railing as well. The Laughing Man wouldn't escape that easily.

With a single grimace, Eisenstein pulled himself over the railing. He poised over the precipice for just a second and then released his hold. He dropped, plummeting straight downwards. Eisenstein's trench coat billowed around him. He reached to his head and clamped a hand on his fedora, struggling to hold it in place. Wind tore at his face, ripping at his skin and nearly dislodging his spectacles. The elevated train drew closer. Eisenstein reached out and hoped.

His fingers gripped the edge of the nearest carriage. Eisenstein increased his grip, his legs dangling down as the train rumbled down the track. Passengers below must find it odd to see a pair of legs dangling past their windows. Eisenstein's arms twisted. His muscles stretched and then he pulled himself up. He used his elbows to help him and then lay on top of the train carriage as it rolled along. Eisenstein lay flat on his belly. The train roared along and the rumble hummed through his skin. Eisenstein looked up, staring down the train. The Laughing Man stood on the roof of another carriage, about two or three train cars over. He hadn't run yet. Eisenstein returned to his feet. He rose slowly, his legs shaking slightly as he stood, and reached into his coat for his pistol. The Laughing Man watched him. Eisenstein gritted his teeth and gave chase.

He ran down the carriage, his boots slamming against the metal roof. The gap drew closer. Eisenstein jumped it, leaping up and slamming down on the next carriage. The Laughing Man remained, watching him from his perch on the far roof. He was close enough to shoot now. Eisenstein brought up his pistol, struggling to take aim as the train continued speeding along. Eisenstein looked down the sights and squeezed the trigger.

The Laughing Man lunged for him, just as the pistol cracked. The shot blazed through the air, humming past the Laughing Man's shoulder but the killer had moved too quickly. Eisenstein had not expected him to jump and he missed. The Laughing Man pounced, leaping nimbly over the gap between train carriage and landing right in front of Eisenstein. His claws came down, slashing through the air and aimed toward Eisenstein's body. Eisenstein raised a hand to defend himself. The claws cut through his trench coat and slashed his skin. Blood stained his sleeve. He stumbled back and tried to fire again, but the Laughing Man grabbed his wrist with another clawed hand. The claws scraped against Eisenstein's wrist as they pushed the pistol down. The Laughing Man raised his free hand. He would drive the bladed tips into Eisenstein's throat and finish him for good.

He paused for just a second. "You were wrong." He leaned closer, revealing his needle teeth. "I don't want people to be happy. I don't care about the people in Metropolis, because they don't care about me. I make them smile so that they know what it's like." His own grin grew. "I want them to know what it's like to always laugh…when you really want to cry. You're going to learn that now."

"I'd rather not." Eisenstein lunged for the Laughing Man and tackled him. It was a wild tactic but it beat receiving a claw to the throat. He forced his weight against the Laughing Man. The deformed killer lost his balance. They crashed down together, the Laughing Man's back slamming hard against the roof. Eisenstein drove his fist into the Laughing Man's gut, slugging him hard. The Laughing Man's mouth opened, his needle teeth scraping the air. Eisenstein slugged him again even as the tip of a claw jabbed into his shoulder. He struggled to raise his pistol. If he could get a shot off, he could weaken the Laughing Man and finish him before those claws did any more damage.

Eisenstein pushed up the pistol, ramming it into the Laughing Man's chin. The muzzle of the gun pressed against the Laughing Man's pale skin, jabbing his head back and making his smile fade. Eisenstein struggled for the trigger. It would just take a little pressure and the Laughing Man's brains would spray on the carriage. He would never kill again.

But the Laughing Man slammed two sets of metal knuckles into Eisenstein's chest, striking with terrible speed and surprising strength.

Eisenstein rolled over, struggling to hold onto the pistol as he tumbled toward the edge of the cartop. The Laughing Man sprang back. He raised a boot. "I'm a sick man." He moaned slightly, his teeth once again forming a garish grin. "I need to see a doctor." He stared at Eisenstein. "You're a monster." He almost whispered the words. They were scarcely audible over the clatter of the rolling train.

"No," Eisenstein said. "No. That's not…"

"You know it," the Laughing Man replied. "Just as I do."

His boot lashed out before Eisenstein could stop him. He kicked Eisenstein; a mechanical blow like a striking piston. The force rippled through Eisenstein's body and knocked him back. He rolled over the edge of the train and slipped off. His hands stretched out, reaching for the train. It proved futile. Eisenstein fell down, tumbling from the train and falling down. The train blurred as it roared past him. The Laughing Man stood up and watched him fall, following him with his dark eyes. Eisenstein flailed his arms as he zoomed downwards. He would fall for miles before something hard broke his fall, and then he'd splatter all over the cement. They probably wouldn't even find his body.

+++

He thought quickly as his trench coat flapped like a flag in a storm and the wind rushed over him. He turned to the nearest building. Windows rushed by…solid glass, but they were his only hope. Eisenstein angled his body. He pressed his legs together, grabbed the edges of his trench coat, and extended them. For just a second, he would have to be like one of Hildy's biplanes and learn to fly. He gritted his teeth as the wind caught him and shoved him to the side.

The office building drew closer. Eisenstein reached out. His fingers brushed brick and cement and then caught hold of some crenellation. He swung down, his boots extended. Glass shattered under his weight and then he fell through, flying over the sill and into a small office. He tumbled through the window and struck the floor. Shattered glass landed next to him, some pointed shards jabbing into his legs. He winced at the pain. Soft carpet scraped his fingers. Eisenstein groaned as he sat up.

He had smashed through a window and landed in a small corner office. An office worker, one of the thousand clerks who kept Metropolis running, looked up from his typewriter. Electric panels of arcane economic data and several stylized clocks clicked away behind him. Eisenstein sat up. The office worker, a thin fellow with dark hair split down the middle and a neat suit and vest, gingerly stepped out from behind his desk and approached Eisenstein.

The clerk stood over Eisenstein. "Sir?" he asked. "Are you well?"

Eisenstein gave him a quick smile. "I'm fine, thank you. May I use your radio? I have to send a quick message."

"By all means." The clerk pointed to the radio at the edge of his desk. Eisenstein struggled to his feet and stumbled to the radio. He dialed in the frequency he and Hildy used. She kept a radio in her biplane. Eisenstein placed a quick call to her, asking the clerk for his address. He made the transmission quickly and then switched off the radio. The clerk continued to watch him wide eyes. "Do you need anything else? A glass of water or some coffee, perhaps?"

"No, thank you." Eisenstein offered him a quick smile. "Sorry about your window."

"Easily repaired." The clerk offered his hand. Eisenstein shook it and then turned and walked out of the office.

He took the automated lift to the top floor of the skyscraper and the landing dock. He sat down on a bench near the airstrip and did his best to see to his wounds while he waited for Hildy's biplane. After a few minutes, it soared down from the sky and rumbled to a halt. Eisenstein stood up with a grunt and walked over to meet her. Hildy hopped out of the cockpit and ran to his side. She pulled back her goggles, revealing eyes full of fear.

She gripped Eisenstein's shoulders. "My God, boss…what happened?"

"I found him," Eisenstein explained. "I found him and he got away."

Hildy covered her mouth. "The Laughing Man? Who was he…how did he…"

"He's a monster…as I expected." Eisenstein waved his fingers. "But he's not alone. We're looking at something larger, Hildy. I'm not certain what it is, but it's big. It infects all of Metropolis like some Biblical plague." He patted the back of his hand. "The Laughing Man had mechanical claws and metal teeth. Someone paid a lot of money to turn a deranged, malformed man into a killing machine. He said that he had no choice in what he was doing." Eisenstein paused. "He said he was being controlled by a doctor. I'm wondering if this doctor isn't the same person who gave him his claws and is now sending him loose into the city to seek out victims."

"Who would do something like that?" Hildy asked.

"In this city?" Eisenstein considered the question. "Someone ruthless. That doesn't narrow it down, much." He reached into his pocket. "What about you? How'd your trip to the Worker's City in the Depths go?"

"Not so good, boss. You know how the workers are." The lower caste of Metropolis, the workers who slaved to keep the great Heart Machine pumping and powering the city, lived together in their own city. Vast tenements housed them and they trudged to their work in the factories through vast tunnels, so that no one from the upper city ever had to look at the dirty coveralls or smudged faces. As a result, they tended to keep to themselves. Hidy stared at her shoes. "I asked around. Some of them seemed like they wanted to chat, but most were just too frightened, of the bosses and their security teams as much as the Laughing Man." She perked up. "But I'm working on one fellow, and I think he's willing to chat."

That was good news. "He got a name?"

"Georgy. He works in one of the big factories next to the Heart Machine. Spends his day spinning arms around on a giant dial. Apparently, he knows quite a few of the other workers and suspects a pattern to the killings. He promised to meet later, apart from the other workers, when his shift ends. I'll bring you along and we can talk…but he didn't promise anything."

Eisenstein patted her shoulder. "That's good. Whatever we can learn from the workers will be helpful. The Laughing Man's focusing on them, apart from the chorus girl from Yoshiwara, of course. There's a reason why he's killing the poor. Or at least, someone is giving him a reason. He didn't strike me as a man in charge of his destiny."

"There has to be a great reason," Hildy agreed. She sighed. "I guess neither of us were very lucky."

"Maybe not." Eisenstein withdrew his hand from his pocket. He held a matchbook between thumb and forefinger. "I'm a decent pickpocket. I gave it a try on the Laughing Man when we tussled. He kept his pockets empty, apart from this." Hildy and Eisenstein both looked at the matchbook. It bore the symbol of a stylized spider, an insignia of a black arachnid with its legs extended through silver strands of web. *Spider Club* had been etched under the spider in shimmering letters along with an address. Eisenstein flipped it over and handed it to Hildy.

"The Spider Club," she muttered. "The name's familiar. Is that one of the places in Yoshiwara? Like that Blue Angel place?"

"No," Eisenstein explained. "Look at the address."

"Near the Club of Sons and the New Tower of Babel." Hildy snapped her fingers. "Oh, I know. It's this gentleman's establishment. Popped up a few months back. I've flown by the sign a dozen times. Great big spider in a web, looking like it's about to swing down and wrap up the whole city. It's the kind of place where men go to have drinks and talk about business deals in quiet rooms. City Fathers would like to go there before wandering into the Eternal Gardens." She examined the matchbook. "But why'd a freak like the Laughing Man have it? He doesn't strike me as the type to care much about international finance and civic projects."

"So he went there for another reason." Eisenstein smiled slightly. "We're gonna find out what it is."

"You're just gonna waltz in to the Spider Club?" Hildy stared at him. "No offense, boss, but you don't really look like one of the City Fathers; you look more like you went twelve rounds with a steak knife. You think those uptown types will just let you head in and ask your questions? They could end up tossing you out, and it's a long way down."

"So I've heard." Eisenstein offered Hildy a broken smile. "Don't worry. I can be persuasive." He walked to the back of her biplane and hauled himself into the rear seat. Hildy spun up the propeller and moved to the cockpit. "Take us up. Straight to the Spider Club. You can drop me off and then pick me up at nightfall and take to me see this Georgy fellow of yours."

Hildy got behind the controls. She pulled back the throttle, sending the biplane taxiing to the runway in the center of the roof. "You sure about this, boss? The Laughing Man roughed you up pretty good. You don't want to rest or anything?"

Eisenstein slouched in his seat. He pulled his fedora low, shading his face. "Monsters don't get to rest. Now fly."

She sent the biplane speeding down the runway, up the ramp, and into the air. They soared through the sky. Eisenstein opened the side compartment, revealing a few rolls of bandages. He did his best to patch up the wounds, rolling up his sleeves and sliding the bandages over the cuts of his arms and legs. The jagged slashes remained, left by the Laughing Man's claws. The Laughing Man had declared that he couldn't help what he did; that someone forced him to kill. Eisenstein could say the same thing about this case, thanks to Boss Moroder's promise to wipe away his gambling debts. He leaned back in his seat, wondering what sort of revelation waited for him at the Spider Club.

✠✠✠

The biplane rumbled to a halt in a large rooftop runway opposite the Spider Club. A slim bridge led across from the runway to the club and Eisenstein left Hildy to cross the thin causeway. He trudged across, his eyes staring through his mirrored spectacles at the Spider Club. It towered above him, a diamond-shaped structure on a large spire, under a massive sign resembling the insignia on the matchbook. A large, stylized spider rested in a shimmering silver web with sharp angles, all looming down from the top of the round tower. Wooden doors led into the lobby. Eisenstein pushed his way through and stepped into the Spider Club.

The place had the smoky, warm feel of a parlor where a fireplace had been crackling away for some time. The cavernous lobby featured a deep, maroon carpet, and red and black checkered walls. A large desk stood at the end, where a receptionist flipped through a copy of the *Courier*. Eisenstein started for the reception, ready to ask about the matchbook when two guards blocked his path. They sported black and red checkered livery and pillbox hats, which made them look more like clowns than bruisers. But Eisenstein noted the bulges in their muscled arms and the glare in their eyes. One sported a broken, misshapen nose, and the other had a thin scar crossing his cheek. It was probably their job to make sure that the members of the Spider Club were not bothered by people like Eisenstein. He offered them a sly grin.

The guard with the broken nose pointed at Eisenstein. "The place is members only, my friend."

"Then why don't you give me a membership?" Eisenstein asked.

"Hah. Funny guy." The guard with the scar drew closer to Eisenstein. "How about we break a few of your ribs, toss you out onto the causeway, or just drop you off the building and watch you fall. You gonna laugh about that?"

Eisenstein sighed. He had hoped to do this the easy way. He let his hands swing at his sides, his thick fingers curling into fists. "I've had quite enough laughter for the day, friend. I'm not in the mood for any more; especially from fellows like you." He glanced over his shoulder. "You can show me the door all you want. I'm not leaving."

A fist swung for his face, the knuckles aimed against his chin. Eisenstein let it approach and then grabbed the guard's wrist and twisted it around. The guard moaned as he tried to free his arm. Eisenstein slugged him, driving a series of rapid blows into his belly. Ribs bent under his walloping and the guard folded as his buddy approached. Eisenstein ducked his first swing and came up with a rapid uppercut. He bashed the guard in the jaw, upsetting him, and then grabbed his shoulders and drove the fellow's face into his knee. The guard's nose crunched, spraying blood on the carpet. His body slumped on the ground and he crawled back. Eisenstein raised his boots, preparing to kick and stomp until he had finished both of them. His heart pounded. Maybe losing the Laughing Man earlier had gotten to him more than he wanted to admit. Maybe the monster inside of him was getting stronger.

"Sir!" A curt, authoritative voice made Eisenstein pause. He pulled back his fists and turned. A tall fellow in a charcoal-black suit, vest, and tie stood next to the desk, his eyes focused on Eisenstein. He had slicked-back hair, gray and spiky, and a hawk's nose. He crossed the carpet, his eyes turning to the guards. "Why were you attempting to remove this fellow?" Eisenstein recognized him instantly. Any Metropolis citizen would. This was none other than Joh Fredersen; the Father of Metropolis. It felt strange to see him in person. He belonged on signs and pictures in the newspaper, not in real life. Eisenstein struggled to compose himself.

"He's not a member." The guard with the broken nose pulled himself up.

Fredersen shook his head. "You did not even ask his purpose. Or his name." He approached Eisenstein and offered his hand. "I'd like to know both. I believe you already know my name. Is that not correct?"

"It is." Eisenstein paused. "My name's Eisenstein. I'm a private investigator. I was wondering if I could talk to you, for just a few moments. It wouldn't take long." He paused, wondering how much he could trust Fredersen. "It concerns the Laughing Man Murders. If I can ask my questions somewhere in private..."

"Of course." Fredersen pointed down the hall. "We'll retire to the smoking room. We can talk there." He walked away from the guards and moved down the hall. Eisenstein was surprised by his cooperation or maybe he was just saying that he had nothing to hide. "Come along, Mr. Eisenstein. Don't keep me waiting."

"Thank you." Eisenstein followed him down the hall, trailing a little after the famous industrialist. "I do have one question I need to ask now."

"Oh? What is it?"

"Why didn't you just have me thrown out immediately? I did barge into the Spider Club and attack two of your guards."

"Hmm." Fredersen let out a light smirk. "Mr. Eisenstein, I have no regard for weakness. I am a strong man. I have built a strong city. You defeated my guards with ease, demonstrating your strength. That alone warrants a meeting." He moved down the hall, his hands folded over his vest. Eisenstein followed at a slower pace, trailing behind the industrialist. He should have expected this. Fredersen had built Metropolis on the broken backs of his workers, the huddled poor in the Depths. His businesses dominated half the globe. Such a man would respect only strength.

They arrived at the smoking room at the far end of the hall. Fredersen led Eisenstein inside and then to a massive armchair to sit down. An

*"Eisenstein raised his boots..."*

automated cigarette machine, a tall glass case filled with rows of packs, sat near the chair and it provided Fredersen with a lit cigarette. Comfortable, shaggy armchairs sat around the smoking room, some occupied by other industrialists, factory owners and City Fathers, as they talked quietly and made important deals. Stuffed hunting trophies rested on the wall, leering bears, snarling lions, and tigers reared up on their pedestals and snarling their rage out at the world. They had been built with glowing neon eyes, which sparkled as if they were still alive. Portraits looked down from the wall, showing the City Fathers with their families. Eisenstein's eyes drifted to the picture of Fredersen, his arm on the shoulder of his smiling son. The boy smiled but Fredersen didn't.

Fredersen formed his fingers into a steeple. He smiled slowly. "Now, Mr. Eisenstein, you mentioned that you were investigating these dreadful Laughing Man murders? It seems rather unnecessary. The police are already fully engaged in hunting down the killer. I have no doubt in the Metropolis Police Department's efficacy."

"Somebody does," Eisenstein replied. "And they hired me." He looked at the portraits and the hunting trophies. "This place hasn't been in Metropolis for long…has it? The Spider Club, I mean. It just opened its doors a few months ago."

"That is correct," Fredersen agreed. "I was approached by the founder and he told me that he wished to help create a sort of informal meeting place for businessmen and the City Fathers, a refuge near the New Tower of Babel, where important men might go to discuss important matters in privacy. There is no chance of nosy reporters overhearing private conversations here. We can talk about business plans and tactics. Consider how free enterprise might better benefit the hard-working citizens of Metropolis, all without outside scrutiny."

"Like me?" Eisenstein asked.

"Precisely." Fredersen matched Eisenstein's slight grin.

"Who founded the club, if you don't mind me asking?"

The question hung in the air for a few moments. "A doctor," Fredersen explained. "A foreigner, but a doctor of note." Eisenstein perked up slightly. The Laughing Man had mentioned that a doctor was seeing him and controlling him; using him for his own ends. A skilled doctor would be needed to create the mechanical claws and metal teeth and attach them to the Laughing Man's body. Fredersen's smile faded. "This is a private club, Mr. Eisenstein. I don't really feel obligated to divulge the fellow's name. He's a very private man, you see."

"I understand." Eisenstein tried to change the question quickly. He couldn't let Fredersen know about his suspicions. "Well, thank you. This has been very helpful for my investigation."

"I'm happy to be of assistance," Fredersen replied. "But may I ask why you've come to the Spider Club?"

There was no getting around that. Eisenstein decided to try a little of the truth. He produced the matchbook. "I encountered the Laughing Man, actually. Ran into him today in Yoshiwara." He spoke casually as he held out the matchbook. "We struggled. I managed to get a hand into his pocket and I found this. Now, the Spider Club seems rather exclusive. I was wondering how a monstrous serial killer would get his hand on something like this?"

Silence filled the air. Some dignified conversation between businessmen droned on in the background. Fredersen's smile faded, slipping away bit by bit. "Well, I suppose there's any number of ways, young man," he explained. "The Laughing Man could have taken it from one of his victims, perhaps."

"His victims were all from the Worker's City," Eisenstein said.

"Then perhaps the Laughing Man found that matchbook in the gutter where he dwells." Fredersen spoke too quickly. He stood up, suddenly. "I'm afraid it really isn't my concern. If you believe there's some connection between the Spider Club and these terrible murders, than I must say that you are gravely mistaken." His eyes glared down at Eisenstein, anger etched across his features. "Now, I believe you've spent quite enough time in the Spider Club. Shall I have someone show you out, Mr. Eisenstein?"

"That's fine, sir." Eisenstein stood up. He bowed politely. "I think I can find the exit."

"See that you do."

Eisenstein turned and walked away, leaving Fredersen in the smoking room. He went down the hall, striding easily across the checkered carpet. The hall led back to the lobby and the exit but another portion curled around, leading further into the Spider Club. Eisenstein glanced at the clerk and the two guards in the lobby. They didn't notice him. He turned around and walked down the second hallway, his fedora in his hands. He didn't fit in the Spider Club and he hoped that he could turn something up before he was thrown out. He would have to work fast. Eisenstein glanced at the ornate wooden doors, each carved with the imprint of a spider web, as he walked past. Brass labels rested on the doors, showing that one contained billiards, another offered a viewing gallery, and a third housed a conference room. None of them seemed promising. Then Eisenstein stood before the door at the end of the hall.

He looked at the label, marked in brass above the spider. "M." Eisenstein said it aloud. He rubbed his hands over the label and then reached for the handle. It was locked. That was strange and what did the 'M' stand for? Maintenance, perhaps? "Murder." Eisenstein whispered the word, though that made even less sense. He had to know.

Quickly, Eisenstein withdrew an automated, electric lockpick from his coat. He slid the metal pipe into the keyhole and worked the miniature crank at the side. The lockpick whirred and turned. A single spark flew from the lock. Eisenstein looked up the hall, hoping that any errant members of the Spider Club wouldn't see him. Seconds ticked past. The automated lockpick whirred and then clicked. Eisenstein gave the door a gentle push and it swung open. He stepped inside and closed the door behind him.

The place looked like an office, with a desk in the corner topped by a neat stack of papers. Scientific equipment covered the table in the center; vials of strange substances, glowing electric coils, and syringes waiting to be used. Eisenstein picked up a vial and glanced at the bubbling material inside. He didn't know much about them, but they looked like some form of narcotics, perhaps used to drug victims. The Laughing Man had talked about a doctor. Could he have been drugged and manipulated, perhaps hypnotized to commit his terrible crimes? It seemed too mad to be true. Eisenstein carefully set down the vial and turned to the desk.

A letter rested on top of the files, topped with a strange name; Dr. M. Eisenstein flipped through the other papers. He didn't have time to read them in detail, but the name 'Dr. M' popped up again and again. Some of the notes had come from Fredersen, while others were addressed to places in Africa and Asia, asking for certain herbs and rare chemicals. Dr. M had amassed quite the collection of drugs, though he didn't seem to have any patients.

He couldn't find much in the papers, so he turned back to the office. Eisenstein's eyes fell on a large wooden case, standing just as tall as a man. At first Eisenstein thought it was a coffin, but it was much too square. No, it was a cabinet, with large wooden doors bolted shut with a simple lock. Eisenstein undid the bolts and set them aside. He swung wide the cabinet doors and peeked inside. Empty space greeted him. The cabinet could have housed any amount of equipment. A man could have stood inside, with his arms folded and his head down. The cabinet could easily be turned into a coffin. Eisenstein shuddered suddenly. What was Dr. M's mysterious cargo? Where had it gone? He closed the cabinet lid and replaced the lock.

More mysteries doubtlessly awaited him, but Eisenstein didn't have time to search everything. He had to move quickly. He reached into the pocket of his suit coat and withdrew an electric bug; a small circle of steel no bigger than a button. Eisenstein had used those minute electric bugs before, to great effect. He searched for a hiding place and chose the velvet cushions of the couch in the corner. Eisenstein pulled up a cushion and slid in the bug. He replaced the cushion. The bug would transmit to a receiver in Hildy's biplane. Hopefully, that would give him some more information. Eisenstein stood back, ready for a final pass of the apartment when the door slammed open.

Fredersen stood there, accompanied by a tall fellow in a stiff black frock coat, formal collar, and somber cravat. Eisenstein recognized him instantly. The Thin Man, the only name he had, worked as Fredersen's personal bodyguard, enforcer, and all-purpose Angel of Death. The Thin Man looked like a shark coaxed into a formal suit, with a wide-brimmed black hat tucked under his arm and a constant smile on his cylindrical face.

They stared at Eisenstein. "You were told to leave," Fredersen said.

Eisenstein gave them his best guilty smile. "I needed to find the Water Closet." He lied carefully.

"That's not so." Fredersen stared back, all good humor gone. "I just made a telephone call to a very close friend of mine, Mr. Eisenstein. You never need to use the Water Closet, just as you never drink or eat." His eyes traced Eisenstein's body. "You will leave this place immediately."

"I think I will." Eisenstein glanced at the Thin Man. "Will you be following me?"

"Pray I'm not ordered to," the Thin Man replied.

"I'll keep that in mind." Eisenstein walked past them, brushing by the pair of men as he stepped into the hall. Fredersen and the Thin Man remained, watching his departure with eager eyes.

He moved down the hallway quickly, waiting until he reached the lobby before breaking into a run. He hurried outside, charging through the open doors and then over the causeway. Fredersen knew him. The Thin Man did too, and they knew his case. Suddenly, the Laughing Man wasn't the most dangerous force in Metropolis. Eisenstein hurried across the bridge, scrambling back to the landing dock where Hildy waited with her biplane. She leaned against the side of the plane, flipping through a magazine as Eisenstein hurried over. Hildy glanced up and noticed his panic. She folded her magazine quickly and gave the propellers a spin.

The engine of the biplane rattled. "What's happening, boss?"

"We need to be airborne. Orbit the Spider Club. I've got a bug I need to listen to." Eisenstein hurried around to the back while Hildy pulled herself into the cockpit. "This case, it's worse than I thought. It's worse than I could ever imagine."

"Worse than the Prince Achmed case, boss?" Hildy asked.

"That's right." Eisenstein settled into his seat. "Now start flying."

The biplane rumbled down the runway and hit the air. Eisenstein settled into his seat. He opened a compartment and withdrew the receiver for the bug, which he placed to his ear. Only static and faint voices crackled through. He'd need to wait until someone entered the room. After his visit, he hoped that wouldn't take long. Eisenstein glanced out of the plane and examined the city. The skyscrapers flickered to life, neon signs adding a colorful tinge to the night. In the distance, the New Tower of Babel glowed like a great candle. The biplanes and zeppelins flickered as well. Darkness never really reached Metropolis, but the colorful lights only seemed to deepen the shadows. Eisenstein listened and waited as the biplane spun around the Spider Club.

✝✝✝

After a quarter of hour, the receiver picked up the door opening. Eisenstein crouched low, pressing the receiver to his ear. He could imagine the door of the office sliding open as two sets of footsteps clicked on the floor. "Dr. M." It was Fredersen's voice with an almost strange hint of deference. "You have my thanks for coming so shortly."

"You said our operations may be in jeopardy, Mr. Fredersen. That summoned me. Your gratitude is unnecessary." "The voice made Eisenstein shiver. It seemed to sneak from the receiver, slide down Eisenstein's ear, and tickle his insides. The voice had a cold emotionless quality, a gentle drone like it was almost bored with what it was saying. "Now, what is the trouble? Our little sleeper has not been caught. Your Metropolis Police stand little chance of finding him." The sleeper; that had to be the Laughing Man. "But you think this private detective will succeed where they have failed?"

Fredersen paused. "He knows, Dr. M. He encountered the Laughing Man already. Battled him and lived. He found a matchbook from your club in the Laughing Man's pockets and came here. He almost accused me, doctor. I never liked the idea of employing a murderer. This is all the more reason to end this operations immediately." He paused. He sounded regretful. "I should never have agreed to your proposition. I should never have allowed that monster loose in my city."

Dr. M didn't respond for a while. "It doesn't matter. Blood has been shed. My interests have already been served."

"*Your* interests?" Fredersen asked.

"The interests of Metropolis; of your legacy." Dr. M continued speaking without the faintest trace of emotion. "No, even if the Laughing Man is caught, it will not matter. The terror of his crimes will accomplish what bloodshed alone cannot. You don't have to worry about this meddlesome private investigator."

"Nonetheless, I intend to take precautions."

"By all means...wait." Dr. M sniffed the air. The intake of air, sharp and powerful, echoed in Eisenstein's ears in an almost painful burst of static. "There is something here." Eisenstein heard footsteps and then something scratching. The couch cushion must be lifted aside. How could Dr. M do that? Could he simply smell out the bug? It didn't seem possible...unless he had used those strange drugs and experiments to increase the power of his senses. "Yes." Dr. M's voice grew in Eisenstein's ears. "Are you listening to me, little detective?" Eisenstein shuddered. Dr. M had pulled out the bug from the couch.

Fredersen became panicked. "He's bugged the room? You must destroy it..."

"I believe you are." Dr. M continued. "Do you consider yourself an intelligent man, Mr. Eisenstein? I rather think you do. Of course, you're not a man at all. Not really. You're a monster and you will die." Dr. M's voice dropped to a whisper. "Goodbye for now, detective. Death will reach you shortly." The bug died, smashed by Dr. M. Only static filled Eisenstein's ears.

Hildy glanced back at him. "Boss?" Her voice squeaked through the speaking trumpet. "What's going on?"

Eisenstein's mind raced. "It's a conspiracy. Fredersen's using Dr. M, or maybe it's the other way around, and Dr. M controls the Laughing Man. He's using hypnosis, narcotics, brainwashing, or just strange science to make the Laughing Man do his bidding and kill the people of the Worker's City."

"But why?"

"That's the question, isn't it?" Eisenstein drummed his fingers on his knees. "Take us down, Hildy. We need to visit your pal in the Depths. We need to find out why." He reached into the second compartment at his side and withdrew another firearm; a machine pistol, resembling an automatic with an extended clip. "And hurry." Hildy pushed down on the throttle. The biplane descended. Eisenstein held on as they swooped past the skyscrapers, the city turning into a gray and neon blur around them. They were getting close to the answer, to all the answers, and Eisenstein could only hope that they'd survive to learn the truth.

The biplane dipped past the skyscrapers and entered the shadowed base of Metropolis. Garbage and detritus, the wreckage of the greatest city in the world, lay in disorderly piles around crisscrossing avenues. Bits of old newspaper and handbills for forgotten nightclubs caught the wind of the biplane and fluttered in the air. Hildy drove through the garbage and flew to a great round platform above a series of tunnels, which led deep underground. She brought the biplane to a halt. From there, Eisenstein and Hildy rented a small, puttering automobile. Hildy drove; she was as good with autos as she was planes, and they rolled down the largest tunnel. Eisenstein took the passenger seat and tucked the machine pistol into his coat as they drove along. Hildy didn't comment. The tunnel sloped downwards and finally came to a stop behind the first block of worker's barracks.

Hildy and Eisenstein exited the car and walked into the empty town square. The gray cement barracks where the workers and their families lived stood all around, lit by only a few lanterns and candles. The workers slept restlessly, waiting for the screeching alarm in the early morning that would begin their ten-hour shift. They would stumble home, fall asleep, and then wake up again the next morning to repeat the process. Eisenstein and Hildy walked past the silent buildings. A vagrant; a little tramp with a shabby bowler hat and shabbier moustache, crouched in the shadow of one tenement. Eisenstein tossed him a few dollars and he nodded his thanks. Hildy led him past the town square and then into a large alley, between two of the apartment buildings.

She raised her voice still speaking softly. "Georgy? Georgy – it's me?"

A worker emerged from the shadows, his eyes frightened. Like all the workers of Metropolis, he sported the shapeless gray coveralls and round cap marked with his number, 11811, stenciled above the brim. Georgy looked to be a younger fellow, but his eyes had the hollow look of a tired and old man. All the workers were like that. He clutched his hands, staring into the square with frightened eyes. Hildy walked over to him. She offered her hand and Georgy took it.

He offered her a weak smile. "Hello, Hildy. This is your boss?"

"That's right." Hildy pointed to Eisenstein. He walked over and shook

Georgy's hand. "He's a good man, Georgy. He can help put a stop to this. Tell him what you know and he'll put it to use against the Laughing Man."

"I need to know about the victims," Eisenstein said. "They were all from the Worker's City, apart from the chorus girl, but they had to have something else in common." Georgy looked away, unwilling to meet Eisenstein's eyes. "Georgy, the Laughing Man is being controlled. There's a method to his madness. I need to know what it is."

"I can't...if the bosses find out..." Georgy started.

"They won't," Hildy assured him. "Don't worry. Eisenstein won't let you down."

"So what's the connection of the victims?" Eisenstein asked.

Georgy glanced back over their shoulder, into the square. "Union." He whispered the forbidden word. "The victims were the relatives of workers who talked about union, about rights, about revolution. The chorus girl was the daughter of one of the ringleaders. She managed to escape from the Worker City, but the Laughing Man still found her." He leaned closer. "There's rumors about a woman in the catacombs, who will teach us a better way. But as long as the Laughing Man is around, I doubt that anyone will be brave enough to visit her."

So that was it; the Laughing Man was just another weapon used by the bosses to keep the workers of Metropolis oppressed. Eisenstein should have known. Everything in Metropolis revolved around industry. Why not murder as well? He clenched his hands into fists. "They won't have to be afraid for long," he told Georgy. "The Laughing Man's not going to be around soon enough."

"Boss?" Hildy asked.

"The Laughing Man has his own enemies. I'm going to make sure they find him." He would head back to his office, call up Boss Moroder and tell him everything he knew. Soon enough, the Laughing Man would show and Boss Moroder and his gangsters would finish him. Eisenstein patted Georgy's shoulder. "But thank you, for what you told me. It means a lot. I'm going to make sure that the Laughing Man never takes another worker's life."

"I hope so," Georgy said. "Now, I better get going before..."

Something clicked at the end of the alley. Eisenstein, Hildy, and Georgy turned. The tramp from earlier stood in the alley. He had tapped the stone wall with his thin cane. He pointed to the center of the town square, nodded quickly, and hurried away. Eisenstein peered past him. A half-dozen figures, clad in black, approached them from the square. The

*"Don't worry, Eisenstein won't let you down."*

Thin Man stood in the center of the six men, his broad-brimmed black hat shading his shark-like face. They all carried high-powered precision rifles, and they leveled them as they stepped closer.

Eisenstein reached for his machine pistol. "Against the wall...hurry!" He pressed himself against the stone wall, going flat as the rifles cracked. Hildy pulled Georgy to safety as well. They crouched as the rifles thundered. The Thin Man and his goons opened fire, hurling lead at Eisenstein and his friends. The bullets tore into the street and ripped through the cement walls. Fragments of gray cement spun through the air as the gunshots echoed across the Worker's City. Eisenstein wondered if any of the workers would even be wakened by the noise of the barrage or if they would sleep like the dead through any noise. Either way, they knew better than to go outside. The bullets roared past them and Eisenstein readied his machine pistol. He didn't stand a chance against that many guns. They needed to get out of the Worker's City and get Georgy to safety, before he was identified.

The precision rifles paused in their fire while the Thin Man and his gunmen reloaded. Eisenstein popped out and unleashed a blast from the machine pistol. Bullets roared through the air and the Thin Man and his goons fell back behind the decorative gong in the center of the square. Eisenstein turned back to his friend as he paused his shooting. "Down the alley. We need to get back to the ramps and get out of here."

Hildy grabbed Georgy's arm. "Come on, buddy. Let's go."

They darted back from the alley, their shoes clattering on the stone. Bullets hummed behind them. Eisenstein ducked as shots whistled past his head. The alley ended and turned, moving down another passage cut out of the stone. They continued running, pausing occasionally to take cover from the rifle fire. Eisenstein fired behind him with the machine pistol but he doubted that he hit anything. They kept running, and then neared a tunnel leading further into the earth. Stone crosses rested on the walls of the tunnel, showing that this led to the catacombs beneath the city.

Georgy pointed to the tunnel. "That leads into the catacombs. I can go there. I can hide. When the boss's men are gone, I can sneak back."

"You're sure?" Eisenstein asked. "You'll be safe?"

"No one goes into the catacombs...not amongst the dead," Georgy explained.

"Well, all right." Hildy patted his arm. "Be careful, Georgy. And thank you."

"Just stop the Laughing Man," Georgy said. "Life is dangerous enough for the workers of Metropolis. We don't need more killers, besides the machines that we work on." He turned away and raced down the tunnel, quickly vanishing into the gloom of the forgotten catacombs. Eisenstein watched him go. Georgy was right. Metropolis was a city built on oppression. The Laughing Man was just one symptom of a greater industrial disease.

A gunshot cracked. Eisenstein turned to see the Thin Man leading his riflemen down the alley, their guns raised. Eisenstein gave them a burst with the machine pistol. They crouched down, ducking the roar of bullets. The machine pistol clicked empty and Eisenstein reached in his pocket for another clip as he and Hildy turned to run. They sprinted down the alley, more shots careening past them, and then reached a short tunnel leading to the slope. Hildy stumbled on the smooth cement incline. Eisenstein reached down and grabbed her hand. He helped her up and they raced up the tunnel, scrambling to where their car waited.

Hildy hopped into the driver's seat. She turned the key and the ignition rumbled. Eisenstein stood guard, aiming his machine pistol down the tunnel. Rifles shots blazed past him, smashing into the automobile. One shot shattered the window, sending glass spinning through the air. Another slammed into the dashboard, and Hildy winced at the sparks. Eisenstein fired back, but the Thin Man had them outgunned.

"We need to motor out of here, Hildy!" Eisenstein cried.

"I know, boss...I know. I just need to...there!" The motor of the auto roared. "Hop in!"

There wasn't time. The Thin Man and his men raced up the tunnel, their rifles clattering away. Eisenstein leapt onto the runners of the car. He gripped the edge of the door with one hand and extended the machine pistol with the other. "Go!" he roared. Hildy hit the gas. The auto shot down the tunnel, bouncing and rumbling over the slope. Eisenstein fired from the runner, shooting madly at the Thin Man and his riflemen. The shots echoed through the tunnel, the muzzle flash sending shadows dancing across the alabaster stone. The Thin Man ducked down, holding their fire. Eisenstein spent the entire clip, shooting until the machine pistol clicked empty. He pushed open the car door and slid inside next to Hildy.

She glanced at him. "You're all right, boss?"

"They tailed me," Eisenstein explained. "The Thin Man tailed me as soon as I left the Spider Club. I should have known better. I should have been prepared for this." He lowered his eyes. "The Laughing Man. Dr. M., Fredersen. Maybe it's too much for a cut-rate PI."

"That's not true." Hildy kept her eyes on the road as they zoomed out of the tunnel. They rumbled to a halt on the landing pad, where her biplane waited to take them aloft, back into the rest of Metropolis. "You've cracked the case, boss. You've found out the truth. There's something rotten in Metropolis, but it's not you." She paused. "When you hired me as a secretary, I figured you were just another jerk in a city full of them. You'd want me behind a desk, clattering away on a typewriter and looking pretty for the clients. But you let me fly. You financed my plane." She squeezed his arm. "You're a good man, boss."

"I'm not a man," Eisenstein muttered.

"No." Hildy smiled sadly. "You are. No matter what anyone else says."

The automobile rolled to a stop. Hildy and Eisenstein hopped out and clambered into the biplane, after a quick push got the propellers humming. Hildy got into the cockpit and sent the biplane rumbling down the runway and then into the air. They soared upwards, flying back to the neon hive of Metropolis. Eisenstein looked over his shoulder, staring at the entrance to the Worker's City. Hopefully, they could make those people's lives just a little easier.

The biplane shot into the sky. Hildy glanced back at Eisenstein as they ascended. "So, where to, boss?" she asked. "Any more investigations?"

"It's late enough, already. Take me back to the office, Hildy. I'll make a call to Boss Moroder and let him known that his money isn't going to waste. Then you better head home. Get some sleep." He returned the machine pistol to its compartment. He'd need to buy an additional magazine for the weapon. If he was going to be taking on the Laughing Man and the Spider Club, he'd need plenty of firepower. "And good work today. From you, at least."

"I'm happy to hear it." Hildy made the biplane go level as they reached the peaks of the skyscrapers. In the distance, the New Tower of Babel loomed over everything. Its countless parapets and ridges stood out in the night, lined in neon. Metropolis seemed different this late; a ghost city, formed only in glowing light. Eisenstein watched it blur past as the biplane rumbled along and brought him home. He was eager for this day to end.

✛✛✛

Eisenstein's office rested in an upscale skyscraper, a great tower across the gap from the Eternal Gardens where the young and wealthy of Metropolis could enjoy the only space of greenery in the city. Eisenstein could peer through his window and look at the fantastic, curved tree trunks and flowering groves of the Eternal Gardens. He had even taken Hildy there, once or twice. For now, she brought the biplane to a halt on the skyscraper's landing dock. Eisenstein clasped her hand. "Goodbye,

Hildy. I'll give you a call in the morning." She nodded her agreement. Eisenstein doffed his fedora to her and headed for the stairwell. He went down one flight and came to an unmarked gray hall. At the end of the featureless hall, a glass door bore his name in white letters, along with his profession – Eisenstein, Private Detective. He leaned against the door and pushed it open, then stumbled inside.

His office didn't have much in the way of furniture. A desk rested in the corner, with a typewriter, a radio, a line of ticker tape to receive messages sent from all of Metropolis, and a few other supplies. A leather armchair sat across from it, a place for clients to rest. Eisenstein got behind his desk and rested his hands on the keys on his typewriter. Almost as an afterthought, he reached for the cord of the graceful lamp curved above his desk, and gave it a tug. The office flooded with light. Eisenstein stared at the leather armchair. He wasn't alone.

A strangely small man in a black opera coat sat in the armchair, his gloved hands resting on his lap. He wore his top hat low and the collar of his opera coat upturned, hiding his face completely. Only his eyes gazed out, red and hateful. The Laughing Man stood next to him, his gloves gone to reveal his claws. They dangled down at his sides. Eisenstein stared at both of them. They must have picked the lock to his office, stepped inside, and waited for him to return. He could easily understand what they meant to do.

He didn't say anything, but simply sat down and stared. The man in the opera coat pointed at him with a stubby figure. "Mr. Eisenstein. I believe we spoke previously." Eisenstein recognized his voice. "I'm the man called Dr. M."

"Is that so?" Eisenstein asked. "You founded the Spider Club, then approached them with the Laughing Man; your pet murderer. You convinced Fredersen to unleash the Laughing Man on the poor in the Worker's City. I'm sure he's paying you quite a lot of money. But you have other goals, Dr. M. Goals which Fredersen can't imagine. I don't think your plans will benefit Metropolis."

"Metropolis is nothing," Dr. M replied. "I watch this city with a thousand eyes. I've seen its weakness. Such a place, so large and so divided, cannot exist for long. The workers will rise. The wealthy will attack them. Metropolis will vanish into the savagery that is the most basic state of the human race. I will be there for this cataclysm. I will rule what is left."

"What if the cataclysm isn't what you imagine?" Eisenstein asked. His hand reached to the radio on the side of his desk. Maybe he could make a distress call; send a desperate message for help. "What if something different rises from the chaos, like a better city which will never respond to the terror and fear which you bring?"

Dr. M nodded to the Laughing Man. The Laughing Man's claws slammed down, stabbing into the radio. Sparks flew through the air as the machinery crackled. It wouldn't be sending anymore messages. "You have a very optimistic view of human nature which is very strange, given your own nature, Mr. Eisenstein."

"What makes you say that?" Eisenstein asked.

"I told you. I have seen this city with a thousand eyes. I know everything. I know what you are, Eisenstein. I know your electric soul." He whispered the words. "It will have to be snuffed out. For my plan to succeed, there must be more death at the Laughing Man's hands; more hatred and fear between worker and boss. You would stop me."

"I would kill you," Eisenstein said calmly.

"I cannot be killed." Dr. M nodded to the Laughing Man. "I could make you like him, I think. The proper drugs. The proper amount of hypnosis. The proper alterations." He patted the Laughing Man's coat. "I could find a cabinet for you."

"I prefer my office."

"You'll die here, then." Dr. M glanced at the Laughing Man. His eyes blazed again. "Kill!" His voice echoed across the office, seemingly coming from every direction. "Kill for your master! Obey your commands!" The Laughing Man winced as he stepped closer to Eisenstein. He raised his claws. "Give him a smile. Gut him and then grant him a smile ear to ear and beyond!" Dr. M roared out the order. The Laughing Man charged to obey.

Eisenstein was ready. He slammed his boots into the underside of his desk and knocked it over. The desk tilted and smashed into the Laughing Man. A blizzard of papers flew through the air. The typewriter crashed down as well, making musical clangs as it rolled on the floor. Eisenstein sprang up and ran, already reaching into his coat for his compact automatic. He had to get out of the office, get the Laughing Man somewhere out in the open and call for help. He ran for the door, firing the pistol behind him. The Laughing Man ducked down, avoiding the shots. He hissed and sprang for Eisenstein, who had already reached the door to his office.

The order from Dr. M echoed in the air as Eisenstein slammed open the door. He hurried into the hall, then pressed the door shut. The Laughing Man's claws punched through the glass. Eisenstein's name and job description vanished as the frosted glass shattered. Eisenstein couldn't look back. He ran down the hall, hurrying madly for the stairs in the corner. He reached the stairs and scrambled up, already breathing heavily. The Laughing Man's footsteps clicked on the tile behind him. He could almost see that grotesque smile.

The stairs led back to the roof. Eisenstein scrambled onto the landing dock and searched the skies. He spotted the colorful outline of Hildy's biplane, and waved with his fedora. The biplane buzzed in the sky above the apartment building. Hildy was making a quick pass before beginning her flight home. "Hildy!" Eisenstein had no idea if she could hear him over the roar of his engine. He ran to the center of the roof, still waving his hat. "Hildy…I need a pick-up!"

The Laughing Man emerged from the roof and charged toward him, swinging up his claws. Eisenstein turned. He raised his pistol and pulled the trigger only for the gun to click empty. The Laughing Man lashed out at him, a claw scratching his arm and making him drop the automatic. The Laughing Man kicked it away and then grabbed him by the shoulder with one hand. The other claw pulled back, preparing to plunge into Eisenstein's chest and gut him. Eisenstein wriggled and tried to free himself, managing to deliver a crushing punch to the Laughing Man's face, but the killer's grip on his shoulder remained.

Then an engine's rumble roared close. Hildy swooped low on her biplane, flying just over Eisenstein and the Laughing Man. The wind from the plane knocked them both down and bought Eisenstein some time. He kicked the Laughing Man and he ran after the plane as Hildy flew low. His boots pounding on the pavement he reached out, grasping for the wing. His hand clutched the wood, then he reached with the other and caught hold. The end of the rooftop drew closer. Eisenstein struggled to increase his grip, his feet flailing. The biplane buzzed over the roof and flew in the open air, with Eisenstein dangling from the wing. Hildy called out to him as he tried to keep the biplane level. He couldn't hear her over the rush of wind.

He pulled himself up and reached into the back seat. Eisenstein grunted as he pulled himself in and collapsed in the seat. The speaking trumpet blared Hildy's words in his ears. It took him a few moments to realize what she was saying. "He's on board!" Hildy cried. "He's on board!" Eisenstein turned around. The Laughing Man had jumped at the biplane too and now clung to the tail. His claws drove into the metal and wood, pinning him in place. The Laughing Man crawled closer, grinning with his metal teeth as he neared them.

Eisenstein thought quickly. "The Eternal Gardens…land there." He needed to get the Laughing Man out of the sky and away from Hildy, in a place with no easy exits. "Use your radio to call up Boss Moroder's frequency. Get him to the Eternal Gardens, with as many as guns as he can bring, as fast as he can. Tell him that the Laughing Man is there."

"You got it, boss." Hildy fiddled with the radio dial as she twisted the biplane around. It zoomed over the Eternal Gardens and started to dip preparing for a rough landing. Eisenstein turned around. The Laughing Man had crawled closer, pulling himself up the tail and toward the back seat. The claws reached out, aiming for Eisenstein's throat. He ducked down; avoiding the slashing claws, and then twisted around and gave the Laughing Man a powerful punch. His knuckles brushed against steel teeth. The Laughing Man hissed and started to make strange, panting noises. After a few seconds, Eisenstein realized that he was laughing.

The biplane ducked and drooped. The wheels smashed into a tree, shattering branches and sending flowers spinning through the air. Then Hildy dropped the biplane down into a slight meadow, before a wide fountain, a grove of trees, and a flowerbed all overlooking the edge of the Eternal Gardens and the city below. The biplane's wheels struck the dirt and rolled to a halt. Grass and soil flew through the air. The plane bounced and rumbled, knocking Eisenstein about in his seat. The Laughing Man somehow held on. Then the biplane came to a halt.

There was no time to think or strategize. Eisenstein simply had to get the Laughing Man away from Hildy. He pulled himself out of his seat, perched on the tail of the plane, and dove for the Laughing Man. They crashed down from the plane and rolled into the meadow, spinning end over end in the grass. The peacocks inhabiting the Eternal Gardens fluttered away, crying in panic as their colorful tails waved in the air. Eisenstein and the Laughing Man rolled to a stop in the grass and came apart. They pulled themselves up, both men tired and weakened from all the battles they had gone through. They stared at each other. The Laughing Man raised his claws. Eisenstein raised his fists.

The claws struck first, a blinding flurry of slashes that sunk into Eisenstein's shoulder and chest. He moved back, trying to avoid the flashing claws. His boots crunched in the grass. The Laughing Man pressed the attack. Eisenstein tried a punch, but the Laughing Man weaved out of the way of the blow and slashed his arm, cutting his sleeve and skin. Eisenstein tried to pull back, but the Laughing Man's claws came again; this time aimed at Eisenstein's face. The steel claws slashed across his cheek and reached his mirrored spectacles. The glasses fell away.

Eisenstein's true face stood revealed to the moonlight. He had no eyes, only round circles of metal. The Laughing Man paused his attack. "Machine Man." He rasped out the words. They were true. Eisenstein was a Machine Man, a mechanical being built as an experimental prototype by a mad scientist named Rotwang, who lived in the center of Metropolis in a decaying mansion. He had created Eisenstein, found him wanting, and cast him out in the world. Eisenstein had found employment as a security guard before becoming a detective. Some days, he almost forgot about his true nature. Now, the Laughing Man reminded him.

"A monster," Eisenstein said. "Just like you."

He attacked the Laughing Man again, this time allowing fury to drive his fists. He rammed a devastating right hook into the Laughing Man's head. Several metal teeth flew from the killer's lips, the needles spinning as they vanishing into the night air. Then he grabbed the Laughing Man's arm and yanked him to the nearby fountain. He slammed the killer's skull against the fountain's stone edge. The Laughing Man's claws darted out wildly. One finger carved into Eisenstein's shoulder, sinking in deeply. Eisenstein stumbled back. The Laughing Man reared up. They faced each other, right on the edge of the Eternal Gardens. The Laughing Man prepared for another attack. This one might bring them both down. Maybe Eisenstein wouldn't mind.

Then Boss Moroder's harsh voice cut through the night. "Destroy the freak!"

He stood on the meadow, along with Rondo and several of his men. All carried high-powered shotguns with drum magazines. The Laughing Man turned to look at them. His smile faded. For just a moment, he was the sad, hapless creature who had been forced to commit his murders; brainwashed into craving and enjoying bloodshed. Then the automatic shotguns roared. Shells tore into the Laughing Man's body. The Laughing Man's thin arms danced and shook. His mouth fell open. The shotguns blasted him apart and what was left fell off the edge of the roof and plummeted downwards. He didn't get a chance to cry before be fell.

Boss Moroder approached Eisenstein. He held out his hand and Eisenstein shook it. "Your debts. They're forgiven." Eisenstein didn't reply. "Your girl there says he was working for someone; a doctor. Are you expecting trouble from that?"

"I don't think so. He's the kind who sticks to the shadows. He needed the Laughing Man for his plan and now the Laughing Man's gone." Eisenstein stared into the distance. "He was right about one thing, though."

Hildy pushed her way through the gangsters and ran to Eisenstein's side. "What's that?"

"This city." Eisenstein looked out of the gleaming towers of Metropolis. "It's rotten. It's based on exploitation. It makes monsters of us all and a day will soon come when every monster will face his fate." He and Hildy looked out at the gleaming spires, the endless lights of the Metropolis skyline. Eisenstein leaned on her and she helped him stand. "Take me home," he said, his voice weak and with a mechanical whine.

They limped back across the meadow to the plane, leaving the gleaming skyline behind.

# THE END

# METROPOLIS & ME

Sometime in high school, I became obsessed with silent movies – and German Expressionism in particular. I think the impermanence of the art of Weimar Germany entranced me, this vast outpouring of dark, subversive and creepy art that was all destroyed by the Nazis. It was like looking at the relics of some forgotten kingdom, but these relics had motion, an austere black-and-white beauty, and a surreal sense of danger. I loved *Nosferatu*, *The Adventures of Prince Achmed*, and other silent flicks from that era, like Sergei Eisenstein's Russian Revolution body of work, but *Metropolis* was instantly my favorite. I loved the art deco designs, the still impressive special effects, the apocalyptic imagery, and the overall message, while melodramatic and a little weird (The Mediator Between the Head and Hands must be the Heart!), which remains vital today. When I heard about Ron Fortier doing an anthology of stories set in the Metropolis Universe, I knew I had to submit something.

At first, I wasn't sure what. I didn't want to do a direct prequel. I grew up with the Star Wars prequels, and those soured me on the idea of adding back story to cool characters and settings. I wanted to do an Expanded Universe-style story, one which would tangentially involve some characters from the film, but be mostly original. I thought that a detective and serial killer yarn might be interesting, but still needed something else to make it worthwhile. Then I remembered how much I enjoyed pastiche literature – stuff like Kim Newman's *Anno Dracula* or Alan Moore and Kevin O'Neil's *The League of Extraordinary Gentlemen*. These are great stories that stand up on their own, but they're packed with cool 'Easter Egg' references to other works, while creating fascinating crossovers and even a little bit of social commentary about the fiction of the era. That's what I wanted to do, but with references to other Fritz Lang movies, German Expressionist works, and silent films in general.

I'm no Kim Newman or Alan Moore, but I hope the story I created offers some cool tidbits for readers who are a little familiar with the era. Eisenstein (named after the director of the *Battleship Potemkin* and other seminal works) was originally supposed to go up against Count Orlok from *Nosferatu*, but Ron wisely pointed out that a vampire didn't fit into the sci-fi setting of *Metropolis*. Instead, I made the Laughing Man a fusion of Orlok's freakish appearance, mixed with Conrad Veidt in *The Man Who Laughs* (the inspiration for Batman's Joker) and Cesaere (also played by Veidt) in *The Cabinet of Dr. Caligari*. The villainous mastermind controlling the Laughing Man is Dr. Mabuse, a hypnotist super-criminal from several of Lang's other films. There are quite a few references to other silent movies, particularly in Eisenstein's previous cases, and I hope you enjoyed picking them out as you read.

I also hope you enjoyed the story as a whole. I know that there's no way a writer like me can top *Metropolis*, which has influenced pretty much every sci-fi story to date, but I can at least pay some tribute to Fritz Lang and those other great German Expressionist artists. Their world crumbled and they either escaped to Hollywood, languished in exile, or suffered terribly under Nazi persecution – but their art lives on. It has inspired me and countless others, and I hope my little story follows the tradition that they started.

✝✝✝

**MICHAEL PANUSH** – at twenty-six, has distinguished himself as one of Sacramento's most promising young writers. Michael has published numerous short stories in a variety of e-zines including: AuroraWolf, Demon Minds, Fantastic Horror, Dark Fire Fiction, Aphelion, Horrorbound, Fantasy Gazetteer, Demonic Tome, Tiny Globule, and Defenestration. He published his first novel, Clark Reeper Tales, for his high school senior project. A graduate of UC Santa Cruz, Michael currently serves as a City Year Corps Member at Rosa Parks Middle School. His books with Curiosity Quills include *The Stein and Candle Detective Agency, Volume 1: American Nightmares, Volume 2: Cold Wars*, and *Volume 3: Red Reunion*, all featuring a pair of occult detectives in the 1950s, *Dinosaur Jazz--* where *The Great Gatsby* meets *Jurassic Park* -- a story about a Lost World battling against the forces of modernization; *El Mosaico, Volume 1: Scarred Souls, Volume 2: The Road to Hellfire*, and *El Mosaico, Volume 3: Hellfire*, a Western about a bounty hunter whose body was assembled from the remains of dead Civil War soldiers and brought to life by mad science; and *Dead Man's Drive*, a 1950s urban fantasy about a hot rod-riding zombie. Read excerpts from his work at http://curiosityquills.com/published-authors/michael-panush/ and follow him on twitter at https://twitter.com/Michael_Panush

Michael began telling stories when he was only nine years old. He won first place in the Sacramento Storyteller's Guild "Liar's Contest" in 2002 and was a finalist in the National Youth Storytelling Olympics in 2003.

In 2007, Michael was selected as a California Art's Scholar and attended the Innerspark Summer Writing Program at the CalArts Institute. He graduated from UC Santa Cruz in 2012 and attended the School of Education for the Loyola-Marymount University.

# METROPOLIS: SERVO-SURROGATE

## KEVIN NOEL OLSON

Rasp joined his three-wheeled sedan with traffic. The automobile became a single, shining scale of the kilometers-long snake as it slithered over the elevated motorway. Its gleaming and segmented torso glided serpentine toward the New Tower of Babel in the center of Metropolis. The vastness of its width and breadth imposed its presence over the city. It stood a spacious and magnifying monument to the zenith to human architectural ingenuity. Enormous pilasters and columns incrementally lifted roads and rails to encircle the base of the Tower, appearing as vipers wrapping about the tree of knowledge in a synthetic Garden of Eden.

Variously-sized and shaped aeroplanes and airships flitted as gadflies and fowl among the vast forest of imposing concrete skyscrapers. The structures were Pantegruelian in size. Such largess shrank with envy in the shadow of the New Tower of Babel at which Rasp arrived.

He drove into the expansive garage set aside for employees. He stepped into the Pater-noster, the never-stop passenger lift, its identical, rectangular cells moving up and down in unceasing succession. He disembarked in front of the grand doors leading directly to the offices of Joh Fredersen.

Rasp entered the room. Joh Fredersen sat at his imposing desk. Professionally-attired underlings furiously wrote in notebooks, running calculations on the translucent numbers descending through the roof from on high. Ostensibly, these numbers represented reports from overseas stock exchanges, delivered instantly and indexed vibrationally through the mechanisms of Rotwang's trans-ocean trumpets. The Master of Metropolis approved and rejected by caressing the sensitive plate of blue metal with his right hand. The room remained deaf to the outside world as the Rotwang process drowned the cacophony of Metropolis into mute submission.

On seeing Rasp, Joh held up his left hand as if taking an oath while removing his right from the round controller plate. Freezing midair at the unspoken command, numbers remained still and ephemeral. The assistants filed out of the room.

Joh Fredersen spoke. "Josaphat."

Joh Fredersen's first secretary shut the door behind the exited assistants. "Yes sir."

Joh stood to his feet, placing his hands on the desktop. "Retrieve Freder from the waiting area. Rasp needs hear firsthand what my son relayed to me." Rasp smiled slightly at being called Rasp. His name was Rasp, though he chose not to share it with many. Not even the Master of Metropolis for whom he worked. To the dark-clad thin man of bone white features, it served both as affectation and appellation.

Josaphat left the room. In short time, Freder appeared, leading Josaphat.

"Hello father," the handsome Freder said.

Joh said, "Tell Slim what you have told me. Leave nothing out."

Freder breathed deeply. "Though a member, I am not often an attendee of the Club of the Sons. There is no need to go into the facts regarding the young ladies selected mostly from the worker's city to entertain the favored sons of Metropolis in the Eternal Gardens. For their services, these girls are handsome rewarded. Hope rests in the hearts of many they may become joined in marriage to one of the blessed sons of Metropolis.

"Last night, while receiving playful attention of one such sprite, she broke into tears. I listened to her tale with sympathy. As happens with some of the exuberant sons, she found herself with child but no husband. She hid her pregnancy, and was allowed to take extended leave from the Eternal Gardens. She spent the time below at the home of her parents, where she discovered her father had developed a severe drinking and gambling disease, and her parents now owed a great deal of money to his creditors. Her father quit the gambling and swore off alcohol. Her parents wished to become right again.

"Her pregnancy was difficult, and the care she received in the worker's hospital put a great strain on her finances. She hoped to see her parents free to heal from the great burden and threat. With that in mind, she approached one of her father's creditors. The creditor suggested, rather forcefully, a selling on the black market the only commodity she had of value. Her infant child. When realizing her parents could be murdered by any of her father's creditors, she agreed.

"The creditor was not directly involved in the buying and selling of babies. While in the hospital, she caught word of the illicit sale of infants to interested residents of Metropolis who could not have children of their own and failed to navigate the adoption process.

Rasp spoke in grave tones. "I garner such activity is highly organized, predatory, and conspiratorial, requiring a great deal of obfuscation. While this girl was party to the events, it has become common for newborns to be taken from cribs with impunity."

Josophat nodded. "There have been serious grumblings among the workers reporting such stories to Grot, their overseer. It is true, that some women feel compelled to sell their babies, either willingly or through difficult circumstances, though this is an insignificant number. This has created an increase in kidnappings to fill the void in the supply. How these thefts are accomplished remains a mystery to the investigators serving the Worker's City. There is great suspicion of the force and growing unrest and distrust for the wealthier citizens of Metropolis. Grot fears such a climate will foment a revolution. If it were just women selling their own children, it wouldn't be such a problem. This issue is garnering support for those who desire violent unrest against Metropolis. Should it be put to rest, it may allay such action."

Joh Fredersen stiffened his shoulders. "This matter has been known to me for some time. The recent bomb plots against the Tower, while unsuccessful, have set Desertus, his congregation of Gothics in a tenuous position concerning the continued existence of their cathedral. It is time to concentrate efforts on pacifying the workers in the kidnapping matter.

"Slim, you have proven yourself masterful in fighting industrial espionage in the past, using subterfuge and force to magnificent effect. I say this not to bolster your ego. I state fact. I need you to go to the Worker's City and discover who is behind the infant thefts and stop them by using any resources necessary. Josaphat will function up here to design a relations campaign to allay the fears of the workers. The Council of Citizens will make recommendations on placing social improvements. We are at the dawning of an important epoch for Metropolis. Destructive actions must be stopped at their source. You are to connect with and report to Grot in the machine room if necessary. Grot will relay any messages to me."

Freder stepped forward. "I wish to go with Rasp, Father! I want to help this girl!"

Joh Fredersen firmly yet gently took Freder by the shoulders. "Rasp is more experienced in these matters. He will succeed. Your inexperience would be a hindrance to his efforts. You have already helped her by coming to me. Leave it my hands."

Freder dropped his head on his chest. "Yes Father."

The recently loquacious Rasp, bowed slightly, tipped his hat, and left the room.

+++

Rasp entered the Pater-noster, descending to the parking level. He retrieved clothing from underneath the back seat his car, and changed into a worker's uniform consisting of a dark-blue jumpsuit and matching cap. Designating numbers '71917' rested on the brim of the cap, removing instantly a lifetime of identity from the workers, boiling them down to be counted among the living. He slipped into hard black shoes. Rasp maintained the uniform from previous assignments. The Master of Metropolis ensured that number be saved for Rasp's usage alone.

After descending further into the ground by special overseer's elevator, he exited into a long corridor. This found him at the entrance to the lift that daily brought the workers in long single-file to the heat-grueling machine rooms. The lock-step of the men matched evenly as they strode two-by-two. The river of people moved deliberately. They swayed on the balls of their feet, tilting first to the left, then to the right. The mechanical motion imitated a funeral march. The image mirrored as the workers getting off shift walked by on a matching corridor on the right, separated by a gate, yet joined in drudging resignation.

None of the workers noticed the single figure at the end of the line. No one questioned that there may be a worker missing, and fewer still thought there was anything odd about an additional laborer where the casualty rate moved as steady as the Pater-noster lift. They entered the lift and descended into the brutal heat in the depths below.

Arrival of the lifts was regulated so only a regular number of workers would fit on one. The right number of workers arriving and replacing the men still on shift minimized mechanical inactivity of the lift. Only for mere moments did any station remain idle during shift changes.

Observing the massive Pater-noster machine, with its elephantine features and barrel-shaped legs, Rasp saw the workers pushing arrow-hands back and forth over a white-face wheel with black numbers. An odd parody of passing time. Slim realized that he would not be allowed to stand around long, and he would look out of place without a station for him to attend. As the whistle blew to indicate a shift change, Rasp walked down the row of tired workers. The whistle would blow several more times at intervals matching the arrival of the lifts. Glad to see his replacement with worker 17971, a man sweating profusely at the hands of a machine relinquished his position.

Rasp took the dials of the machine. With no intention of remaining long, he pulled the sharp lever. The action caused the clock-hand to slice deeply into his right calf. The gash in his flesh appeared as a painful and apparently serious injury. Blood poured profusely from the wound, though he insured it was superficial.

In the din of the roaring machinery, Rasp could not be heard as he screamed in pain, so he put little effort into that portion of the ruse. Falling to the ground and cradling his leg, his face became a horrid expression of pain and fear. It took a few moments for anyone to notice him before a foreman saw and rushed to the first-aid station. The medical attendant came and knelt to examine the injured leg. Wordlessly, the diagnosis indicated the wound a dangerously deep one, and additionally either dislocated or broken. Rasp created this illusion through manipulation of muscles and tendons. His joints and muscles he made taut or loose to serve his will with long and deliberate hours of training.

In the din of the ear-deafening room, the foreman used hand signals to direct worker 11811 to take Rasp's erstwhile machine. After bandaging the wound and using a splint to steady the bone, the medical attendant determined to place worker 71917 on a gurney for transport to the worker's hospital.

In the hospital, with its stark grey and joyless walls, Grot, a stout, bearded man of short stature, came to see the patient in his position of overseer of the workers. Though the emergency doctor determined the injuries of Worker 71917 proved slight, Grot demanded in colorful language that the hospital would keep him until fully healed. A wounded worker proved a hazard to others, he argued. The doctors consented to Grot's demands, though not without protesting of the bed shortage the hospital operated under.

"The intensive care units are full of injured workers," a doctor explained, "and the quarantine floor is full. The burn wards could not take another bed with steam injuries, and the screams of the patients would threaten his very sanity."

"Place him in the Maternity Ward, then! A private room too! This worker was at the Sirius Machine. Do you know the importance of that machine? Do you EVEN know what it does, damn your pretentious attitude? Do you not know that we do not have enough men to operate that machine as it is?" Grot huffed angrily, rocking side-to-side and stamping his feet. "We can get by for now, but I need this man in full health soon! Work it out, or I'll make sure you are all worked out the door permanently!"

Grot stayed, ensuring they found a place for Rasp. After the nurses filed out and shut the door behind them, Grot looked at Rasp. "How are you feeling?"

"I feel just fine," the gaunt man replied. "The injury is superficial."

"Even the doctor thought it more serious than that."

Rasp nodded. "That is just as I had prepared it to appear. I assure you I am fine."

"That's good. Joh Fredersen told me what you're doing down here." Grot held out his hand. Rasp took the grease-covered appendage with a seal of trust.

"Let me know if you need anything. I'm not afraid to throw my weight around." Laughing, Grot held his belly in both hands. "I've plenty of weight to throw too!"

Rasp nodded. "Good. Tell the attendants I need a good night's rest, and under no circumstances are they to disturb me."

✚✚✚

After Grot left the room, Worker 17971 locked the door. Rasp discarded his hospital clothes. He examined his worker's uniform they'd left in the room. Pulling it open by means of a recessed zipper, he extracted a black set of tight-fitting pants made of nylon, along with a shirt and domino mask made similarly. He put this stealthy costume on. He pushed the bed under the air vent, stood on the mattress, and carefully extracted the vent cover with a small tool. In moments, he slipped into the air vent. In this fashion, he received unobserved access to virtually the entire hospital.

Equal in width and height to form an ugly grey cube, the building was 33 stories high and woefully inadequate for the great number of workers it was created to serve. Rasp headed for the first floor where the newborns were kept. His familiarity with the hospital comprised only a small portion of his knowledge of the worker's city. He had studied every blueprint, street layout, sewer system, and a plethora of so many other facts, minutiae, and figures retained by the archivist department office in the New Tower of Babel. He had done the same for the city of Metropolis itself and its inimitable new Tower. He knew the designs and workings of the vehicles, grounded or airborne, and the engines and purposes of the organs and nerves that drove industry in Metropolis. The position held by Rasp made it his business to collect facts and use them to their fullest service of Joh Fredersen. His photographic memory and quick mind permitted remarkable storage of facts, figures, names, dates, addresses, mechanical construction, architecture, and all the knowledge written down about the twin cities, settled above and below.

The newborn warehouse, as Rasp saw it through air-grate slits, was a wonder to behold. No book might describe the experience of seeing it. Infinite rows-upon-rows of sealed rectangular cribs, evenly set to movement along a conveyer belt at regular intervals, displayed a genius concurrently diabolical and angelic. Rasp noted unmistakable similarities to the Pater-noster in appearance and function.

In several dual, motor-conveyed rows of enclosed 'cradle-coffins,' each compartment containing infant boys and infant girls separated ever by sex, the Moses Matriculator machine rolled. With precision, a belt-paired set were fed mechanically. Cleaned and washed mechanically. Offered toys mechanically. Reached the end of the right-journeying belt mechanically. Lowered in the tiny 'cradle-coffins' into holes beneath the floor into complete darkness for the chemical-mist induced sleeping period mechanically. All timed to regularity of life lived by their fathers and mothers, designed the children to someday replace their fathers and mothers. Ten-hour shift changes. Engrained. When to laugh, love, cry, sing, dance, learn, play. Engrained. No loving touch soothed these children. It was not until months of this treatment had passed that parents might hold their child again. The children, theoretically no worse for the wear, became model youth. In keeping with experimental psychological science of a psychologist named Doctor Skiffling, now long-dead. His legacy long tested, now approved.

All this treatment offered to the parents as entirely optional. True in word. If parents denied the children this treatment, the children would be unlikely to find work and receive social services. The children without the benefit of the Skiffling treatment were often enough incorrigible and futureless. Often enough, they were relegated to an orphanage or orphaned to the street. Unspoken punishments for resistant parents caused a lifetime of injury to their children.

All these facts sat hard in Rasp's mind. Knowing deed done proved pale in the face of deed in action. As the workers slog in pairs through ten-hour days in oppressive heat, so attend the machines to their children in a ten-hour day of mechanically-delivered wonderment. As the worker trudges home for his meal and relaxation, the infants are cleaned and given sustenance. As workers fall into bone-weary sleep, so do the infants fall into exhaustion induced by a misted sleeping drug and darkness for that time. The infants float the dreaming river of Lethe, the efficacy of the process is unquestionable. At least it is, as yet, unquestioned. Ethics belonged in the domain of the politicians and pedagogues of Metropolis who discuss them as passing entertainment. "Someday, they say, the light of day will lay, even away in the Subway." So goes a popular children's recess song.

Rasp observed the movement of the many nurses, clad in grey ankle-length skirts, grey hats, and black capes as they came and went to observe the health of the infants displayed through the one-way viewing glass of their enclosed coffin-cradles. Rasp spent hours observing each of the nurses individually. They checked the functions on the various gauges, clocks, tubes for air, water, pap. The babies could not see outside of their box, though some seemed to notice they were being observed.

Rasp's gazing eyes stopped on one nurse. A nurse with a strikingly-beautiful face with the hat number 58311 caught his eye. She set off unfamiliar sensations in him without apparent reason. Nurse 58311 slipped lightly out the room. Drifting as mist, this Nurse carried with her Rasp's attention. Following her through the vents all along, Rasp watched as she entered the *Regina Caelorum*, the medical sister to the Pater-noster. He did not seek to follow her in the serpentine device drifting up and down to and fro from Metropolis to the world below. Rasp returned to private convalescence. Dressed again as a workman, he walked into the corridor.

None challenged Worker 17971, Rasp, as he strode the corridors of the hospital. An air of authority unlike any other worker, any approach met with Rasp's penetrating eyes worlds-upon-worlds deep. He entered the *Regina Caelorum*, descending to where the workers lived.

He arrived at the school building for children of the workers. A quite beautiful woman sat on the lower five steps of the building, reading to the children.

Rasp allowed his shadow to interrupt the veldt of yellow grass populated by lions, tigers, monkeys, elephants, giraffes, colorfully printed on the page of a book for children. "Maria."

Smiling, Maria gently fluttered her eyes as she looked up to see the imposing figure of the not-workman-in-workman's-clothing. "Hello. May I help you?"

"I am not in need of assistance. I am here to help the children you raise." Rasp's shadow grew longer as the air grew graver. Maria closed the book on her lap.

"Children, go and play for a minute," she said serenely and kindly. "We will eat soon. I will finish this story."

The children left to play. "I hope to know what you mean," Maria stated to Rasp, her lips stern, yet kindly and motherly.

"Newborns disappear from the hospital. They are surreptitiously and illicitly sold to desiring residents of Metropolis. The frequency of said practice rises sharply. Mothers wishing to adopt out infants and supply the need are not maintaining the supply. These children are being stolen. I am here to break this practice. This will stave off the fomenting revolution."

Maria smiled lightly, her eyebrows raised. "Is it such an unkindness to move a child from a stygian pit to the rewards of living above? Of course, I think it is reprehensible to steal children from their parents. That is done daily down here, where mothers lose their sons daily to the great Moloch beasts, the insatiable machines of Metropolis. Orphans live without homes, treated as the lowliest of creatures, forced to steal and sell their pride to fill their bellies. Even to kill or be killed, forced even to the depredations of predatory individuals. They take drugs that change in name and composition daily, and die for their sole transgression of being unloved. I do not blame them. Nor their parents, who are crushed, burnt, bled to death to keep smiles on their brothers and sisters above."

"I know the life of an orphan." Rasp said, "Not one so cruel as you express, yet it is difficult for an orphan to find their way in life without parents to guide them."

Maria sighed. "I despair a loveless, lightless world as is thought to be here below. Except I cannot. Love down here is not so rare. Kindness is not hidden away in darkened doorways. The loam that creates the beauty above is rich with loving kindness, though too often unrealized. Whether knowing drudgery below compares more or less favorably to witless pursuits above, never filling and always pursued, is a question for the heart. Who to pity more? A man who knows he's destined to a life of slavery or one blindly slave to his unquenchable passions?"

Maria shook her head, dispelling the cobwebs of thought. She stood to her feet. The light blue dress she wore over her white blouse seemed severe, yet the innocent, radiating love of her face and gestures belied such sentiment. "I will, of course, help in any way possible."

Rasp nodded his confirmation. "I am looking for a woman. A nurse at the hospital. She was an age where she would be schooled here recently. Her number is 58311."

Maria dropped the book she held. "I know her! I knew her! Jael Stordahl! She was a student of mine. Jael died when a sanitation boiler exploded, slicing her in half with heated metal!"

"It is as I now recall. This was a year ago. Her number has been retired and not revived. Someone is using her number now. Now I am aware." Did you see the body of Jael?"

"None of us were allowed. We were told the sight was too horrific. I laughed at the time, as horror is too common in the machine rooms."

Rasp touched his cap with slender fingers. "Indeed. I leave you now to attend the children." Rasp walked away quietly. A long shadow stretched behind him as he turned a corner.

In a doorway, Rasp changed into the clothes he wore when set upon the mission by the Master of Metropolis. His flat, wide-brimmed black hat appeared on his head, the worker's clothes obscured in a long coat of stygian hue, the worker's cap disappearing into a pocket.

Again in his natural appearance, Rasp cut an imposing figure. He returned to the machine rooms to meet Grot. He used the overseer lift to return to Metropolis.

+++

On the rooftop of a prodigious Metropolis skyscraper, leaning toward the welcoming sun as statues on the island so-named Easter, Freder walked past the walnut tree. A walnut fell at his feet as Prometheus dropping to earth to deliver fire to human hands, as an apple struck Newton, as Milton's Lucifer fell from grace. Freder took no notice. None of the cornucopia of flowers, full of livid pinks, twilight-dim purples, sun-brilliant yellows, could hide from him the farmhouse built upon the shoulder of the Rabalais' giant Pantagruel.

On the porch sat Freder's grandmother. When she said she would never leave the farmhouse, her son Joh Fredersen had the house moved here, for her to ever see the triumphs of her son. She so loathed the view of the New Tower, and every inhuman and inhumane sickness it represented. Holding her Bible in her lap, she pursed her lips.

"Hello, grandmother." Freder said.

She turned, her grim demeanor instantly lightening. In her wheelchair, she thrust her arms to the sky, pulling the corners of her lips with them into a smile. "Freder! Come here, my beloved grandson!"

Freder obeyed her wishes, giving her a long, deep embrace. "I love you grandmother!"

The embrace over, her gaze returned to the New Tower. "It was some joke your father played on me, having this house and walnut tree moved at great expense to rest next to his one love since your mother passed. The New Tower of Babel is a blight on the spirit of the world!"

"In his way," Freder said, "Father loves you and I both."

She nodded. "In his way. The pain he felt at losing your mother Hel never healed. We provide a memory of that pain. It causes him to envy Hel her death, and it causes him torturous guilt to love Hel so greatly that her memory injures the love of us. The edifice he designed overshadow the entire city. Even I am allowed diminished hours of sun, overshadowed by a representation of his love, both lost with Hel and continuing for us. He thinks he can't love us enough, he knows he can love Hel no more, so he erects white elephants we cannot help but to notice. It is all a bit smothering."

Freder considered the New Tower. "That is all too true grandmother. Hopefully, it will be a discussion for the two of us at another time. Now, I come to you for advice."

"You come to me for aid against your father?"

"Not this time. Mine enemy I may need help against is myself. I fear I may have erred."

"You do not know? That is in an error in itself."

"A slight error compared to that which I may not recall. I told my father the truth about an incident, yet I did not tell him the entire story. I met a girl at the Club of Sons. She told me she sold her child to the black market."

"It does not seem to concern you."

"It may be that she sold my child the same moment."

"Your child?"

Freder hung his head as he dropped pleadingly to his knees, taking her hands in his. "Yes, Grandmother. After an argument with father, I engaged in a drunken dalliance with the girl. Too great a bacchanal it was, that I do not recall it a bit. She told me she thought it may be mine. I do not blame her, yet I cannot tell father of this. He may not forgive her. Please, forgive me."

"There is nothing I may forgive. Only God, the girl, and any child of yours may forgive the possible offence." Freder's grandmother smiled kindly, clutching the Bible resting in her lap.

Freder placed his head in his grandmother's lap. "If the child is recovered and is mine, I will do my best by it and her. I promise."

"If you love her, and she you, if you love the child, then it will not matter whose child it is. Do not love her to destruction either. Your father loved Hel thusly, and left himself alone when she died as he made her alone in life. Do you love her, Freder? Does she love you?"

Freder shook his head. "I do not know if I love her. I think not. I could learn."

*"…if you love the child…it will not matter…"*

"Love is not a thing to be learned. It is a matter of the heart. If you wish to help her, help her not be confined to a loveless marriage."

Freder sighed, standing again to his feet. "Thank you, Grandmother. I will do my best." He walked off the porch and away.

"It is no more than anyone can ask of you," she whispered. "Do well, Freder. Do well, my grandson."

✝✝✝

Rasp returned to his car and drove it through the streets of Metropolis until he observed a neon sign proclaiming XANADU LOUNGE in a rainbow-coloring of flashing lights. The establishment had two requirements of its members; only fun ruled and only boredom outlawed. The "Club of Sons", with its Eternal Gardens, remained exclusive to the sons of the most powerful Masters of the great city. The Xanadu Lounge held entertainments for the not so privileged sons of those not so powerful, yet still proud in significant success.

Rasp entered the darkened room. The velvet couches and chairs circled large round tables, rich in deep maroon colors, all furniture supported by ornate, shiny brass legs and backs. The young men were as young men are. Most of the youths were quite handsome. Where looks did not come naturally, streams of money made up for the majority of appearance deficits.

A bevy of young women, invariably attractive, populated the lounge. They hung off the young men like jewelry. The girls engaged in entangling the boys and men in laughter, enfolding them in perfume. The girls clutched the young, membership card-carriers with their long legs and enwrapped them in slender arms. The males soaked up the premium of attention spent on them. Occasionally, a fist fight erupted over a particularly lovely female or an argument between women over the attentions of a prize specimen of masculinity.

In the Club of Sons, all the girls were hired, primped, and assigned to the Sons in regimental fashion. The Xanadu Lounge appeared a cavalcade of working girls and hunting young women all vying for the attentions and affections of the males in a raw display of animal passion. Nearly a zoological exhibition of virile manhood and sensual womanhood among humans presented itself. The war waged on boredom in Metropolis proved heated with lust and boiled in liquor.

Rasp breathed deeply the scents, listening intently to the babble of conversations as he observed the various scenes reflected in the mirrors proliferating throughout the darkened lounge. He swept the floor with his gaze slowly to the left, again to the right. Raised his head and repeated the action. He gauged too the bar, at the waitresses moving deftly through kissers, dancers, fighters, and tables. Rasp's narrowed eyes moved easily over the multitudinous faces. A wolf seeking prey, a hawk searching for rabbits over prairieland, no visible detail escaped his gaze. His brain indexed, categorized, identified. Catching an insect in the web of his vision, Rasp impelled his legs along a translucent, silvery spider-thread none except him saw. He floated past the chaotic revelers to an empty seat at an occupied table and sat down.

The man at the table, striving to maintain a youthful appearance of twenty though he was nearing thirty-five, sat with an attentive girl aged seventeen years or so. The man looked at Rasp. "May I help you?"

Rasp let his eyes fall to the table, his fingers dismissing the question with a wave of his gloved fingers. "Sometime, you may help me. Tonight I am not seeking your help."

"Why are you at my table?" The man demanded. "What do you want of me?"

Rasp smiled sleepily. "I am not here for you. I want nothing of you excepting a speedy lack of your presence. I am here for the girl."

The man stood up, pushing the girl away. His muscles flexed the seams of his suit. She looked at Rasp with surprised curiosity. "The girl is with me!"

Rasp chuckled quietly, almost below perceptibility. "I assure you, I am not here to challenge your claims of property. I also assure you that if that was my purpose this night it would be a simple matter for me. I suggest you retake your position at head the table if you can. If not, allow me to converse with Charlotte Cady before you forfeit your opportunity with this girl nearly half your age."

The man clenched his fist, staring into Rasp's eyes for a short moment. Shaking lightly, he pursed his lips to silence and regained his seat.

"How did you know my name?" The girl said, covering her mouth with the slender fingers of her left hand; half in surprise, more in coquettish flirtation. She sat across the table, engaged in the mystery, finding Rasp terrifying and intriguing. "How!?" she demanded.

"I am the only one to perform any interrogation," Rasp assured easily. Charlotte sat back in her chair, leaning toward her escort for unconscious protection.

Rasp retrieved a slender cigarette from the inside pocket of his jacket and placed it in his mouth. His fingers moved like spider legs to deftly retrieved a match. His long arm reached toward Janette and struck the incendiary stick to blazing blue life as he retracted it over the surface of the table. He lit the cigarette.

"You work in the Eternal Gardens, Miss Cady. I understand moonlighting is grounds for termination at the Club of Sons."

Charlotte shook a bit. She shivered as pallid tone infected her olive skin. "How…"

Rasp put his head back. "I tire of such inquiry. Please."

Her lips shook as she spoke. "You won't tell."

"It is of no concern to me. If you are not forthcoming in your answers, it may become a concern to you. Ask the gentleman to leave."

Charlotte turned. "Please…"

"Excuse me." The man's face turned red as he walked away.

"Now, Charlotte. I understand you spoke to Freder Fredersen about a recent sale."

Charlotte put her hands to her chest. "How did you know? Freder wouldn't talk to anyone!"

The tall man shook his head. "Freder means you no harm. Your story concerned him greatly, and he hopes to help you. He did not mention your name. It was a simple matter to discover your identity. You do not then deny it was you," Rasp affirmed.

Charlotte thought to do just that. She stared into Rasp's enigmatic, steel-blue eyes and sighed. "No."

"Tell me who approached you for the transaction."

Eyes fluttered beneath beaded strings falling from Charlotte's headdress, a rain of artificial tears to express an inner pain, suggestive of a real vulnerability. A blouse of sheer material meant to tease and titillate exposed her strength, inferring weakness in young men. Her lip trembled. "I do not know."

"You will not say," Rasp replied in gentle hiss, fraught with kind venom.

"How do I know I can trust you?"

"You know you can trust none other than me. I can destroy or rescue you in a single revolution of the Pater-noster. None other has such power."

She removed her headdress. Real tears flowed. "I…cannot!"

Rasp nodded. "You cannot fail to give me what I request."

"You're the devil!" She shouted, standing to her feet. "Go to Hades!"

Rasp smiled. "You rose from Hades. There is no moment a rose cannot be returned to wither and die. No need for a scene. Return to your chair."

Charlotte looked about. The nearby tables turned in to watch her outburst. She sat.

"Better. I am not your enemy until you choose to make one of me."

Charlotte looked for rescue at the door, at her escort who rested fuming against the bar, sipping on clear bronze liquid without ice. The other tables offered no respite. Her shoulder fell into dejection. Calmly she repeated. "You are the devil."

"If you prefer. An angel, if you wish. Speak."

Unconscious fingering of lips. "I don't know what I can tell you."

"You can tell me who approached you about selling your child."

Rubbing shoulders as if chilled. "One of the nurses."

"Nurse Number 58311."

Eyelash flutter. "I don't recall."

"You do, and I appreciate your unspoken candor. Thank you." Rasp stood from the table.

Eyes widen. "Will you report me?"

Wordlessly, Rasp placed the flat-brimmed hat on his head. His eyes gleamed. Turning, he walked out. The man Rasp interrupted at the table came quickly in front of him, accompanied by six other men attempting to bar his exit.

"You're not going anywhere, Tall Man!" The man Rasp slighted earlier said. "I don't care if you are working for Joh Fredersen!"

From behind the bar, two tall, stocky bouncers approached the scene, standing on either side of him. "Are these fellows bothering you?"

Rasp smiled. "They are not. I am bothering them."

"If you are causing trouble, perhaps we can show you the way out?"

Rasp laughed deeply. "I know the way out. Perhaps you can help me in another way."

Quick as a cobra strike, Rasp deftly punched one of the men in the chest, to the sonorous sound of cracking ribs. As the man staggered away, breathing heavily, Rasp punched the side of the other bouncer's nose. Blood gushed over Rasp's black glove as the bouncer fell backward into a table. Revelers sitting there shrieked their surprise as the furniture broke, spraying a chaotic color-wheel of alcohol drinks that rested thereon.

The six men and their leader looked on in astonishment, making no movement on Rasp. The events happened so quickly they hardly had time to react.

"I trust you will be kind enough to let me allow you to go in peace. A round for everyone bartender. On me."

Rasp parted the Red Sea of incredulous youth in his exit.

✝✝✝

Joh Fredersen stood alone in his office. The numbers fell around him. Down the walls a '441' dripped. From the ceiling, a '77' became a meteorite plunging toward the ground before ascending once more. A displaced '2' here, a drifting '90' there. Joh pushed the large button to interact with the cascading digits.

A side door to the office opened. Rasp quietly entered. "Report." Joh Fredersen said.

"I have discovered a connection. A nurse involved in the theft of infants."

"Who."

"A nurse. Dead to the world for some time. One Jael Stordahl."

Joh watched a number fall toward the floor. Its reflection danced in his eyes as a burning angel plucked from the ether with the push of a button. "She is dead."

"Yes. Purportedly. A steam explosion. A funeral. No body to view."

"Confront her and have her arrested."

"It will not cease. We must find out who is behind the skein. If we arrest her, the arachnids will disappear to their dens."

Joh Fredersen nodded. "Find out who is masterminding this. Use every resource at your disposal."

Rasp nodded as he backed out of the room. A blink from the Master of Metropolis created a brief moment for the dour spy to disappear from sight. Joh allowed himself a brief moment of wonder, then returned to the task of capturing firefly-digits and releasing new ones to flitter as butterflies into thin air.

✝✝✝

Far beneath the New Tower, and quite directly beneath the Workers Hospital, rested a great cistern of water used for cooling the great machines of Metropolis. This reservoir, one of many, also sustained the voluminous supply of the precious liquid so invaluable to quenching the thirst and aiding the hygiene habits of its citizens. Steam created by the machines in laborious functions returned to Metropolis for heating and use with pneumatic systems. Once cooled, the steam returned to condense to drip and cool in the vast network of pipes. These pipes returned the still-warm liquid dripping into the lake below.

Stygian gloom presented itself on the surface of the underground lake. Rare occasion found anyone standing on its sterile, concrete shore. Water testing happened at the outgoing pipes to check their individual designated purposes. A pipe used to cool the vast machinations required different testing than potable water. The water was treated at outer facilities.

The dripping sound from the condensed water made a steady, light rain of tiny drops and mists accompanied by larger droplets falling from the ceiling ten meters high. The soft hum of the Moses Matriculator gently conveyed rows of infants sleeping in their enclosed cradles to float on the water. This portion of the machine was designed to allow the infants a sensation reminiscent of their recent journey through the womb. A spot on of one the infant cases glowed in the dark. A door nearby opened, allowing a dim light to escape. For a brief moment, an outline of a woman dressed as a nurse appeared in the illumination. The door quietly shut out the light, permitting the deep blackness to resume. From the nurse's hat, the numbers 58311 glowed a dim blue. A flashlight clicked to life, revealing a nearby raft made of amber, translucent Bakelite tubes floating on the dark water. The figure, now obscured more by the beam of the flashlight in front of her than the surrounding blackness, stepped onto the raft. She picked up the paddle resting there and directed the raft over the water.

The oar directed the small boat to keep pace with the slowly-moving and brightly-glowing mark atop the coffin-cradle. She leaned over the Moses Matriculator to click four hasps holding the cradle into place. She deftly lifted the baby, cradle and all, onto the top of the raft. The conveyor chain of the Moses Matriculator slowly and mechanically closed the gap left by the absent infant with finality. In its inhuman absent-mindedness, it quickly forgot the presence of the infant it carried mere moments before.

The raft continued. The flashlight lit parts of the concrete wall surrounding the cistern as the nurse piloted the raft over the water. A sloshing sound grew as the small craft drifted lazily along. The sound never grew very loud, yet the flashlight dimly revealed its origin. The last portion of Pater-noster lift compartments ended here to be washed out after their long descent deep into the bowels of the earth. The conveying chains and the compartments were revealed as never in Metropolis, where the riding portion alone was seen by commuters. Behind the riding section of each box, a second section rested for maintenance access, half the depth of the main compartment. The conveying chains took up a middle section the area, and a designated numeral identified each compartment.

Slowly, the raft came along to a stop in the still water in the area between the descended and ascending compartments. The cells created a slight stir in the water. In the dark, the glowing cradle was gently lifted and placed in the access space on a returning compartment numbered '14'. A blue light illuminated the compartment with introduced pressure. The nurse stepped off the raft into the access space numbered 13. Once she alighted, a blue light illuminated the cell.

She climbed up the ladder through a square hole and into the space with the cradle. She sat with her back to the rear wall, her long skirt covering her legs as she brought her knees to her chest.

✛✛✛

Freder left the elevator to his penthouse suite to walk in a daze. Mechanically, the son of the Master of Metropolis took steps toward the elaborate keyboard organ to lose his muddled thoughts in music. As soon as he neared the keys, he struck a violent minor-7$^{th}$ chord, releasing beautiful tones in the steam escaping from the long, prodigious brass pipes towering over him. He sat in the organ bench with his fingers still depressing the chord. He began to play a fugue. It fit his mood, Freder thought, smiling sardonically. His mood felt angry. His anger needed release. Alcohol would not fill the holes he felt in his life. More and more, nothing but music managed to alleviate the deep pain he felt. The wealthiest sixteen-year-old in Metropolis, he felt he was also the most miserable. The loneliest boy at the dance. How can he have the world at his fingertips yet feel as if he held an empty, deflating balloon? His right hand danced over the keys to form a strange melody as his left continued to push down the chords, holding them to near-suffocation of notes. Eerie the tune, mad the player. Lost in the music, Freder smiled insanely, delighting in the sweating battle cry erupting volcanically from the massive, shaking pipes. Building to crescendo, the organ threatened to bulge and burst at the last. Last notes played, Freder stood from the instrument seat. The insistent knock on the door continued, though Freder heard it now for the first time as his performance drowned out all other auditory incursions.

"Who is it? I'm quite indisposed!"

In hushed tones, the female voice came through the heavy door. "It is Charlotte, Freder!"

Freder rushed to the door and placed his ear against it. "Charlotte? What are you doing here? How did you find my flat?"

"Please, Freder! Let me in. I am in trouble!"

Freder pushed away from the door, biting the knuckle on his left fist. He waited for long moments before Charlotte's voice returned. "Freder!? Please!"

Freder moved to the door. "This is a security building! How did you get in?"

"A girl has her ways. Please, Freder! I'm in trouble!"

Freder tilted his head back, his eyes staring down at the lock on the door. His hands moved forward and performed the unlocking.

Charlotte rushed in, pushing the massive door away. She threw her arms over Freder's neck. "Oh Freder, I'm so frightened! Someone is following me!"

Freder moved to the door to push it closed, pulling Charlotte with him. Pressing the wood-grain, he met with mechanically irresistible force. He recoiled protectively as a voice came through the door as it opened further. "Nobody is following you any longer, my dear." Through the door appeared a nurse, identified by her cap and uniform. The nurse with the number 58311 brandished a sleek, black pistol. "I do not intrude too greatly."

"What's this about?" Freder demanded. "Get out of my apartment, or I will call security!"

The nurse laughed. "If you would look at the visual monitors, you will see the fate of your much-vaunted 'security'." Freder pulled Charlotte, still clinging to his neck, with him as he moved to the security monitor and turned it on. The lobby of the edifice displayed in black-and-white. The picture on the screen showed three unconscious security guards, their black uniforms and pillbox hats ruffled, tilted, and torn from significant violence as their bruised, bleeding and battered faces confirmed.

Freder turned to the nurse. "What is the meaning of this? Who are you?"

"Someone you would not know. Someone who died at the hands of your father's brutal and heated Jaganatha of machinery, making slaves to be crushed beneath its cruel, unstoppable wheels. Someone returned to life as a broken toy of the madman magic man of Metropolis, Rotwang, then tossed on a trash heap like a forgotten and broken child's toy."

"What are you talking about? Why do you persecute Charlotte?"

"Once, I took pity on Charlotte over her situation. I made a mistake to think I could help financially, rather than just taking her child. The worst came from not knowing the identity of the child's father. That father, my dear Freder, was you. The child already gone to another city, you threaten the trade in the worker's children. Your father can crush the black market. The only way to dissuade Joh Fredersen is to threaten you, his son."

"What will you do now?" He demanded.

"I will take you captive."

"What of Charlotte?"

The nurse turned her pistol toward the distraught woman. "This."

Freder leapt to place his body between Charlotte and the inevitable slug of hot, melting metal. He slumped to the floor with his unfortunate charge, both of them shot and bleeding. Freder sat up, holding Charlotte in his arms. "NO!" he raged. "No!" Tears welled in his eyes, rage pulsed in his heart. He laid Charlotte's still form on the floor. "I will kill you!"

He rushed at the nurse. With a springing motion, her fist flew out. Freder took a powerful blow to the forehead and fell unconscious to the floor. Reaching down and lifting him, the Nurse slung him over her shoulder. "Come with me, dear boy."

Male and female Gothics ascended and descended the stairs of the massive Cathedral, imitating angels on a helix-ladder of dreaming Jacob. Rasp ascended the stairs to Cathedral. He paid no heed to the stares of curious fear that bore into his frame as the Gothics poured out blinking into the shade of the New Tower of Babel.

Through the massive, metal doors, far too large for any human to lift yet amazingly balanced on hinges that any child might manage with effort to move, Rasp walked toward the altar. The massive structure held a dim form clad in black robe. "Welcome Brother!" the prodigious voice filled the massive cathedral. "It is too little your countenance is observed to attend the House of the Lord!"

Rasp nodded. "I come for guidance, Father."

Desertus shook his head as he descended from the pulpit. "You never called me such in your childhood. I never deigned to take such a position with you either." The priest nodded. "I have never been your father. For the representation of a father, such as he is, it would be necessary for you to walk across the square. As much as I would be your spiritual Father,

*"I come for guidance, Father."*

you have withheld such access to me of yourself. My attempts to offer paternal guidance you denied. I managed still to offer you a sense of self that molded you into a person of uncanny ability and strength of will."

"Do not depreciate your impact on me, Desertus. It is significant."

"I most certainly do not. I place a sober judgment on our relationship. You as my ward in agreement with your mother's wishes to not permit your father or stepfather know your ancestry. I raised you as *a* son. I could not raise you as *my* son. You would not so permit. Nor would you accept my council."

"You gave advice I neither needed nor requested."

Desertus laughed. "Fair enough! I acknowledge a habit of kibitzing. It does not often go unheeded amongst many and is intended well. If I thought myself your father in some way, it was done of love for your mother."

"Love?"

"Of course I once found love. I was not always a priest you know. I had youthful attractions as any young man might. Your mother caught my heart as it caught the heart of many men. God did not intend her for me. Created to serve His will, romance would only interfere in my calling. I never stopped loving her to this day, though our paths in life diverged. My path dedicated to a love of God's people. Her path followed the love of another. Your father. Then, it followed yet another."

"Both men you despise."

"Their inhumane actions I despise. I despise no man for falling in love with your mother. Even I gravitated toward her great beauty, strength, and wisdom. No, to fault another for falling in love is folly and conceit."

"Yet you have ever refused to speak their names in my presence."

"Out of love for your mother, and a promise she elicited from me. I agreed you would never discover your father's identity from me."

"I discovered it."

"I never revealed it."

"You did not intend to. No matter. The past is in the past. I require knowledge of the present for a future requirement. Has anyone confessed to you during confession regarding the black market infant kidnappings?"

"If they had, the authorities would know already. I am a priest of the Most High. I do not protect murderers or kidnappers from justice, however the Master of Metropolis would suppose of me. It is not my purpose to absolve crimes. Not even you in your dark dealings for the Master of Metropolis."

"I am prepared to explain myself to the proper judge for any sin. I absolve you from culpability in my actions. Mother gave me orders. I was to protect my brother Freder from undue harm. Not even his father knows the solemn oath I pledged to my mother in front of the seven deadly sins. Few people have a singularity of purpose as the one that possesses me. You are one who has such a singular will, Desertus. You do not comprehend my heart or even know the complexities of my actions. I absolve you from your responsibility for my soul. You are not my judge, temporal or spiritual."

Smilingly, Desertus nodded. "I am only your kibitzer."

"Still, I do wish you had heard something about the matter. The fact you have heard nothing tells me something important."

Across the nave of the cathedral, the massive door opened. In came six workers from the machine rooms. The men whispered prayers, stopped at the fount of holy water, and crossed themselves. Desertus and Rasp watched as they crossed the massive sanctuary. The thickly-built man in the lead spoke for all. "Father Desertus, why have you not spoken to Joh Fredersen about the children disappearing from the worker's city?"

"I have just heard of it from a representative of Joh Fredersen," Desertus admitted, passing an open hand toward Rasp to indicate. "It seems the Master of Metropolis knows little more than I."

The man turned to address Rasp. "You are Fredersen's Tall Man! Maybe the leaders of Metropolis are responsible?"

"I see you think it a possibility," Rasp returned, "but no. The leaders are as perplexed as yourself. What profit would be in it? Selling children is not the business habit of Metropolis. My investigations will bring a conclusion to these matters, I assure you."

"Certainly, your assurances did not protect Joh Fredersen's own child from being kidnapped!"

Rasp's face turned to stone. "What?" he asked. "WHAT!" he demanded. The worker back stepped back, shriveling from Rasp's demanding gaze.

"Freder Fredersen was kidnapped," the worker said quietly. "I'm surprised you haven't heard, though it's only just happened in the hour. There was a girl with him. A person disguised as a nurse single-handedly beat three guards at Freder's apartment. The guards fired guns at the figure but it was unharmed. The figure confronted Freder, and beat and shot him and a female visitor. The figure took Freder and left the woman to die. They had a special report on the radio. They are taking the girl to the hospital."

Uttering not a sound, Rasp strode toward the door. He walked down the steps and walked toward the inimitable New Tower, offering a glance toward the dark house belonging to the scientist and magician known as Rotwang. House and owner remained shrouded of mystery beneath the ever-present shadow of the New Tower. Rasp turned to the house, approaching it. He walked toward the door, sigiled with a red Solomon's Seal. The door opened noiselessly to admit him. A dwarf of a man, wearing a juggler's costume in height, appeared in the doorway. He turned and announced, "Slim is here!" the man said before turning back to address Rasp. "Rotwang will be here momentarily."

As the dwarf said this, a shadow rose behind him in the corridor. The face of Rotwang drifted through the gloom, growing larger as the Faustian scientist approached. "I anticipated your arrival, Slim. You won't come in?"

"Said the spider to another spider the first spider assumed to be the fly," Rasp quipped. "As you likely know by now, Freder Fredersen has disappeared. I was investigating matters on my own time. I have questions. I believe you have answers."

"Perhaps I do," Rotwang said. "I will need to hear the questions first."

"I will ask them on the way to the hospital floor of the New Tower. We need to see what the woman knows. She was with Freder."

"The woman is Charlotte."

"I admit to being surprised as to your knowledge of the woman," Rasp said. "I assumed it already, yet I hope to never assume too greatly."

Rotwang fell silent. Rasp agreed with the attitude as they walked toward the New Tower. They found the moving sidewalk and stepped on its surface. It smoothly moved them along toward the Pater-noster lift. The dark pair stepped into the Pater-noster. It lifted them toward the hospital floor on the fifth story. The substantial size of the hospital floor caused no consternation to Rasp. He knew who to ask at the front desk, and in little time the pair stood over sleeping Charlotte. Plasma and medicine stored in glass bottles pumped through an accordion device through clear, pliable celluloid tubes to deliver the precious liquids into syringes in her arm.

"Charlotte," Rasp said softly.

Charlotte's eyes fluttered open. She looked at Rasp drearily. "The Tall Man. I thought you would let me be."

"I did. I need to know what happened to you."

"The cameras…"

"Caught everything kinoscopically. They recorded none of the words. They tell us too little. You were there. Tell us exactly what you saw."

"Let me tell it," a woman's voice came from outside the room. Nurse 58311 entered, brandishing her pistol. "I know the occurrences far better than Charlotte. I came here to silence Charlotte, yet I am pleased to find Joh Fredersen's Tall Man. It is extraordinary luck to find Rotwang in your presence as well!" She stared at the scientist. "How I have hated you for what you have done to me, Rotwang! All the people I need rid the world of are sitting in this room." Nurse grinned.

"The nurse reveals herself," Rasp said. "Kidnapping children to sell them on the black market is not a task generally attributed to your profession."

"Would you rather I let the children be relegated to a lifetime of mindless drudgery? Taking them from the workers gives them an opportunity. I think even their parents would wish for their children to be in an environment where their potential might be fulfilled."

Rasp's jaw clamped for a moment before he spoke again. "No. You have removed opportunities from their parents to give their own children a home when you steal the infants from them. You judge those workers unfairly."

"Judge them? It is your Master of Metropolis, Joh Fredersen, who condemns them to servitude! He passes no judgments except to keep their tongues and push the torturous Catherine's Wheels of Rotwang's mad designs! Those with ability need never know nor concern themselves with the damnable pit where those workers toil, are injured, and die daily!"

"You make more thoughtless inhabitants of Metropolis, blind to the workers."

"And you, Tall Man? What do you do for the workers? You are nothing more than Joh Fredersen's stooge!"

Rasp laughed easily. "You know nothing of me. I work for Joh Fredersen, yes. I am dedicated to Metropolis and its workers. If the workers destroy the city, they will have nothing. I stand between them and the destruction of Metropolis. Wanton savage anarchy has never solved anything. In fact, it is how all of this began. The savage wars and brutalities of the past have been the result of the lawless, with none to protect the defenseless from abuses unimaginable. That is a state of blindness. That is the unfettered state of mankind. To create a motion toward ultimate justice it is necessary to create justice itself. Anarchy is not the answer; it is the antithesis. Despotic governments are not governments at all. They are anarchical and place the power in the hands of the few. The workers have representation, whereby they will attain means of working toward a brighter day that will free all. The burdens of the Masters have their own weight."

"The burdens of the Masters do not compare to the deadly machines below, created by this madman!" She pointed her white-gloved index finger accusatorily toward Rotwang. "I know the pains and tortures which your machines mete out to the workers! I am a monument to that pain!"

Rotwang's eyes dilated with his broad grin. "I created the machines to create a new world! One where my name will live on forever! Not alone in your condemnations, Nurse! On the lips of the people will be praises for the genius of Rotwang! I give birth to the machines because I must release them! My machines do not destroy." Rotwang held his mechanical fist up high. He stared at it to create an impact. "They create!"

"As you created me?" Nurse snarled. "As you destroyed me? As you discarded me?"

Rotwang peered through eyes cleared of sanity. "Jael! I know you! I *saved* you! I saved your life!"

Jael howled with rage."Madman!" Her gloves came to her chest, tearing violently at the clothes. The frock and blouse ripped way in her attack. An empty metal ribcage showed naked beneath. Her spine fashioned a model of the Pater-noster. Tiny metal boxes moved up and down on a pair of opposing conveyors in a fashion reminiscent of a Mobius strip. The descending glowed a green light, the ascending a yellow light.

"Beast!" She continued. "Is this life! Is this salvation!"

With glee, Rotwang danced a jig. "Yes! Yes! A thousand times yes! As you live and breathe! You are here to chide me! I will not be goaded for my brilliance! No remorse for giving you life, though you intend me death! You should thank me! You should praise me! Murdering me will attest to the triumph of genius!"

"You didn't give me life-you have made me my own Iron Maiden! You're no genius-you are a sadist! You stole my identity! I am no longer a woman! I am no one! You did this! Better death than this torturous existence."

"Why, then, your persistence?" Rotwang mocked.

"To ensure no child grows to suffer the tortures you design!"

Rotwang laughed. "Attitude makes curses of gifts, or gifts of curses! You choose!"

Seething, Jael vacillated on Rotwang's insane pronouncements and the conundrum they emulated in her mind. Rasp took advantage of her indecision. He moved toward the pistol on the floor. She swung at him. He ducked and knelt to pick up the gun as her fist met with the brick in the wall. The force of the blow shattered the brick wall, shredding her gloved hand to reveal the metal appendage below. Gun in hand, Rasp moved to avoid another blow. He pulled the trigger as his back hit the corner wall. She shrieked as the bullet tore at her cheek. The superficial wound bled. Wailing, she turned and fled the room. Rasp rushed after her, leaving Rotwang to continue his maniacal ravings.

Jael moved with machine-induced accuracy. Challenged to keep up, Rasp reached the corner of one corridor just in time to see her turn another. Acknowledging he could not keep up with her artificial speed, he moved to anticipatory tactics. Jael attempted to double-back and lose him in the confusion of corridors, though her initiatory direction suggested the hospital Pater-noster as a destination. Rather than heading directly to the machine, the lanky figure continued on as the pursuer in the cat-and-mouse game. He cut time through knowledge of the Tower.

Finally, he let her think she had lost him. He headed toward the Pater-noster, as did Jael. In this case, she became the follower, though unwittingly. Rasp now headed for the Pater-noster, careful to avoid allowing Jael to know she was following him. He slipped into a janitor closet to observe the Pater-noster from a distance.

He looked on as Jael approached the Pater-noster. In her journey, she had found a white hospital overcoat to cover her chest. Rasp wondered if her appearance had escaped the notice of the people she encountered along the way. The soft thrum of the eternal passenger lift continued as she stood next to it. She observed as people ascended and descended in the boxes. She timed the moment as the view of the ascending and descending compartments to exactly when neither person in the Pater-noster would be likely to have a clear view in their journey. This floor was not the emergency floor, nor was it the common area, so it was the least likely to receive many exiting visitors. In that short amount of time, she plunged toward the stark-white wall and opened an access panel next to the lifts by pressing an obscured and recessed button. The door closed after Jael disappeared through it.

Rasp rushed down the hallway and slipped into the maintenance access area. He needed to discover which lift Jael took. He would not allow her to slip through his fingers.

Peering quickly at the ledge whereby the maintenance compartments were accessed, he noted a slight, red mark on the nearer ascending portion. The mark seemed to be blood of recent origin. Assessing the spot, he chose the descending side.

Stepping onto a downward cell, he peered closely at the dim shaft. Making little noise, all of it covered by the increased volume of the clanking chains of the machine, Rasp descended the ladder.

The inner concrete walls and exposed steel girders of the New Tower moved by. Soon the Pater-noster travelled through the basements and sub-basements of the Leviathan structure. Doors on the passenger side pushed the back wall out to force any passengers persisting beyond the last floor to exit at this level. The paired conveyors split from each other at the end of the rectangular shaft into the vast cavern below. The chains of the seemingly-infinite eternal lifts spiraled around each other loosely while the remaining cells, resting on a single, strong pivot, remained upright. The ascending compartments snaked around the descending ones several times, dimly lit in the abyss, a mechanical love-dance of cobras around Mercury's caduceus staff. Rasp observed this in the descending and ascending bodies he rode. At the closest points the ascending cells slid by moved two meters from the descending.

Mixed with the overt cacophony from the multitudinous Pater-noster lifts, Rasp heard a metallic sound below, moving toward him. He stopped in his lift and waited. In the ascending lift, he saw Jael appear. Clothes discarded, the creature's entirely mechanical body revealed itself. Utilitarian gun-metal gears acted as pivot points for the skeletal metal arms and legs. With her back turned to Rasp, he could see the full Pater-noster model, glowing blue in its continual Mobius strip fashion. The incongruity of her soft, beautiful face juxtaposed with the apathetic metal frame seemed a poignant reminder to Rasp of his own life. Her intricately-devised metal fingers and extended toes designed for extreme functionality wrapped around the ladder rungs as she moved swiftly higher, passing Rasp's position.

"You thought I could not detect your movements, Tall Man!" She shrieked over the abyss as she progressed swiftly higher. "On earth as in heaven, I am as one with my father, the Pater-noster! I felt the treads of your feet as you walked over its spine!"

She leapt to the descending lifts, landing deftly in the access compartment above. Rasp waited for her to climb down the ladder. "Where is Freder?" he demanded.

"Freder is hidden where you cannot go, Tall Man!" Jael rushed toward Rasp with the force of an automobile. She swung a deadly fist, yet he ducked readily. The powerful blow struck the compartment wall with a sonorous ring. Being smelted of extremely strong alloy, the metal lift remained unscathed.

"I grant you are tireless. I am relentless. I will hound you to no end until Freder is safe."

Jael pressed her attacks. Though swift and powerful, Rasp found them mechanically predictable. Filled with rage, Jael persisted. "I am tireless, Tall Man! You have not the stamina!"

Rasp dodged the pistons thrown at him. He came in close to Jael, and gently placed his hand on her cheek, caressing it. Her eyes fluttered, willfully pressing her cheek into his hand. "Perhaps we need not battle to my inevitable death. There is another way. Your creation is a tragic event, yet it does not define your essence."

Her eyes met Rasp's. "Rotwang has done this to me." A tear fell from her cheek. "Taken away my beauty and taken away everything that makes me human!"

"He has left the only thing that makes a woman beautiful. Rotwang's a madman. Madmen have no conscience nor fear of death nor life. In his madness, he was able to salvage your beautiful brain and your face."

"He replaced my body with a network of crowbars and gears!"

Rasp continued to soothe Jael. "Mechanical wonders that your mind causes to move in ballerina grace and ease. You, your mind, makes it beautiful beyond compare."

"I have no arms! No legs! No chest! There is nothing for the touch of a lover to know. Nothing where a child may grow!"

Rasp ran his thumb over her full lips. "Nothing? I find you beautiful in simplicity. "

"I have no heart! No organs!"

"Hearts and organs are a system to run the arms, legs, and the organs themselves. The system exists largely to keep itself going. It nears superfluity. Propagates superfluity. A woman is a beautiful creature. It can create love beyond understanding. Its genius can exceed the comprehension of man. You have your infants in the children you help. You love them, do you not?" Rasp embraced the cold frame, drawing closer. "The mind is where love happens." He leaned forward, kissing her lips with passion. "Can we do this together, Jael?" he breathed deeply. "You have done so much by yourself. I can assist."

Engaging in the kiss, Jael breathed deeply while the Pater-noster passed into the roof of the Worker's Hospital, once more regulated and confined by steel girders and concrete. Her metal fingers clasped Rasp's throat and pushed him away. "Do you think me a fool, Tall Man? I could snap your neck right now!"

"Do you really think so?" Rasp took out a thin, brown-papered cigarette. He wrapped his left elbow over her arms and put the cigarette between his lips. She allowed this as he struck a match on her metal hand holding his throat and lit it.

*"Nothing? I find you beautiful in simplicity."*

Jael's eyes slowly fell. "You made two mistakes, Tall Man. You thought you could trick me with our Casanova whispers! I am no heaving-chest Juliet! I have no use for foolish Romeos. Your second mistake is to think I did this alone."

To punctuate her point, Jael turned as the lift-box moved passed to a recessed wall. Jael lifted Rasp into the air and into the recess. A door slid open in the wall as the Pater-noster continued downward. Behind the door stood Charlotte's date at the Xanadu Lounge brandishing an outlawed steam-driven repeater pistol.

"Hello, Tall Man. How rude that you didn't allow me to introduce myself at the Xanadu Club. I'm Sydney Oosthuizen. That is my name, but you may call me Sid! You can be on speaking terms with your death!"

"You made one mistake, Jael." Rasp grasped Jael's hand with his right. With powerful fingers, he spun the screwed-on thumb loose, and pulled I it easily away from his neck. Using her surprise, he pushed her into the ascending lift. Sydney's steam-repeater chattered hot teeth of molten lead. Rasp jumped through the still-open door. The projectiles tore at the descending cell, emitting a haze of warm mist. The bullets left not a mark on the cell's metal surface.

Syd rushed to the next passing compartment, to be met with an unexpected hand punching him from the side. The gun clattered against the metal floor as Syd imitated its fall.

"Introductions were not necessary, 'Syd.' I knew who you were. If you must, you may call me Rasp." Rasp wrapped his fingers around Syd's neck. Dragging him out of the compartment, he threw the man to the floor, arranging Sydney Oosthuizen's neck to the edge of the floor and the descending lift. "Stop! It'll cut my head off! This is murder!"

"It's the least I can do. Where's Freder?"

The edge of the lift came to within inches of Oosthuizen's neck. "In the lake! FOR GOD'S SAKE HE'S IN THE LAKE!"

The edge of the lift slid over the back of his head, shaving his hair as Rasp pulled him out. He continued to hold onto Oosthuizen's neck. "If you are lying, the next time will be murder."

"It's true!" Syd's eyes were wide. "Only Jael knows where! It's true, you blasted devil!"

Rasp smiled thinly. "You are lucky if I am not. Where is Jael going?"

"I don't know!" Rasp tightened his gloved fingers around Syd's neck. "Believe me!"

Rasp nodded. "I believe you. You are more lucky than you know." Rasp picked up the steam-pistol from the compartment floor, throwing it and Syd into the Pater-noster.

Rasp descended on the ladder, following Jael. "Jael!" he shouted, his sonorous, deep tones reverberating throughout the shaft, though inaudible by design of the Rotwang process to those on the passenger side of the lift.

Lantern flashes tore the fabric of darkness. Rotwang lead Charlotte through an underground maze of caverns and tunnels. These pathways and natural caves were built by ancient people eons in the past. They used the catacombs to live, hide, worship, bury, and defend. These wounds and veins of the Earth remained unknown and unmapped. Exploited and plundered for the hidden metals Earth held in its bowels, the ancient mines still hid untold wealth of kings and nations.

"Where are you taking me?" Charlotte asked, brushing a dark spider from her shoulder.

"To where are you following?" Rotwang chuckled. "I take you to nowhere. I only lead."

"Where are we going, then? No riddles, please."

"We are nearly there, my dear." They carried on in silence a few minutes longer. Rotwang moved the torchlight over a rugged entrance. "There! While that wolf Rasp follows the bird, we arrive at its nest!" He led her through the opening.

"What is in here?" Charlotte asked.

The lantern illuminated the large cavern. Discarded machines, some of obvious design, others of indiscernible purposes, rusted away in eternal darkness. "Everything you seek is in here to discover. Patience!"

A soft hum of machinery reached their ears.

Rotwang furrowed his brow. A smile stretched over his mad countenance as he picked up the pace. "We have found it!"

Rotwang and Charlotte picked through the discarded constructs and machinery. They came to an area, dimly-enlightened by the torch Rotwang carried, with rows in the dozens of mechanical cribs from the Moses Matriculator Machination. Charlotte rushed to the nearest one and peered in. "There's a baby in here!"

The infant sleepily open its eyes and offered a smiling coo. The sound could not be heard throw the Rotwang process treatment of the glass, yet the expression of delight on the child drew a tear from Charlotte's eye. "It is alive!" Rushing around to look into the cribs Charlotte wept with joyful bitterness. Her relief and her pain informed her expression. "Where is my child? Is it here too? I see no identification on the cradles."

"Should there be?" The voice came from behind them. Rotwang and Charlotte slowly turned to see Jael holding her antiquated and deadly pistol.

"I want my child!"

"I see there's an issue. You want your child, yet the couples who asked for an infant just want a child. Perhaps they are more worthy as parents? Certainly they are better equipped financially to care for a child. However, your child is not here, and I will not return him to you."

Sneering, Charlotte stepped toward Jael. The nurse reminded her by shaking the pistol. "I have already told you the child is not here. Would you die for something you cannot have?"

"If I cannot have my son, I cannot live with myself."

"You gave him up for money. You gave him a chance for a better life, free from the slavery offered in the worker's city."

"I was desperate. Estrogen raged through my body, I feared for my family's lives. I will live with that regret for the rest of my life. I won't allow another regret to compound it. I want my child back. Free to choose which city he inhabits. Even a gilded cage is still a prison."

"You are so blind, Charlotte! I offered a chance to build a life for your son and yourself. I offered life for your parents too!"

"You offer us life? What do you know of life? You don't know what it's like to be a mother. You are hardly alive."

Jael gasped to silence. When she spoke again, it was soft and deliberate. "I know life precisely because I am nearly dead. I know the love of a mother precisely because I can never, ever be one. I can carry children from those who do not desire them to those who will love them. I live because I was given love in the womb. Is there any more to life than this? Is there any greater love than that of a mother? You see me as a monstrosity. I see the culture creating me as the true monstrosity. I believe in children; in their ability to change the monster. If I did not, I would have ended my cursed existence long ago."

"What will you do about me, then?" Charlotte demanded. "Return my child or kill me!"

"Those are options," Jael admitted. "I have already given you life, as I have already taken it away. You are persistent. I discover today persistent opposition." Jael shrugged as she raised the pistol to aim at Charlotte's head. "I suppose the only choice is to be persistent myself."

Charlotte stood stock still, defiant. The hammer fell. The blast resounded throughout the cavern. The bullet exited the barrel.

Jael let the gun fall to the ground. "I cannot. I am sorry."

Charlotte realized the bullet had whizzed past her left ear. She touched her head, the side of her face. "You...you didn't kill me!"

Jael sighed. "How I wish I could. I cannot. Not now."

Rotwang laughed. "Of course you will not kill her! You are no monster. You are a nurse. I created you as such!"

Jael spun and lifted the pistol on Rotwang. "She is safe from me for now, but you're another matter! You're the monster!"

Rotwang erupted raucously in guttural mirth. "I welcome your judgment! Metropolis now deems me a mad devil! Kill me; you make of me a saint! You had your chance to kill both of us! You have not done so before. I doubt you will do so now. If Freder had not tried to rescue Charlotte from the bullet, I surmise that shot would have missed too! Well-meant as the action of the beloved Son of Metropolis was, she was in no danger from your gun until he thrust both of them into its path. That is what happened, is it not?" Rotwang returned to performing his mad jig as he had earlier in the hospital.

Jael dropped the revolver once more to her side. "It is true. I planned to shoot, but I couldn't. Perhaps you programmed that in me. Rotwang."

"Not I," Rotwang smiled. "That is all on you."

"So you'll return my baby," Charlotte pleaded.

"I will not. It's true I can't kill you, but I have other ways to subdue you."

Charlotte rushed toward Jael, inhaling the stream of green gas the latter exuded from her fingertips. Rotwang held his breath, yet it was too late.

"Airborne anesthesia." Jael smiled as Charlotte's fingers slid down the nurse's dress into unconsciousness, her fingers clutching for the infant. Rotwang fell backward into a pile of his own failed, broken, and discarded creations. "Your genius knows no bounds, Rotwang."

Jael went to one of the cradles and opened it. "I will keep the child." She said, lifting the infant into her arms. "This matter is done."

"Not yet, it ain't." The voice of Sydney Oosthuizen sounded before he came into view around a pile of broken machinery. "We've got a sweet setup. I'll kill you and the kewpie dolls before this letting the tail go on this cash cow."

Jael looked at Syd. "Thank you for telling me that, Syd." She stepped toward him, cradling the infant in her arms. "It gives me the chance to kill someone." She cocked her head to her side as a bird. "You will do to relieve frustrations."

Syd leveled his steam pistol. "Stay back Jael! We can still make a lot of dough!"

"You see, gentle Sydney, you engaged these endeavors for the money alone." Jael continued to advance. "I see now that our purposes, while for a time complementary each to the other, were crossed from the beginning and never meant to last long."

The intensity of her emphatic gaze burned the gangster deeply. "If that's how you want it, sister!" The steam repeater fired projectiles cacophonously. Jael continued to advance; her metal arms were stripped of clothing, leaving the naked metal arms exposed. In her encompassing embrace, Charlotte's infant remained safe from the frightening clatter of bullets. Striding up to Mister Oosthuizen, she grasped his gun in her right hand and pulled it from his grip. He backed away. "You ain't human!"

She smiled lightly. "I am more human than you." She swung the butt of the machine gun at his head with great force. The sickening crunch accompanied the crushing inward of his skull. He rocked back and forth for long moments, blood mixing with brain fluid. His broken neck leaned awkwardly to his right shoulder. Sydney Oosthuizen fell to the dirt, and out of the river of life.

✠✠✠

Having descended, the cell of the Pater-noster arrived at the massive underwater lake. Rasp stepped out of the Pater-noster into the Stygian, machine-warmed amniotic fluids of the lake nourishing Metropolis. Few ever descended to the far depths to reach the tail of the great, mechanical Tiamat, the world-encircling snake threatening the end-of-days battle against the hero Marduk. The serpent whispered lives and lays both in its smoothly humming engines, all but muted to the ears of its passengers. Blue lights shown from the Pater-noster helped to illuminate the rectangular concrete shore.

The tails of Rasp's black longcoat floated lazily behind him as he swam for the shore. He pulled himself out of the water. The deeply-gloomed, six-foot walkway disappeared into the receding pitch blackness engulfing the lake.

Water dripped from his jacket, drying quickly to leave no residual trace. He surveyed the vast expanse, searching the lake's placid surface. The shore stretched on for miles, he knew. A quick discovery of where Jael might have placed Freder proved a hopeless task.

Rasp listened to the ever-present sound of dripping from steampipes, reverberating incessantly throughout blackness. Shrugging, he reached into his coat and removed a long, cylindrical flashlight. He switched it on, affirming what he knew already from reading the original blueprints. The enormity of the lake proved daunting for search. He flashed the light over its enigmatic depths. It was designed at a depth of 150 meters; about the distance possible for a human to dive and return. Very few humans alive ever managed such a feat. If Freder was being kept alive at the bottom of it, Rasp came unprepared. If Freder was dead at the bottom, Sydney Oosthuizen and Jael would both be unprepared for Rasp's wrath.

Rasp shined the light over the Moses Matriculator as it gently floated the infant cradles in the water. Freder may be in such a cradle beneath the water, yet the question remained as to where.

Rasp's eyes narrowed as a bright, white light suddenly appeared farther done the shore. He moved behind a nearby pillar, though he was quite invisible to viewing in the inky blackness. The light shut off with the closing of the door.

He saw Jael's hat glow bright blue in the distance. He followed the light as it moved away from him, watched as she stepped onto the surface of the water. Jael floated over the surface as he looked on, headed back toward the Matriculator.

"Jael!" Rasp shouted. "It's Rasp! I have come to find Freder."

Jael looked for Rasp. She was disappointed in her search, yet still she laughed at his words. "Oh, that is a coincidence!" She reached out to the Moses Matriculator. "I am here for the same purpose."

Arriving at the machine, she touched it several times. The actions added a hum to the silent-by-design operations of the mechanism.

Rasp left his hiding place, heading down the shore toward the water-borne Jael. "Do we really have to play?"

"Not at all. In fact, I am finished playing."

Rasp neared the line of floating cradles as a larger version of a coffin-cradle lightly disrupted the surface of the water. He could not see inside it from his vantage point. Jael pulled a lever on its edge, causing the casket to open. She leaned over it to lift the unconscious or lifeless Freder out of the box. "With Freder and Freder's son, none will challenge my designs."

Rasp let his flashlight illumine her. She cradled the infant in her right arm while pulling Freder along under her left.

"You are simply mad, Jael. As discussed earlier, I am mad as well. So too, Joh Fredersen. There is enough to go all around. Of course I will challenge you to my dying breath. Or yours."

Jael smirked in the gloom. "Joh Fredersen will never forgive me the kidnapping of his son, nor his grandson." Freder stirred to dull consciousness. Jael grasped him about the chest.

The door opened once more, interrupting their conversation. The forms of Rotwang, Charlotte, and Joh Fredersen appeared in the sudden light.

Jael's eyes widened at the revelation. "How did you return to consciousness so quickly?"

Rotwang laughed. "Immune to the anesthesia, I awoke in short order. I designed it, after all! Consciousness returned to me just in time to observe the pleasant display of the death of Sydney! After you left, I awoke Charlotte and informed Joh Fredersen."

The voice of the Master of Metropolis, Joh Fredersen, imposed itself into the echoing chamber. "Let me have my son back, Jael, and all is forgiven and forgotten. I am a business man. You will be rewarded for the return of my son."

"I have no reason to believe you, Joh Fredersen, 'Master of Metropolis.'" Her tone carried undeniable and spiteful facetiousness. "I have no need of your blood-money. What you call progress has stolen from me a possibility of a child of my own and my very life! What amount of recompense would equal the portion you have taken from me in the name of 'progress? You are not even concerned for your grandchild!"

"I have no great concern for the child. It is not of my loins."

The words shocked Freder to full awareness. "Father! How can you say that?"

"I do not say. Charlotte has told me she lied to you about your paternity."

Freder looked at Charlotte. "Charlotte?"

Charlotte nodded. "I would say I am sorry, Freder. I am not. I would not have received the help if you had not believed my lie. As you can see, your father has no concern at all. The baby was not yours. Sydney Oosthuizen fathered him as a payment for my father's debts, and agreed to take the child to pay for the balance. The only way to retrieve him, I imagined, was to have you think it was yours. With Syd dead, a matter I do not mourn, there is no need to maintain the ruse any longer. I used you Freder to defeat Sydney and retrieve my child. I meant you no harm, yet it was the only way I saw to freedom for myself and my family."

Rasp looked to Jael. "Release Freder and the infant Jael. It is over."

"The child is mine!" Jael demanded. "Freder's life ensures my custody!"

"No!" Charlotte rushed to Jael, climbing over the coffin-cradles to a point that allowed a leap of some distance to the floating raft, and grasped her infant child. Surprised by this action, Jael let go of the infant to hold

Freder with both arms as the conveyance tilted. Jael slid forward to sink into the liquid abyss. Charlotte swam away clutching her child.

Rasp instantly leapt into the water, swimming downward toward Jael, laden with the struggling Freder. The three descended some distance. As strongly as Rasp swam, he could not catch up to the pair. He swam to meet Jael as she came feet-first to stand on the floor of the lake. He let his flashlight illuminate the area. He looked imploringly into Jael's face. The nurse looked at Freder with realization, and let the young man's body free of her grasp. Freder swam upward, his face red.

Rasp gently placed his hand on Jael's cheek as if to wipe a tear from her frightened face. The couple knew she could not be saved, and would soon drown. He kissed her with passion, leaving her only after her eyes closed. He followed the ascending bubble of her last breath upward, coming upon Freder who had fallen unconscious in his attempted ascent. Not allowing himself a deadly breath of drowning water, his lungs near bursting, Rasp clutched at Freder's shirt as he swam up to the too-distant surface.

Exhausted, Rasp reached his hand up, breaking the surface tension of the water, and fell unconscious. The last thing Rasp saw was a black glove reach into the water and grasp his arm, pulling him up with marked strength. .

✝✝✝

Rasp opened his eyes to see Joh Fredersen looking down upon him. "Welcome back, Slim. I owe you my gratitude for safely returning my son to me." Freder held his hand out to Rasp, pulling the Tall Man of Metropolis to his feet.

"I owe you my thanks as well," Freder said.

"As do I," Charlotte chimed in. "An apology to you Freder, for I nearly caused you to lose your life. I hope you can forgive me that, at least."

Freder shook his head. "No, Charlotte. You have given me an introspection of life. I must go on a search to discover what kind of man I want to be. Never again do I want to not know what wrong I may have done. For that, I thank you."

All fell silent, listening to the gentle lapping of the waves against the stygian shore and the coffin-cradles of the Moses Matriculator.

# THE END

# CITY OF HOPE

People often shy away from silent films as laborious and outdated. For me, it is not a judgment that applies to Metropolis. The film is full of life and the characters leap from the screen to this day. I have likely seen this movie more than any other film, and I feel a resident of the streets and sensations of Metropolis.

Re-reading the novel by Thea Von Harbou, I tried to incorporate some of the concepts and characters from there as well. The technology is left as an alchemist's mystery, very befitting of something invented by Rotwang, himself being a mechanical wizard in more ways than one. The 'Rotwang process' renders a soundproofing for rooms, 'Rotwang's trans-oceanic trumpets deliver messages between continents. Little clue is given as to how these technologies actually function. Perhaps that is by design.

Many of the characters are as left to the imagination as explanations of Rotwang's creations. Freder's grandmother proved so intriguing a character in the book, it felt necessary to include her. There were characters that would allow far greater extrapolation. I found Desertus-spiritual leader of the Gothics, quite intriguing. Grot-the overseer of the workers, September-the manager of the Yoshira nightclub, the girl Freder is playing with when he first encounters Maria, and many others present fields ripe for investigation. Even Rotwang's butler, who only shows up briefly, adds to the shadows and breath of Metropolis.

In choosing a central figure for this project, there was no other choice for me than the Thin Man of Metropolis. In Harbou's novelization, he is called Slim. His real name in my story is Rasp, the name of the actor Fritz Rasp who played him in the film. He's certainly a mysterious figure in Harbou's tale, not coming off as a mere lackey of Joh Fredersen. Creating a back story for Slim proved rewarding, as the more the character reveals himself, the more of an indecipherable figure he becomes. In the novel, Harbou writes that Hel, Freder's mother, often came to the cathedral to worship. Obviously a devout woman, it struck me that she may have an additional reason for her visits. These cues proved integral in helping me weave the novel and film together into a cohesive picture.

In the 'American version' of Metropolis, it says the film represents no class, creed, or political party. It represents no specific time or place. Given the 'placelessness' of Metropolis, I chose to base parts of my story on portions of my own mining town of Butte, Montana (which is locally called Butte America). The analogy is imperfect, yet there's a building called the Hotel Finlen. It is quite dwarfed by the New Tower of Babel, yet worthy of mention. Far below Butte rest the old mine shafts, where workers would descend and ascend daily. Daily, if they were lucky, in some instances. If one watches the film or reads the book with their city, town, or village in mind they may find the analogy quite functional.

While Metropolis is a dystopian story, it is an optimistic one compared to stories that would come later and more realistic than Utopian novels preceding it. Aldous Huxley's Brave New World shows a society unsentimentally trapped in unabashed, self-serving consumerism. 1984 shows a dour world where people are hopelessly caught under an oppressive boot. In the optimistic book by Sir Thomas More's, Utopia, Francis Bacon's New Atlantis, and Edward Bellamy's Looking Backward, we see societies based on experimental naiveté. While these societies may or may not function, they place an enormous amount of their wager on the ability of humans to function on absolutes not generally recognized as within the ability of many humans to fulfill. At best, such societies seem prone to failure as the Brooks Farm experiment and others like it have too-often failed. B.F. Skinner's Walden II served as the basis of experimental communes, all of which failed. Skinner, by the way, had theories with similarities to the Moses Matriculator Machine. Back to the point, all of these books offered either dour pessimism or unbridled optimism, as most dystopian and utopian literature seems to take one stance or the other.

Metropolis takes a more even-keeled view to my estimation, Harbou recognizes the ills and abuses of society and the positive points as well, leaving the viewer with a message of hope, yet finally offering no conclusive way to achieve this hope but to lay aside our differences and work toward a goal for the benefit of all. If anything gives me hope for the future of the human race personally, it will only come from us working together.

✚╍✚╍✚

**KEVIN NOEL OLSON** - lives in a charming bungalow in Butte, Montana with his wife Amelinda. He writes pulp and children's adventure fiction and pulp adventure fiction along with sundry articles. Included among his works are the TOCSIN CODEX middle-grade series and BUK BAKUS IN DARN NEAR THE FIFTIETH CENTURY. He is also a citizen of Metropolis and a loyal airman on Airship 27.

# THE MAN FROM AIR TOWER 12

## Erik Franklin

The view from the elevated train that morning was stunning. The sunrise caught the steel and glass of Metropolis's skyscrapers, causing a golden hue to blanket the entire city. Even at that hour of the morning, aircraft were flying around the sky like worker bees to a hive. Planes dove and soared while great zeppelins moved through the clouds, each with neon advertisements displayed on their robust bodies, competing with each other to catch the city's attention. If one looked down, he could see the city's pleasure gardens. Each of them was a miniature Eden in this synthetic world, planted high atop the penthouses exclusively for the enjoyment of the wealthy. This was the view atop the highest elevated train in the city, and it never failed to impress tourists or first time commuters. They would stop and gawk, overwhelmed by the beauty of man's architecture and technological advancement. It was impossible not to be impressed…

…Unless your name was Martin Galeen, and after twenty five years taking the same route, you were bored and thoroughly bitter. Occasionally he would glance down at the gardens and grow resentful that he never saw anyone awake at this time. Of course, the rich could afford to sleep in; he never could. He unfolded his paper and lazily scanned through the headlines. There were rumors of some female prophet attempting to lead the underground workers in a revolt against the government. "Good for them," Martin thought to himself "the poor will become less poor, the rich will crumble, and nothing will happen to the rest of us. Life will go on, dull as before."

It was not that he was unsympathetic to their plight, on the contrary, he felt that there were many people like them *above* ground. People thought only of the rich, beautiful people when Metropolis was mentioned, but the truth is that there is a whole group of people who exist somewhere between the elite and the underground slaves. The servants, chefs, doormen, bouncers, pilots, taxi drivers, shop clerks, and people like himself were only a fraction of this group. Martin considered his position only slightly better than the slaves he was reading about. True, he was able to enjoy the sunlight and his accommodations provided by the city were better than the subterranean world, but that is where he drew the line. He had to wake up at an ungodly hour every day, work for ten hours, and then, if he could afford it, (which he almost never could) try to find a few hours of amusement before going to bed. In Martin's mind, there was no difference between himself and the slaves.

"Mama, look!" a little girl said pointing to one of the massive zeppelins that soared over the train. The mother proceeded to tell her daughter what she knew of the ship. Martin scoffed as he thought bitterly to himself: "Without me, little girl, there would be no zeppelins or planes for you to gape at. Without me they would all crash into each other. But do I get a thank you? No!"

In this, Martin was not exaggerating. He was the senior air traffic controller at Air Tower 12. This was perhaps the most prestigious of air traffic jobs, for his tower overlooked the majority of the high rises in Metropolis. Martin had started off as a lowly errand boy at an air tower, climbing his way up the ranks. When he first started working at Air Tower 12, he would get excited when he personally guided the planes of the city elite. Twenty five years later the novelty had worn off.

He arrived at his stop. As Martin rose from his seat, the polished metal doors of the elevated train presented him with the one thing he disliked more than his job: his appearance. Nobody called him handsome, nor did he have the money to persuade them otherwise. He was of an average height with a chubby physique. His greying moustache and thinning hair also displeased him. Martin's nose was small and pointed, while he considered the rest of his face to be pudgy. His eyes, once a vibrant blue, had turned grey like the rest of him. His suit was holding up reasonably well, but he was long overdue for a new one. Straightening up, he walked out of the train with his head held high. Regardless of how he felt about himself, Martin thought that, as a supervisor, he needed to set an example for the Air Tower.

Martin had learned to cultivate a gruff manner, and over the years developed a crusty disposition that made his underlings hop to whenever he said a word. Understandably, this made him unapproachable to most, but it was a consequence that Martin had accepted. In spite of this, after leaving the train he was met by a lanky, balding man with a pockmarked face. He towered over Martin, also wearing a suit that was far past its prime.

"Good morning, Martin!" he said. His sunny disposition, especially this early in the morning, had always disturbed Martin.

"Good morning, Hugo," Martin replied. They had said the same thing to each other for twenty three years. Hugo Osborne was the only person that Martin allowed to address him by his first name. To everyone else, "boss", "sir", or "Mr. Galeen" would do… although "sir" was his favorite. Both worked at the Air Tower, and Martin looked to Hugo as his right hand man. Hugo, as per usual, was finishing a cinnamon roll.

"Hey, the boys and I were thinking about going to the Yoshiwara District next week. We'd love it if you could come." Hugo said between bites.

"I can't afford anything in the Yoshiwara District," Martin replied. His default response to life was that he could never afford anything, and it was said mostly out of reflex rather than actual truth.

"Well, Martin, you're in luck! I heard that some of the clubs have been running discounts lately to drum up some more business."

"Discount dancing girls, that sounds delightful," Martin said with a deadpan delivery "I can only imagine what they look like."

"You need to live a little, Martin. You've been looking tired lately."

"I always look like that," Martin replied as they approached the security checkpoint for Air Tower 12. Martin and Hugo went through the usual examination as they carried on their conversation.

"Well, I can't stop you if you insist on being like that. I can't wait to tell you what you missed." Hugo said as he was patted down by the guards.

"I know exactly what I'd be seeing. Chemical addicted dancing girls, not-so rich snobs pretending to be millionaires getting into fistfights over the girls, and a bunch of cheap booze to make the entire experience nothing but a headache the next morning." Martin had never actually been to the Yoshiwara District, but was making an educated guess based on everything he read in the papers. The Yoshiwara District was always in the news; chock full of headlines involving scandal and violence. It was a world he would prefer to sit back comfortably and ridicule rather than be party to.

"Besides it's better to keep your nose clean, Hugo. What if the Air Manager finds out? Do you want to lose your job?" Martin said to Hugo with an omniscient expression.

"The Air Manager? Last time I was in Yoshiwara District, the boys and I had to drag him back to his car and drive him home. He'll be no trouble." Hugo said with a smile, remembering the incident and the great story it made during lunch break.

Passing the security checkpoint, Martin and Hugo made their way towards the elevator that took them to the top of the tower. They worked in a large, copper colored building with a gigantic white "12" stenciled on it. The elevator had a reinforced glass window, so one could admire the view of Metropolis as they ascended the structure. Martin allowed Hugo to press the elevator button as he absentmindedly watched the skyscrapers grow smaller. Many things did not bother Martin, but Hugo's comment troubled him. The Air Manager acting like a drunken buffoon, his men getting drunk… he could not help but wonder. Was Martin Galeen the only person who took his job seriously?

+++

As he entered the tower, Martin was greeted by the ever present smell of stale coffee as he surveyed the situation during the shift change. He glanced around the large, cylindrical command center and looked over each of his men. They were illuminated by various controls and monitors, their voices were a monotone of coordinates and commands. Despite his earlier thoughts, he was satisfied that his men were guiding people in safely. Just as Martin was about to settle into his normal work routine, something caught his eye.

One of the men was jumping back and forth between seats, frantically issuing orders and checking the instruments for two work stations. Gunther was a young man, only recently employed at Air Tower 12. He had worked exceedingly hard to make a good impression with the rest of the team, and they sometimes took advantage of it. This was one of those times. With his attention divided, Martin knew that the fledgling worker would make a mistake sooner or later.

"Gunther, what is the problem here?" he barked, making his way over to the worker.

"There is no problem, sir!" Gunther said, failing to appear calm. "Fritts is sick today so I have to cover his position."

"Do you realize that what you're doing is impossible! It's a miracle that you haven't let some of these rich clowns in their flyers collide!" Looking around, Martin caught Hugo's eye and waved him over.

"Yes?" he asked.

"Hugo, you head over to that budget meeting today and report back to me. You know the material as well as I do. I'll take over here." Gunther was stunned as Martin sat down beside him and rearranged the console to his preference. Hugo looked annoyed at his boss.

"I can take over here if you want to go…"

"I don't, I trust that you'll represent us well."

"You do realize that it will reflect poorly on Air Tower 12 if the senior air traffic controller is not there…"

"And it will look much worse if Air Tower 12 fails to do its job. Goodbye, Hugo!" Martin growled, his unpleasant demeanor in full force. Hugo knew that further discussion would be pointless, so he grabbed the appropriate papers from Martin's office and headed out of the building.

Sighing, Martin looked at Gunther. It was unthinkable to the young man that anyone would lower their status in the workplace. Martin was the leader, not a worker, and according to the unspoken rules he should not be operating machinery alongside someone as lowly as himself. However, Martin was raised by an old-fashioned family. His father taught him that sometimes the best way to get the job done was just to roll up your sleeves and dive right in without a second thought. He was irritated by the young man's gaping mouth, so he offered an explanation to shut it.

"Listen, the only reason I'm here right now is so that none of these rich clowns go down in flames. Now stop gawking at me, you've got lives to manage."

Turning back to his console, Martin placed the binoculars to his eyes and looked out at the city in front of him. The clouds obscured part of the skyscrapers and towers, but the golden radiance of the sun lit them beautifully. Martin felt his spirit rise and his heart flutter slightly, for it had been a long while since he was actually in a seat guiding planes. He had nearly forgotten the joy that he felt at seeing Metropolis from this vantage point, and he made a mental note to come back to this viewpoint more often. It reminded him of his first day on the job, watching pilots emerge from the clouds and the neon glow of zeppelin advertisements illuminating sections of the city. It was a sense of wonder that had been rekindled, and if any of his workers had observed him, they would have been mystified to see ten years erased from his physical appearance. This was the real reason he sent Hugo to that meeting… he wanted to do his old job again.

As much as Martin wanted to fondly remember old times, he still had a job to do. What the clouds obscured was revealed by radar. He got on the radio and began to read coordinates and flight plans to the pilots. He got through the first hour rather awkwardly, he felt, but by the second hour his muscle memory and familiar routine kicked in. He watched his planes soar to and fro, proud to be their guardian angel.

An old annoyance of the job crept back once again, but Martin did not mind. A zeppelin from the Nibelungen Pharmaceutical Company was making its way down the main stretch of the city, its new advertisement campaign painted on its side. Zeppelins, for air traffic controllers, were a necessary evil. They were slow, bulky, and the biplanes constantly had to divert their courses to avoid collisions. Making sure that these diversions did not intersect was the tricky part of the job, but Martin was not the senior air traffic controller for nothing.

Martin talked the zeppelin pilot through the main district of the city. The timing of the route coincided with elevated rail traffic, so commuters could be persuaded to buy pills from the Nibelungen Pharmaceutical Company. The biplane pilots made their usual gripes and complaints, but each safely navigated around the large obstacle.

It was then that Martin observed something strange on his radar screen. A single blip had been moving in a straight line for some time now, and if it kept up on its present course, it would crash into the zeppelin! Fearing that the pilot may be having a mechanical problem, he hailed the zeppelin crew. A quick glance at the radar and lighting quick mental calculations plotted a safe route for the ship. It would be a close call, but it was the only chance that they had!

"Air Tower 12 to Nibelungen zeppelin, we've got a situation here! It looks like a plane is having mechanical problems and is heading straight for you! Recommend that you increase altitude immediately!" Martin ordered into the radio. Everybody in the control tower looked over at the commotion, each ready for action.

"Roger, Air Tower 12, increasing altitude. We've spotted the plane... I've never seen one like that before!" the zeppelin pilot replied.

As the zeppelin rose in the air, Martin grabbed his binoculars and looked out the window. After a moment of searching, he spotted the plane. In all his years of observing aircraft, he could never recall seeing this kind of plane, and he knew virtually every type there was! The plane was of a tri-wing design and painted a solid crimson color. There were no markings, and as far as Martin could see, no visible damage or problems of any kind. Was the pilot deliberately trying to crash into the zeppelin?

Air Tower 12 watched with bated breath as the incident unfolded. Martin, who was not accustomed to calling upon a higher power, prayed that his maneuver worked. The next few seconds seemed like an eternity. The zeppelin, still rising, had only just evaded the crimson plane! Martin was banking on the fact that the plane would have reached terminal velocity, which meant that maneuvering or sudden turns would have been difficult, if not near impossible. The entire tower gave a cheer and sigh of relief as the danger was averted, but Martin ran back to the radio and adjusted the frequency.

Not knowing the plane's frequency, he adjusted the radio for a general broadcast and sent the message out. "This is Air Tower 12, repeat, Air Tower 12, will the pilot of the crimson tri-plane identify yourself?"

There was a moment of silence as Martin waited anxiously for the answer. He was about to repeat his request when the reply came. It was not at all what he expected. A piercing, horrible scream emitted from the radio! It was not a yell of agony or fear, rather it was the angriest, most hate filled sound that Martin had ever heard. Amidst the rage was a warning, like a predatory animal threatening one trying to steal its food.

Martin leaned back in his seat as the yell faded. He watched as the mystery plane flew away from the cityscape and disappeared into a dense cloud. The stunned workers at Air Tower 12 all turned to their boss and hailed him as a hero.

"Three cheers for Mr. Galeen!" "Bravo, sir!" "That was incredible!" These were the words that Martin had longed to hear his entire career… but they felt empty and hollow. He appreciated that his workers meant well and quietly thanked them, but the whole incident left him shaken. Attempting to regain his composure and return to his old self, he barked at everyone.

"Stop the party and get back to work! Just because we stopped one crash doesn't mean we let our guard down. We have a shift to finish!"

The men nodded and went back to work, but there was not one among them who did not feel pride for Martin. As Martin continued to operate the station, he felt his thoughts drifting back to that scream and the plane. Nothing like it had ever happened before in his career, or he doubted, in the career of any air traffic controller.

A short while later, Hugo came back to the control room with a packet of company propaganda, notes, and general rubbish paperwork. He slapped them down next to Martin with a weary smile on his face.

"Here you go. Reading material for tonight. It ought to put you to sleep faster than any pill," Hugo said jovially, and then he got a good look at Martin's expression. Hugo's demeanor changed. "Hey, you don't look so good today, Martin."

"I always look like this," Martin said absentmindedly as he continued his work.

"Listen to me. Let me take over this station, and then you can go home for the rest of the day. I am serious." Hugo dropped the façade of jolliness. Martin looked at him, and knew that Hugo would not go down without a fight.

"Hugo, I'm in charge here. I've already had Fritts call in sick. If I don't show a good example for the boys, then I might as well quit now and go work on the Heart Machine."

"And what an example he gave us today!" said Gunther, turning his head to face them. "You should have seen the boss!"

"What happened?" Hugo said, bracing himself for the incoming story. Gunther related the events with panache and the occasional embellishment, but it was nothing that Martin bothered correcting him over. When he heard the events again, Martin listened closely to the descriptions, but something bothered him.

"And then the zeppelin flew out of the way just in the nick of time!" Gunther finished the tale with a smile on his face. It was evident that this was just a warm up telling, and that his friends and family would hear an even more dramatic version of events.

"That was quick thinking, Martin. I guess that's why they made you the boss!" Hugo said as he patted Martin's shoulder.

"You forgot the scream." Martin stated flatly.

"What? Oh yes, the pilot screamed at Mr. Galeen as he flew away." Gunther added casually, for clearly this part of the story was not that interesting to him.

"What did he say?" Hugo asked.

"Nothing. He did not say anything. Just one loud, long, hateful scream. It was like an animal was flying the plane... Not a man." Martin spoke somberly.

"Well, no wonder you seem all shaken up. If you're really sure that I can't relieve you..."

"I'm sure. I'll meet with you about the budget later today." Martin said, although making budgetary ends meet was the furthest thing from his mind.

✝✝✝

As Martin predicted, the meeting was a crushing bore. He did what he normally did: tell Hugo to use his own sound judgment while he signed whatever papers were necessary to keep things running smoothly. Checking the clock, it was time for them to be relieved by the night shift. The morning workers of Air Tower 12 were free to rest before the next shift.

Martin heard his workers exchanging stories with the night crew about his heroics that day. Despite the lack of acknowledgement that he was complaining about previously, he wished that they would have kept the story to themselves. It turned out that he did not like being the hero. He expected and demanded that any of his men would have done the same thing in this circumstance. Martin would not treat that worker like royalty, perhaps he would give him a recommendation, but he increasingly grew sick of his small measure of fame. "Be careful what you wish for…" he mused.

Riding down the elevator, Martin looked at the Metropolis skyline. The city, which was a majestic sight in the daytime, was even more wondrous at night. The massive spires were illuminated from the various lights within. Neon advertisements and the lights from aircraft looked like moths circling a fire. Spotlights cast beams of light across the buildings and high into the clouds. The headlights of the traffic along Metropolis's superhighways flowed at an alarming rate. Real darkness never exists in a city like Metropolis, yet in the back of Martin's head, he knew that *he* was out there. The mysterious plane and its pilot lurked in the shadows that even the glittering city could not lighten.

As per his routine, Martin declined a chance to go to the Yoshiwara District that evening with Hugo and a few of the other workers. They shrugged and said their goodbyes as Martin made his way wearily towards the elevated train for home. There was only one woman he wished to see, and she would be riding the train as well.

Boarding the train, Martin hunted around until he spotted the woman that he was hoping to see. Her mechanic's clothing was covered in grease and oil stains, which often caused many of the other passengers to sit away from her. That was to Martin's advantage, for he did not wish to be overheard.

The woman's head was stuck in a copy of an aviation magazine, and her hands, though delicate and feminine, were already showing the telltale scars and nicks of her profession.

"Excuse me, miss, but do you know anything about planes?" Martin inquired.

"Do *I* know anything about…" she said putting down her magazine in disbelief. She had a pretty face (although it had a few grease marks on it), black hair pulled back into a ponytail, and large olive green eyes eager to see the world. She recognized Martin and smiled "Oh, hello Mr. Galeen! How are you?"

"Long story Chelsea, I hope you have a few minutes."

She patted the seat next to her and he took it. Martin had considered

Chelsea Berndt the daughter he always wanted. Her mother was a close friend of his ex-wife, and he was there when Chelsea was born. After the usual mechanical conditioning and chemical treatment given to infants in Metropolis, she was brought up by her mother, Martin, and his ex-wife. Her father was a criminal, sent underground to work for the remainder of his natural life. The only thing he ever gave her was an interest in all things mechanical and technical. Her father was part of a stolen car ring, although he told Chelsea that he was a mechanic. They would spend hours on end tinkering with cars. After her father was arrested, she never spoke of him. It was like he never existed. Eventually, Martin became a surrogate father to her, and got her the job she currently held: repairing aircraft.

She listened with great interest to the story, and he watched closely as her brows furrowed at the mention of a tri-wing plane. When he wrapped up his version of events (which was somewhat less melodramatic than Gunther's) he asked her what she thought.

"Well, that's amazing obviously! You're a hero!" she exclaimed.

"Thank you, but that's not what I'm concerned about. Have you ever heard of the plane I've described?"

"In a museum, yes. They were used in the old wars before Metropolis was built, but I did not know that any of them were in working condition. You said that the plane had no markings, correct?"

"No markings. I looked through the binoculars and saw a solid, red plane... I didn't even get a glimpse of the pilot..."

"Well, that's illegal you know," Chelsea stated. "I mean, without markings and labels, how can the tower monitor the plane and signal it?"

"Exactly, we couldn't. I'd say that the pilot was trying to be sneaky except for the fact that he painted his plane a dark red."

"Perhaps it is psychological warfare," Chelsea ventured, her mind going back to her air history books. "Oftentimes, a bold, confident pilot will paint his plane with a clear disregard for camouflage. It is as if he is challenging his opponents by giving them an obvious target."

"But there are no wars anymore, Chelsea. And where would a pilot get an old fighter like that in the first place?"

"Well, I can ask around."

Chelsea then proceeded to tell Martin about her day. It was the usual routine of parts not fitting, her knowing more than her boss, and the latest with her boyfriend. Martin listened with polite interest, doing his best to shove that red plane out of his mind.

✛✛✛

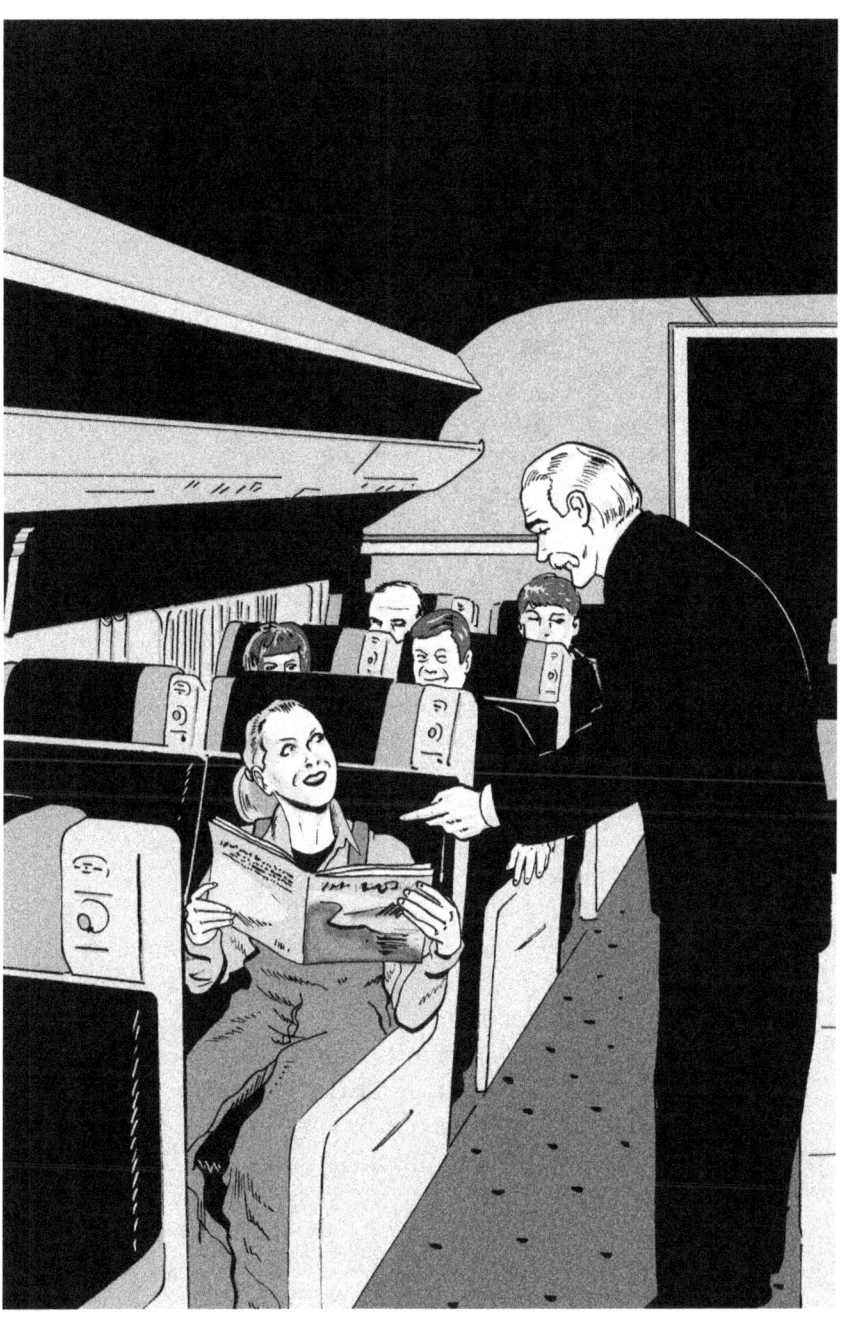

*"Oh, hello, Mr. Galeen! How are you?"*

Martin returned to his apartment after saying goodbye to Chelsea. He looked at the name on the polished sign of the building: The Marine Empress. The designer had sculpted a metal, geometric mermaid heroically posed in the center of neon blue waves. Shaking his head, Martin wished the interior of his apartment matched the opulence of the sign. Walking through the creaking doors, he nodded to the concierge. Her head in a fashion magazine, the concierge gave him the familiar grunt that he expected.

Putting his hands in his pockets, he walked down the empty hallway towards his door. The hallway was polished and clean, but it was not the same as the marble floors that the elite enjoyed. His apartment was too large for one person, and Martin was too tired to put the effort into selling it. His wife had left him a few years ago. Among her many reasons was that she considered him "dull" and his job "boring". If only she were here, then he could have told her how he saved the crew of the Nibelungen zeppelin, and that he was finally the hero of her silly romantic novels.

The divorce had been a bitter one, and they never bothered to stay in touch. Chelsea and her mother came closest to being family, and occasionally Hugo would pop by for a beer, but that was about it. He was preparing for an uncomfortable night's sleep when he opened the door.

He was greeted by a small envelope, slid under the door. Immediately opening it, Martin was faced with the second shock of the day.

The note was typed in crimson ink. The letters were all capitalized, but they were splotchy, as if typed on an old machine. It read:

"DO NOT INTERFERE!"

The color of the letters… the large type as if someone was shouting… the pilot had been to his apartment! Thinking quickly, he raced to the concierge as fast as his feet could carry him. She looked up at him, annoyed at being taken away from her magazine.

"Has anyone been to my apartment today?" he enquired breathlessly. He watched as the woman made a dramatic act of consulting her notes, reminding him of the inconvenience he was putting her through.

"I signed in the mailman, the city health inspector, and… oh yeah, there was a mysterious stranger with a sinister expression on his face. He had a loaded gun and was asking for you."

He glared at her, not enjoying her joke. She shrugged and went on, "Nobody out of the ordinary, Mr. Galeen. You can relax."

"Then who put this letter in my apartment?"

"I didn't see anyone."

"Thanks," Martin said insincerely as he sauntered back to his apartment. She was absolutely useless. Notorious for neglecting her duties, any number of individuals could have probably snuck past her without her noticing.

Lying in his bed, Martin reread the note. He was conditioned to follow orders without question. Whether it came from his supervisor or the president of Metropolis, Joh Fredersen himself, an order was an order. He had heard rumors of Fredersen having an independent enforcer, known as the Thin Man, among his associates. Had the incident that made him a hero interfered with government plans? Was he a threat to Metropolis? Whatever the reason, it made him tremble. Perhaps Fredersen was being merciful. After all, he did not know that he was interfering with the government. Any air traffic controller would have done what he did today. Maybe this was an odd way for Fredersen to warn him.

He looked around at his apartment and personal possessions, all that he had in the world. Martin resolved to keep his nose clean and keep doing his job. He would not interfere again.

+++

It was the usual morning routine as Martin took his accustomed seat on the elevated train, doing his best to forget everything. No doubt his workers would bring up the incident from yesterday, but he would keep putting them off until they eventually forgot the whole matter. Looking out the window, he noticed that the radiance from yesterday's weather had been replaced with a grey, overcast sky. Rain was beginning to pour, and one glance at the clouds confirmed that it was not going to let up anytime soon.

Riding along, Martin watched water droplets streak down the window until he felt somebody sit next to him. He turned to see Chelsea with some papers clutched in her hand. She had not yet started work, so her face was not covered with grease and grime. He knew that someday she would make a beautiful bride, and hoped that he would walk her down the aisle. She wore an expression of delight, but tempered it with determination. She thrust the papers into his lap.

"Is this the plane?" she asked. The papers contained blueprints for a tri-winged plane, very similar to what Martin observed. He felt a cold shiver of recognition, but did his best to play it off.

"Is this what you are doing with your free time? What about your young man?" Martin said, hoping to change the subject.

"I had him help me look through the library. Is this it?"

"I think so, but Chelsea, why are you bothering with this? Surely you have better things to do?"

"Better things to do than investigate planes? You're kidding right? If this is the plane, then you literally saw a relic. It is the Artemis 57, a plane left over from the last war. When war was abolished, production of this and every warplane stopped."

Despite his reluctance to continue this conversation, Martin's curiosity got the better of him. "So, how is it flying around today? Surely they were all scrapped or, like you said earlier, in a museum."

"Well, the Artemis 57 was the best plane ever constructed. Period! I don't doubt that they could still fly today. The simpler a machine, the easier it is to repair. If you look at the blueprints, these planes are the model of efficiency. As to where they came from, well there are many private collectors, many of whom restore these machines for historical research or amusement. The parts are easy enough to manufacture, I could do it myself! "

"Could the Artemis 57 fly in weather like this?" Martin asked, pointing at the storm out the window.

"Well, not many pilots could... but there is always an exception. The Artemis 57 could handle almost any weather conditions. I am sure this has to be the plane!"

"So what if it is? What can we do about it? Why don't we just put this whole thing behind us and not interfere." Martin said, patting her hand in a paternal fashion. He already felt tremendous guilt over getting Chelsea involved in this, and telling her about the note would only make things worse.

"Why is it that any time trouble raises its head, you put yours in a hole?" she said indignantly, shifting her body away from Martin.

"I'd rather be safe than sorry," he offered with a shrug.

"It's possible to be both safe and sorry," Chelsea said defiantly.

"One day, Chelsea, you will understand that life is not like an adventure story. There are plenty of fools out there hoping to be heroes. It's not our place to join them."

Chelsea said nothing for a moment, her lips pursed in anger. He stared at her nervously, waiting to speak.

"If that's true, then why were you a hero yesterday?"

"Well, I had to... it was my job. But seeking danger is a fool's errand. It is best not to interfere."

Martin did not enjoy speaking like this, but he felt that he had to. This was the same advice he would have given his own daughter. To condition the children of the lower classes, the government run schools taught Martin and his classmates the story of Icarus. Icarus was a boy who attempted to compete for the same glory as the gods. He constructed feathered wings held together by wax and attempted to fly to Mount Olympus. As he got closer to the sun, the wax melted and he plunged to his death. The lower class children were taught to not reach too far, like Icarus. Glory and wealth were for people like Freder Fredersen, the son of the president of Metropolis. Everyone else, like Martin Galeen and Chelsea Berndt, were to be content with where they were... and safe.

✚✚✚

When Martin reached the control tower with Hugo, he found that Fritts had returned to his workstation, looking under the weather. Sure enough, everybody had told Fritts about the incident, and one worker brought the newspaper that featured the story for Martin to sign. The headline spoke of a near collision, accompanied by a vivid, artistic rendering of the incident. As he read the story, he found no mention of his name, only Air Tower 12 was recognized. He took some comfort in the fact that nothing ever truly changes as he signed the newspaper.

Sitting back in his regular chair, he observed the men as they went about their business. Air traffic was always reduced during a rainfall, so the work environment was much quieter. Martin watched as the rain grew in intensity, hammering on the windows of the tower. The steel and glass monoliths of Metropolis were cleansed by the downpour, but he could see neon signs glowing through the mist. Amongst them he spotted the Nibelungen Pharmaceutical Company zeppelin and felt his heart freeze momentarily. Despite telling himself that he would follow the letter's simple instruction, Martin could not shake his concern. He called over to Fritts.

"Fritts, how's the zeppelin looking in your section?" He waited anxiously for the answer, squeezing his fist unconsciously.

"Everything seems clear." Fritts replied, sniffing. Nobody in the tower could afford to take more than one sick day.

Hugo approached Martin wearing a concerned expression on his face. Martin looked over with curiosity.

"Have we changed places, or are you the one who should be heading home?" Martin said, his attempt to lighten the mood. Hugo stood before Martin, trying to figure out where to start his story. "Hugo, why don't you sit down?"

"No, this won't take long... Something happened last night..."

"You went to one of those discount clubs in Yoshiwara to watch the dancers didn't you? I told you..." Martin began to scold Hugo. It was not the first time that he would have had a compromising story to tell Martin.

"It isn't that, it's after I got home..."

"Go on..."

"I found... I found this under my door..." Hugo produced a piece of paper, but Martin already knew what it was. The blood drained out of his face as he unfolded the paper and read the same message in crimson ink:

"DO NOT INTERFERE!"

Closing it, Martin turned to Hugo and looked up apprehensively.

"Was anyone seen outside your apartment? Anyone out of the ordinary?"

"I don't know. I didn't think to ask... I wasn't thinking clearly at the time!" Hugo said, running his hand over his bald head and down the back of his neck. On a hunch, Martin took the letter and walked over to Gunther.

"Did you receive a letter like this last night?"

Gunther stared at the message in disbelief and looked at Martin curiously. "Yes, yes I did. But how did you know?"

Not answering him, Martin turned to Fritts and showed him the paper. "What about you? Did you get anything like this?"

"Yes, I did. I threw it in the trash, thinking somebody was playing a stupid joke."

Martin nodded and headed back to Hugo, returning the note to him. He lowered his voice as he took Hugo aside.

"Listen Hugo, you're not the only one. I received the same note myself. It's warning us against taking action, and I have a feeling that it has something to do with the zeppelin yesterday."

"But *me*... I wasn't here! I was at the budget meeting with the other air traffic controllers and the Pilot's Guild chief. I had nothing to do with what happened yesterday!"

"No... but Air Tower 12 does... and that's all whoever sent this message knows... that Air Tower 12 is responsible for interfering... He must have targeted everyone who works in the tower."

"Wait... how did he..." Hugo began, but he never got the chance to finish his sentence. At that moment, Fritts raised his voice in a panic.

"Unknown aircraft! You are heading straight for the Nibelungen Pharmaceutical zeppelin! Adjust course immediately!"

Martin flew to Fritt's radio and spoke into it. He could feel his heart racing as he yelled "Who are you? Why are you doing this? Stop!"

It came again. The scream born of madness! As Fritts covered his ears, Martin grabbed the binoculars and frantically looked through the rainclouds, hoping to spot the plane.

Then he saw it. The crimson plane emerged, fighting through the rain on its course for the zeppelin. Martin had just enough time to focus the binoculars to notice a new detail on the aircraft: machine guns! He did not recall them being there yesterday, and try as he might, he could not see the pilot. What he witnessed would remain etched in his memory forever.

Through the torrential rain, the pilot cut loose with a stream of machine gun fire! Tracers cut through the sky like miniature lightning bolts. Spent bullets joined the raindrops as they fell to the earth. The insane battle cry of the pilot mixed with the sound of gunfire over the radio. Air Tower 12 could only watch as the crimson plane destroyed its target.

The bullets knocked out the neon text of the massive balloon, causing sparks to dance amongst the raindrops. The painted logo and ad campaign were shredded to bits. It was only moments before sparks from the bullets ignited the gasses which kept the zeppelin airborne. A massive explosion tore apart the behemoth, sending flaming debris across the city. The burning carcass of the zeppelin crashed onto the streets of Metropolis, causing chaos and destruction in its wake.

Martin stood still, horrified. He could not think or speak; his mind was overwhelmed by what he saw. He was snapped back to reality when one of the workers bumped against him, struggling to get a better view of the carnage. Snapping back to his work persona, Martin began to holler at everyone in the vicinity, forcing them to resume their work.

"Do you think that fire's going to put itself out?" he demanded. "Get on your radios and help the rescue teams coordinate their movements! Keep the air clear of civilians!" His men jumped to and obeyed orders. Hugo called over to Martin, clutching a phone against his chest.

"Martin, it's the Air Manager. He sounds..."

"I can imagine how he sounds. Listen, Hugo, I want you to go through all the files you took to the meeting. See if anything is missing while I deal with the Air Manager."

"What?" Hugo said, not knowing how searching through files would help anybody.

"Just do as I say and hand me the phone!"

Hugo complied while Martin took the phone. He managed a greeting before he felt the full wrath of the Air Manager. His entire career was brought into question, his competence, his dedication, and every single flaw in his personality was flaunted by his enraged superior. When he stopped, Martin finally got a chance to speak.

"With all due respect sir, can you tell me how an air traffic controller is supposed to stop a plane from machine gunning a zeppelin!"

"...What? I thought they crashed into each other!"

"No! They almost crashed *yesterday*! Today the same plane came back and finished what I stopped! Now if you don't mind, I have a tower to run!" Martin slammed down the phone and a strange exhilaration ran through his body. He would never have thought to question his superior before, let alone defy him. He thought back to the threatening letter, and realized that that single sentence is why he had felt so persistently miserable his whole working life. No more.

"Do not interfere my foot!" Martin thought to himself. There were countless dead outside, not to mention the wreckage and damage caused to the city, and the culprit had escaped. If this is what happens when one does not interfere, then Martin resolved that he was going to be a damned nuisance. He would be a thorn in the side of Joh Fredersen himself if he had to, but that pilot was not going to continue his reign of terror!

He sent out a general broadcast to the rest of the air towers. "Air Tower 12 to all other air towers. Keep your eyes open for a red triplane. It shot down a zeppelin and is flying towards the main district. If spotted, report back to me immediately!" Listening to a chorus of the various air towers responding with "Roger", Martin turned to see Hugo approaching him with a mystified countenance.

"This is the strangest thing," he began, giving the papers one last look "but the duty roster is missing. I brought it to the meeting to show the number of combined hours the tower worked this past month, but I can't locate it."

"I see..." Martin said. He was no detective, and did not enjoy mystery stories, yet somehow he was starting to connect the events together in his mind. "That could explain the threatening notes..."

"What? What does that have to do with any of this?"

"Did the roster ever leave your side?"

"Well yes, we did take a break for coffee."

"When?"

"I'm guessing around nine"

Martin paused, retracing his steps and trying to figure out where he was around that time. The answer came to him.

"So you took a break an hour after I stopped the first incident. That would have been ample time for anyone to steal the duty roster. All they had to do was look up our names in the Metropolis directory." Martin spoke excitedly as he began to move the pieces of the puzzle around.

"Wait... are you saying that someone at the meeting was involved in this?" Hugo said as he motioned towards the disaster area. Smoke was steadily rising from the ruins, eclipsing the grand skyline of the city.

"I stop a crash. Somebody at the meeting gets the message that the plan didn't pan out. They steal the roster, because the pilot of the plane heard me say Air Tower 12. Then we get a note telling us to butt out. The next day the same plane shoots down the same zeppelin. At least that's what I think happened."

"Okay, I can see that, but there is something I don't understand. Why did the pilot attempt to crash yesterday and then choose to shoot down the zeppelin today?" Hugo said, rubbing the back of his neck again.

"I confess that you got me on that one... but let me ask you a question, did anyone at your meeting receive a message?"

"I don't... I don't remember..."

"Think Hugo! Lives are depending on this!" Martin yelled. It was not his typical "manager" bark, he spoke with an urgency and conviction that he never felt before.

"I was... there was... Yes! I remember that before we went to break the secretary brought in a message for the head of the Pilot's Guild, Norma Latour... Martin, you're not suggesting that the Pilot's Guild is behind this!" Hugo stammered.

Martin shrugged "Maybe I am and maybe I'm not. There's only one way to find out. I'm going there as soon as this disaster is cleared up."

"Martin... are you sure? What are you going to do if you're right?"

"Call the police, of course." Martin said as he headed back to the observation window. Down below he saw fire crews pulling bodies out of the wreckage as planes soared overhead, dousing the fires with water. It was a small mercy that the rain was still coming down to dampen the flames, but it would be many hours before the area was deemed safe. He issued orders to a few of his men just before the radio crackled to life.

"Air Tower 12, this is Air Tower 3, can you read me? Over."

"Loud and clear, Air Tower 3. Go ahead, over." Martin said into the radio.

*"Did anyone at your meeting receive a message?"*

"One of our controllers has just spotted the plane you described! It's circling the Siegfried Tower."

A cold sweat appeared on Martin's forehead as he yelled into the radio "Call the police! Evacuate the building immediately! That plane is going to attack!"

✛✛✛

The pilot could hear the blood pounding in his ears. He felt his own heartbeat increasing, his adrenaline kicking in. Everything was in unnaturally sharp focus. He ignored the rain rushing at him as he continued to circle his target. The pilot looked in a window of an apartment as a young man primped in front of the mirror. Hatred raced through the pilot's body as the spoiled child adjusted his tuxedo. The pilot was having great difficulty thinking clearly. He was flying the triplane on muscle memory. The zeppelin was only the beginning, but it was not nearly enough. His life had been ruined, wrecked, and on an inevitable course of destruction. The pilot could feel parts of his rational mind burning away, replaced with primal instincts. Soon he would be nothing more than a raving lunatic, but he was not going down without a fight... Not by a long shot!

Looping around, the pilot adjusted his trajectory until the son of his enemy was in his sights. Handsome, well groomed, opulent. He was all these things once, until he made a deal with the devil. His enemy had tricked him and stolen his life, so piece by piece, the pilot would take his revenge. He had declared all-out war with those who had made him like this, and if they were unable to fight back, so be it. With one final check, he watched as the young man turned to the window to face him. His expression was one of horror, which put a smile on the pilot's face. He would treasure that moment forever.

Giving a barbaric roar, the pilot depressed the triggers on the machine guns. The plane rattled and shook with the force, and his arms strained to keep his aim steady. He watched as glass shattered and the body of the young man was riddled with bullets. The job was completed within a few terrible seconds, but the pilot kept the trigger tightly squeezed until the belts ran out. The apartment, which had been among the most fashionable in the city, looked like a war zone.

The pilot pulled up and soared over the building, allowing himself a barrel roll in triumph. He wanted more blood, feeling that his enemies had not suffered enough. However, he had enough presence of mind to check the dials and gauges on the dashboard. He was low on fuel and ammunition, so he used what reasoning skills he had left to determine that his best option was to head back to base. His hands twitched uncontrollably. All of his senses were under attack, and he could not filter it. It was too much for a human mind to handle! Then he thought of her. Her voice guiding him, telling him to breathe, telling him to relax. He forced himself to take calming breaths as he flew for home.

✝✝✝

An old compact car made its way along the highway with the rest of the Metropolis night traffic. Hugo was still driving the same car that he had when he first met Martin (although it was Chelsea's expertise that kept it running). The two had finished their shift and did their duty helping with the rescue. Stuck in traffic with Hugo, Martin thought fondly of the speed and simplicity of the elevated trains. They went to and fro at their appointed times, no bad drivers to worry about, no flat tires, and no jam ups. Looking ahead, they saw an endless sea of red brake lights. The two had since learned of the apartment shooting and the death of Rich Nibelungen, son of the pharmaceutical kingpin Nicholas Nibelungen. They listened to a speech from Joh Fredersen over the radio. Even though he maintained his usual composure, his voice would occasionally betray signs of emotion.

"This reign of terror will not continue! Metropolis has seen the deaths of over forty people today…"

"Twice that many get killed underground in a week and you don't care," Martin quipped.

"Quiet!" Hugo interjected, wanting to hear more.

"This we cannot stand," the president continued "one of our finest citizens, Nicholas Nibelungen, has lost his son today. Our hearts go out to the families of the victims in the zepellin accident as well…"

"Who don't rate getting their names mentioned," Martin murmured. Hugo shot him an annoyed glance as Fredersen's speech continued.

"I promise you, as the president of Metropolis, our police force will not rest, and I will not rest, until this monster has been brought to justice! I…"

"Sorry," Martin said as he turned off the radio "I've had enough. It's just going to be empty promises and heartfelt condolences for another hour or so."

"Speaking of the police," Hugo said "Why don't we go to them with what you have? They are in charge of this investigation, not you."

"Because I don't really have anything! I cannot even prove that the notes we received had anything to do with the case!" Martin confessed. "Even *you* don't believe me yet, Hugo. When I have something solid, then I'll go."

"It's not that I don't believe you… it's just that the whole situation is hard to grasp!"

"All right, let's work with what we know so far." Martin said, reclining in his seat.

"First the Nibelungen zeppelin and now the son… obviously someone has a vendetta against the company." Hugo said as he merged into a faster lane.

"I was thinking about what Chelsea was telling me, about how pilots in the old wars would paint their aircraft as a challenge to opponents…"

"Yeah?"

"Well, something I also remember her mentioning was that the pilots of old had a code of honor. They were called the noblemen of the skies or something like that. Killing women, children, or any non-combatant was a disgraceful action. This pilot, despite flying an older plane, has none of their ideals." Martin said as he looked out the window. Hugo pulled into the parking lot.

Hugo and Martin stopped outside of an airplane repair shop. The building, despite being washed by the rain, still had a fine layer of dirt hugging the walls. Rows of small aircraft were inside the darkened garages, with welding sparks providing sporadic light. Chelsea was waiting outside for them and walked towards their car. She was wearing a plain dress with a practical handbag, her hair still in a ponytail.

"Remind me to buy you something more glamorous for your birthday," Martin said to Chelsea. She rolled her eyes.

"Mr. Galeen, we are going on an investigation, not to a nightclub. I do not care about looking beautiful right now." Chelsea said as she sat in the backseat of Hugo's car. Martin had called her earlier about the interview with the Pilot's Guild chief, Norma Latour. He thought that while he and Hugo asked the pertinent questions, she could look around the hangars and tell them if she spotted anything unusual. Martin was not used to apologizing, but the truth was that he felt like a fool for the way he talked to Chelsea earlier, and an idiot for discouraging the idea of an investigation. She knew that Martin getting her involved, even in a minor way, was his way of asking for forgiveness, so she accepted.

"What about your young man? Am I breaking up a date?" Martin asked casually.

"No, I think this is more important. Now Mr. Galeen, whatever you do when you are in there, do not antagonize Ms. Latour. A few of the other mechanics worked for the Guild for a short while, and I heard that she is a very disagreeable woman."

"Don't worry about me; I have a few tricks up my sleeve. I think we'll find out who is behind this!" Martin said with bravado. This was mostly for Chelsea's benefit, as he saw her give him a smile in the rear view mirror. He had a sinking feeling in the pit of his stomach; coupled with the nausea he always felt when he got nervous. What was he thinking, getting involved in all of this? He was never one for heroics, so what made him think that he could be a hero now? Catching his reflection in glass, Martin felt that he bore no physical resemblance to a gallant man. His mind drifted to the men of Air Tower 12. He glanced at Chelsea, who, for the first time in a long time, had looked at Martin with pride. As a surrogate father and an authority figure, Martin had always put on a brave face in times of need. He was not about to let them down now.

✛✛✛

The three pulled into the Pilot's Guild building which was located near the edge of Metropolis. The entire complex, which was about the size of a football field, had been standing there before the towers and skyscrapers were erected. When the city was being built, it was used as a depot for materials and workers. Since the skyline of Metropolis was completed, it had been converted into the main offices for the Pilot's Guild. Walking across the tarmac, Chelsea let out a small squeal of delight as she spotted the museum wing. It housed aircraft from every era, each one restored to perfection.

Hugo looked over to the main office building where lights were still on. Despite the traffic, the three had made it there before closing. With no time to lose, the trio briskly walked towards the door. Martin looked at a twenty foot statue of glistening bronze, standing defiantly against the rain. It was a magnificent, expressionist sculpture of a heroic man and a beautiful woman. Both wore aviator outfits and looked towards the sky with determined expressions. A relief at the pilot's feet read "To the skies we belong".

Unlike the statue, the building itself was stark in appearance. The outside consisted of concrete walls and utilitarian windows, somewhat reminiscent of the homes of the underground workers. The only decorations were plaques that indicated where you were. Martin pushed the door open as the three made their way inside.

The interior was lit with tungsten light, casting a warm glow over the office. Despite the late hour, office workers and pilots were still running about. The constant clicking of writing equipment and low whispers reminded Martin of his control room. A distinguished looking receptionist noticed them and walked over.

"May I help you, sir?" the receptionist said looking at the three of them. His expression indicated that their presence, their very appearance (Guild members considered themselves superior), bothered him.

"My name is Martin Galeen and this is my associate, Mr. Osborne. We have an appointment to see Ms. Latour." Martin said pleasantly.

The receptionist was checking his notes when the sharp clacking of heels caught their attention. Indeed, everyone in the room looked over at the sound. Norma Latour was a tall woman with remarkable posture. Her flight uniform was well pressed, and her short hair was styled with a militaristic flair. The few streaks of grey gave her a dignified appearance. Her eyes reminded Martin of a predatory bird, and he felt that he was being scrutinized by her. She addressed the three of them with the calm, controlled air of an officer.

"Mr. Galeen, if you will follow me to my office?" she said as she walked briskly past them. The three followed her up the nearest staircase, trying to keep pace with Norma.

"It is an unusual time for a meeting, so late at night," she stated, her annoyance apparent in spite of her control "but if one asks for an urgent meeting this late… it must be important."

"Yes, yes it is." Martin said as he huffed and puffed up the stairs, making a resolution to start exercising more.

"I met you yesterday, Mr. Osborne, but I do not know you…" Norma said, looking at Chelsea with her piercing gaze.

"Oh, my father brought me along. I'm a mechanic in Metropolis and he thought that I would be interested in seeing how the professionals at the Pilot's Guild do things." Chelsea said as she put an arm around Martin. He felt his heart soar when she called him her father, even if it was only a ruse.

Norma nodded approvingly, the fewer people that she had to deal with the better. She motioned for one of the security officers to come over.

Indicating to Chelsea she said "Take this girl to the mechanic's hangar and museum for a short visit." With a salute, the guard accompanied Chelsea down the hall. She turned around and gave Martin a smile, but her eyes betrayed her subtle concern. Martin nodded back to her with a reassuring glance as he entered Norma's office.

Hugo and Martin took their seats across from Norma's desk. The antique walnut furniture and vintage typewriter added to the history of the room. Old photographs and vivid paintings of famous pilots and aircraft adored the walls. With the exception of her medals and certificates, there were few personal touches of Norma in the room; save for a frame facing away from them. She glanced at the two men.

"So gentlemen, why are you here? I take it this is not a continuation of the budget meeting."

"No, it concerns the incident that happened yesterday and the murders that took place today." Martin said. Hugo was taken aback. He, for one, thought that a slower, more methodical approach was in order. He glanced over to see Norma's reaction, and witnessed something strange. Her eyes, however briefly, grew intense at the mention of the word "murders". It was as if the phrasing offended her. When she responded, though, it was in a manner that was to be expected.

"It was absolutely dreadful, but why are you asking me about it?"

"Obviously you authorize every pilot license..."

"I do not *personally* authorize every license; it is done through these offices. The police came by earlier with the same line of enquiry and searched through the records," Norma spoke quickly, but with authority "so this line of questioning has already been tried."

Martin shifted in his seat and tried again. "It was raining a great deal today. It's difficult for us in the control tower to even see the city sometimes. So how many pilots can fly in those conditions?"

"Not many of the amateurs or hobby fliers, I grant you, but ask any professional trained by the Pilot's Guild and they will tell you that weather is of no consequence to them. Our program teaches them to handle any scenario." Norma said with pride.

"How many have gone through your training program?" Hugo asked.

"Well over two hundred pilots. Some who already have their license come back to hone their skills with us."

"The person who created this course must be some pilot," said Martin, genuinely impressed.

"Thank you. My..." she caught herself "I developed it myself. But gentlemen, I hope you are not trying to play detectives, because the real ones are already on the case."

There was something in her expression that bothered Martin. She obviously did not want them there. The fact was that she just seemed too confident. He was used to putting on a mask to conceal his thoughts, and he could tell she was doing the same. He tried another tactic.

"You know, I'm the one from Air Tower 12 that stopped that maniac from crashing into the zeppelin yesterday," Martin said. "It's too bad that I decided to not interfere, or I could have stopped that monster from massacring all those innocent people today."

Both he and Hugo observed her reaction closely. Every slight towards the pilot met with a small, but noticeable reaction from Norma.

"Quite," was her response. She was about to say more when a buzzing on her intercom prevented her from continuing. She pressed the button "Yes?"

"A gentleman from the city to see you, he said it was urgent." The receptionist said.

Norma looked at the two quickly before answering "Send him into the briefing room, I'll be along in a few moments…" she said. Addressing Hugo and Martin, Norma spoke briefly. "He's arrived early, but this should not take too long. I'll be back." She hurried out of the room before either could speak.

Hugo turned to Martin with an eager expression on his face. "Did you see…" he began before Martin put a hand up to stop him.

"Bugged." Martin mouthed to Hugo, who nodded knowingly. Martin was not sure if this was true, but he preferred to be safe rather than sorry. Hugo changed the subject. He began to describe a show that he watched at the Yoshiwara District, for it would have been suspicious if the two men were sitting there in silence. Martin listened and responded as needed while he stood up and slowly made his way to the typewriter. Taking a blank sheet of paper from Norma's desk, Martin put it in the machine.

"Hang on a second, I have this thought I need to write out… but keep on with your story." Martin said to explain the sudden typing. Hugo finished his humorous tale while Martin typed out three words on the machine. He removed the threatening note from his pocket and held it up next to the newly typed words.

"DO NOT INTERFERE!" was identical to the note slid under his door, down to the crimson red ink.

"Now imagine that happening!" Martin said. It was a response that fit in with their charade, but also with their development in the case. Hugo looked over at the other strange object in the room, the picture frame, and began to turn it over. He showed the image to Martin, who nodded grimly. A major piece of the puzzle was now added.

✝✝✝

To say that Chelsea was jealous was perhaps the greatest understatement one could have made. Her eyes stared longingly at the polished, sophisticated equipment. She longed to get her hands on machinery that was not dented, rusted, or covered with oil and grease. The uniforms of Guild mechanics, though inevitably dirty, were tuxedo-like compared to the coveralls that she had to wear. The security guard that walked her to the hangars left to go back to his duties, leaving Chelsea to talk with the regular tour guide alone. She was floored by everything she saw, but Chelsea did not forget her mission and asked her guide about the various planes.

"We have every model represented here since the dawn of flight," the guide said proudly. "We restore these planes to their exact working order, like they just came out of the factory. Every part is meticulously researched, and if we cannot find the original, then we make it ourselves."

"I see, so you make your own machine guns for the warplanes?" Chelsea asked as she examined one of them.

A quick glance confirmed the guide's next words. "Yes we do, but they're non-firing replicas. Ms. Latour was insistent upon that."

"I see…" Chelsea looked around, but then turned to the guide with a surprise. "Excuse me, sir, but I'm afraid that you're wrong?"

"Oh, what do you mean?" the guide asked, genuinely surprised.

"Well, you told me that you have every plane in existence here."

"We do," stated the guide, firmly but politely.

"Well, I don't happen to see my favorite plane, the Artemis 57." Chelsea said, folding her arms and looking expectantly at the guide for an answer. The guide stammered for a minute.

"The… the Artemis 57… I… oh yes, it had to be taken in for some additional repair work. We tried to move it earlier and I'm afraid it sustained some damage." Chelsea could tell that the guide was lying to her. She glanced back at the work station they had just passed at the beginning of the tour, but saw no evidence of the aircraft.

"But it's not in the work station. Please sir, my grandfather flew one and

*"I don't see my favorite plane, the Artimis 57."*

I have always wanted to see one!" Chelsea knew this plea would have no impression on the man, but it did get him agitated.

"I'm afraid that you'll have to leave!" Not being a physically strong man, the guide looked around for a nearby security guard to assist him.

Chelsea had spotted no one so she took a chance! Grabbing a nearby toolbox, she swung it at the back of the guide's head! It knocked him unconscious. Checking his pulse, Chelsea breathed a sigh of relief. There was a hangar door that the guide was anxious to get past, and she had a feeling that the Artemis 57 was being kept behind those doors. Martin had been right all along! Taking a sturdy wrench from the toolbox, Chelsea headed towards the forbidden door. Martin had demanded proof before the police were called in, and one glance at the plane was all that she needed.

The door was locked, and she did not have time to be fancy. She bashed the lock with the wrench and peered inside the hangar. Her heart skipped a beat. Sitting in the hangar was the crimson plane, the Artemis 57! She rushed over to the nearby phone and dialed the police. Informing them of her location, she relayed the information to them and agreed to stay on the phone line.

Suddenly, she felt a powerful hand close around hers and slam the phone down. Wheeling around she saw a man with a horrifying face! His eyes were red and bloodshot; he was sweating profusely, his hair a mess. He gave a horrific wail as he struck Chelsea across the face. The last thing she saw before she lost consciousness was the man's aviator jacket.

✝✝✝

When they saw the photograph, Martin and Hugo knew they had no time to lose! They stealthily made their way to the briefing room, ducking into corners and shadows whenever they saw anyone. Martin, despite his tough exterior, had not thrown a punch in decades, and he doubted if Hugo was a brawler. They were not about to start a fist fight now.

They crept outside the door where they could hear the raised voices of Norma and a man. Martin took a chance and peaked through the frosted glass window. He saw a man in a disheveled suit pleading with Norma. Even though his view was blurred, Martin recognized the man from the newspapers as Nicholas Nibelungen. Once on top of the world, the billionaire was now tearfully pleading with Norma.

"Please, you've already taken so much from me. My zeppelin... my son... when will it end?"

"It won't, Nicholas. Joh Fredersen's friends are never prosecuted! We want justice... what choice do we have? You must pay for what you did to my husband! We will torment you until you are nothing!" Her exterior control was gone. Norma was seething with venom as she yelled in his face.

"But no one could have predicted the effects of the drug! The tests on the animals went well enough, and your husband signed all the releases. Ms. Latour, you know better than I that pilots are risk takers by nature." he pleaded weakly.

"You make yourself sound so innocent! You sold my husband on the fact that this drug would improve his skills as a pilot. You knew that he couldn't resist the chance to be even better! There were no warnings of any side effects!"

"There were no side effects! All of the animals showed improved coordination and sharper senses. Logically, a pilot would be able to benefit from the same drug. His reflexes would have been heightened and his senses magnified. There was no reason to suspect..."

"Suspect that my husband would become a raving lunatic! No! Your drugs destroyed his mind! He is becoming an animal! James barely recognizes me now; all that he seems to remember now is how to fly..."

"If we can get him help, if we can study him..." Nicholas offered, but Norma was having none of it.

"We both know that he'll be dead in a few days! His first thought was to kill himself by crashing into your damned zeppelin. Obviously he failed, and when he sent me the message saying so, I suggested that he try a different approach. He was flying the greatest warplane ever built, so why not use it to its utmost potential? We built the machine guns ourselves, and we will destroy everything you have before he dies!"

Hugo and Martin exchanged concerned expressions. They were witnesses to her confession, and after they saw the photograph of Norma and her husband, they knew they had their murderer. James Latour was one of the greatest pilots of the modern era. If anyone could fly in the rain and pull off those maneuvers, it was he. What neither of them could decide upon was what to do next. They heard Norma again.

"The next target will be your factories, so you cannot poison anyone else! Then your wife, a woman just as useless as the son she gave you."

That comment tore it for Nicholas. His fear was gone, replaced by vengeance. He struck Norma across the face, and she jerked back. He watched as she swung around to face him, her hawk-like eyes impressed by his anger.

"Multiply that anger tenfold, and you will understand how my husband feels."

Suddenly, the sounds of sirens approached. Martin looked up as he heard the distinctive roar of police aircraft growing closer. Thinking quickly, Martin realized that the only person who could have alerted the police was Chelsea. Was she is danger?

"Hugo, you stay here with them. Don't let them out of your sight!"

"Where are you going?"

"I'm going to find Chelsea and see if she's alright!"

"How will you get past the guards?"

Martin did not bother to answer him as he rushed down the hallway. If everything they just heard was true, then Chelsea was wandering around with a madman on the loose! He ran through the lobby, knocking over a few workers as he screamed at them to make way.

✝ ✝ ✝

Chelsea awoke to the sight of James Latour pacing frantically back and forth in the hangar. She felt ropes wrapped around her, although they were not tied well. Taking advantage of the fact that James seemed oblivious to her, she slowly began to wriggle free of her bondage. Chelsea kept her eyes on James the entire time. One could tell that he once was a handsome man, now ravaged beyond repair. He alternated between whispering and shouting. The topics he discussed ranged from self-loathing and regret, to hatred for Nibleungen, to pleas for his life to end. He would break off from these tangents and stroke his plane, calling it "The Crimson Nightmare". It was evidentially the name that he given the plane.

"We will strike again, Crimson Nightmare, yes we will. Norma will tell us where to attack. She knows where we need to go. She's smarter than us, so the smart thing to do is to listen."

At that moment, the sound of police sirens reached them. James perked his head up, like a wolf sensing danger. He bounded for the window and looked out. He snarled at the lights of the oncoming cars and he made his hands into fists.

"Lights! Danger! They'll ruin Norma's plans! We can't let that happen Crimson Nightmare, we must stop them!"

Running to the hangar doors, James forced them across as he screamed obscenities at the police. Chelsea had wriggled free, but kept the ropes around her to maintain the illusion of captivity. Her hands groped behind her for any kind of weapon. She felt nothing, and looked up to see James watching her. What was left of his brain was trying to decide what to do. Looking from the approaching police lights, to the plane, and then back to her, it was clearly a struggle.

"Norma would tell you to let me go." Chelsea said softly.

"She would?" James said, wondering how she could know that.

"Yes. If you give me to the police, they won't hurt you or Norma. She would not want that."

James thought about this, running his fingers frantically through his hair. Chelsea nervously watched him, unsure if her plan was successful. At the very least, she was stalling him until the police arrived.

"No... No! NO! YOU LIE!" James screamed at her, his face turning red, his veins bulging. "Norma said I must die like a hero! I die fighting the enemy! Nibleungen is the enemy! No mercy! She wants me to die a hero!"

He grabbed Chelsea and tried to force her towards the plane. Knowing that if she was forced aboard she would die, Chelsea swung wildly at James. Her knuckles caught his cheek and her nails scratched his face in a desperate struggle. He stopped to grab his bleeding face and she took the opportunity to flee from the hangar.

The police were at the main building, some distance away from the hangar. She ran towards the lights, knowing that they meant safety. Behind her, she heard the deep rumble of the Crimson Nightmare's engine. Looking back, she saw James climbing into the cockpit. Three police planes were circling overhead, but had not spotted Chelsea yet.

Suddenly, the Crimson Nightmare flew from the hangar and into the night sky! James looped the plane around and began to fly towards Chelsea, starting an attack run. She may not be his main target, but she had hurt him. James wanted retribution, and once he had her in his sights, he squeezed the trigger!

Chelsea dove out of the way as two rows of bullets tore up the ground around her. The Crimson Nightmare flew up into the sky, but this time the police aircraft had spotted him and began their pursuit. Even though the odds were against James, Chelsea knew that the police planes had no chance against him. Their aircraft were inferior to the Artemis 57 in every way, and though the police pilots were no doubt highly trained, James was a force to be reckoned with. She had almost reached the police cars when the Crimson Nightmare began its second attack run.

The rows of bullets raced towards Chelsea, but with nowhere to hide, she was out of luck. Time slowed down for her as she waited to die. Suddenly a great force hit her from the side and tackled her to the ground. She heard bullets strike flesh twice, but felt no pain.

Chelsea looked around to see Martin lying on top of her, his body shielding hers. There were two bullet holes in his back and he was moaning in agony!

"Martin!" she yelled as she scrambled to him. She hoisted him up, and looked at his face. His teeth were gritted as he clenched his fists. The Crimson Nightmare abandoned a third attack run, for the police aircraft had started firing at him. James made his aircraft fly with the grace of a ballet dancer. The police tracer rounds shot past his plane, but not one bullet managed to make contact with the Crimson Nightmare. On the ground below, one could swear they heard James giving his distinctive war cry.

Fighting through the pain, Martin was able to stand, leaning on Chelsea for support. They stumbled inside the main office and closed the door behind them.

The Guild members and workers were all on one side of the room, guarded by two policemen with weapons pointed at them. Norma was among them, but her eyes were staring out the window, watching the air battle raging outside. Hugo was off in a corner as one officer was taking his statement and Nicholas Nibleungen waited nearby to relay his account. Several gasped as they saw Martin and Chelsea stagger in.

"We have to get him to a doctor!" Chelsea shouted.

"With that madman out there we can't risk sending anybody out! He'll shoot them to pieces!" one of the officers explained as they helped Martin into a chair.

Norma took her eyes off the battle momentarily to look down at Martin.

"You foolish, little man. You should have heeded my warning. If you had not interfered, James would be dead now and Nibleungen would still have his son. It looks like you will be paying the price for your meddling soon enough."

"No! You are the monster here! James Latour is nothing but a wild animal, and you trained him to kill!" Nibleungen yelled at her, but she paid no attention to his words.

Martin was not listening to her; instead he was trying to watch the battle unfold. He struggled to focus, fighting the urge to pass out and succumb to his wounds.

The Crimson Nightmare, tired of dodging police plane assaults, started its counterattack. With a plane behind him, James sped straight towards the second police aircraft. At the last second, the Crimson Nightmare performed a perfect loop, which sent the two police planes charging at each other! The pilots banked at the last minute, turning away just in time. This gap in time allowed him to strike at the third police plane. James riddled the plane with bullets! A few of the shots struck the engine causing the plane to explode in midair! The flaming wreck smashed onto the runway, hurling bits of deformed metal everywhere.

Norma beamed proudly at her husband, and then looked smugly at them all. Looking at her, Martin felt a raging fire inside. She must not win, and if it was the last thing he did, he would stop her.

"Chelsea, do the police have any chance against him?"

She regretfully shook her head. Suddenly, he was seized with an idea and forced himself upright. The police officers tried to restrain him, but he shouted for them to keep away.

"Hugo, get me a radio! What are the frequencies of the police aircraft?" Martin said as he sat down. Hugo brought him the necessary components and adjusted them while the police officers got him what he needed. They set up a makeshift control console in the front office. Norma started to grow paranoid and snapped.

"What is this? What do you think you're doing?"

"Somebody keep her quiet!" Martin barked. As soon as he yelled he felt a sharp pain in his chest. Not knowing how much time he had left, he had to make his move quickly.

"This is the control tower to the police aircraft. Break off your attack, you don't stand a chance."

"What are we supposed to do? Just let him go?" one of the pilots snapped back. Martin looked up to see that the planes were far enough apart for his plan to work.

"No, he's not getting away, if you want to stop this, then do what I say! Head away from him now!"

"Just who is this?"

"I'm the only one who knows how to stop this madman!" Martin snapped again. The pain returned, this time much worse. Hugo and Chelsea stepped towards him instinctively, but Martin held up his hand, telling them to stop. He needed to focus.

Reluctantly, the pilots flew away leaving the Crimson Nightmare alone in the sky. Celebrating his victory, he did a barrel-roll as he began to circle around the airfield again.

"How can you stop him? You're just a traffic controller!" Norma demanded. The police dragged her away and locked her in a nearby office. She watched tensely through the windows as the situation unfolded.

Sending out a general broadcast, Martin spoke deliberately and carefully into the microphone.

"Tower to pilot James Latour, this is the control tower. You shot down Nicholas Nibleungen. He stole one of our planes, and went after you to avenge his son. You will run out of fuel and ammunition and the police will shoot you down. Give yourself up before you hurt more innocent people. Your mission is over!" Martin was never a good liar, but it was the only way he could think to stop James. If he was convinced that his target was destroyed, maybe he would surrender peacefully.

A moment of silence filled the control room. All eyes were on the plane, any motion from it might give an indication as to his answer. The radio crackled back to life.

"I will not disgrace Norma! I will die a hero! A hero!" the voice of James Latour screamed back at them. The plane flew towards the control tower with the Crimson Nightmare's guns blazing away! Windows shattered and computer banks were shot to pieces. A fire started, and soon the control tower looked like a gigantic torch against the night sky.

"You fool!" Norma yelled.

The Crimson Nightmare was positioned for another attack run, but no bullets roared from its guns. The plane flew harmlessly overhead while the radio broadcast the nonsensical cursing of James Latour.

"Why isn't he shooting?" asked Hugo.

"He's out of ammunition. I got a good look at that plane and he wasn't carrying much." Chelsea chimed in.

Martin listened to the ravings of James and felt great pity for the man. He was going insane, an attack dog manipulated by a cruel owner. It was not long before the experimental drug ravaged his mind completely. Mustering a commanding tone, Martin spoke into the radio one last time.

"James, we have just received word that Nicholas Nibleungen is still alive. He was spotted trying to climb out of the wreckage. If you can land your plane peacefully..."

"GO TO HELL!" James bellowed over the radio. He screamed again, sounding like a man whose soul was being tortured. The Crimson Nightmare reached its maximum velocity as James flew towards the burning wreckage on the tarmac. Chelsea put her hands to her mouth in shock. Hugo looked from Martin to the impending disaster, terrified and unsure of what to do. Norma was slamming her fists against the window, screaming at James to pull up.

"They can never hurt anyone else again..." Martin said to Hugo. He looked back at the runway to see the results of his plan.

The Crimson Nightmare was annihilated upon impact. It folded itself into an accordion, instantly catching fire and killing James. The flames of both aircraft combined, bathing the area in flickering yellow light. The members of the Pilot's Guild were stunned speechless. The police escorted them outside while Norma was dragged from the office. She was in hysterics, promising to murder everyone in the room.

When she left, Martin fell off his chair and collapsed to the floor. The police rushed him to an ambulance, accompanied by Chelsea who was pleading with him to stay with her. Nicholas Nibleungen walked over to Hugo, his head hung low.

"I wish we never invented the drug. We did all the necessary tests and both he and his wife consented... but that does not absolve me. I've lost my son. This entire disaster was my fault, and I don't know how I'll face it. How can I possibly justify this?" Nibleungen asked rhetorically. Hugo patted him on the shoulder, not knowing what to say.

✛✛✛

Joh Fredersen sat behind his desk, a slight smile on his face. He had just finished reading a summation of events, and he looked at the hero of that night: Martin Galeen.

"You showed great courage that night," Fredersen said as he studied Martin "yet you seem afraid to be here."

"Well, sir, it's not every day that a man like me has a meeting with the president of Metropolis. I feel a little out of place." Martin said as he marveled at the room. It was as large as his control room, with sleek paneled walls and minimal décor. The furniture was austere yet bold in design, the finest of its kind. Martin felt the stiffness of his cheap suit, and wished that he possessed something finer to meet the president in.

"I do not wish to make you feel uncomfortable, Mr. Galeen. Since you have done a great service for this city, it is only fair that the city does something for you in return. What do you wish?" Fredersen said.

Martin was staggered. Not only was the president treating him like an equal, but he was also offering him something! He thought of a new apartment, a new wardrobe, a car of his own, spending money...

"Mister President, there is something that you can do for me. There is a girl named Chelsea Berndt. She is a very talented mechanic and I think that she deserves to work in a better environment. Is it possible for you to maybe give her career a push?"

Fredersen consulted the report quickly. "Yes, it mentions her here. Very well, Mr. Galeen, she will be working for the same firm that services my personal aircraft starting tomorrow."

A smile cut across Martin's face, and, for the first time in years, he was a happy man.

"Nothing for yourself?"

"No. A friend of mine has persuaded me to visit the Yoshiwara District with him tonight in honor of my recovery. That should be enough for me." Martin grinned.

They shook hands and Martin left the office, feeling like a new man. On his way out he passed a shorter, eccentric looking man with wild hair. Martin was feeling too good to notice him, but Fredersen's smile dropped as he entered his office. The man closed the door behind him and wheeled around to face the president.

"I told you it would be a mistake to give that fool Nibleungen funding for his experiments! Chemistry, by its very nature is unstable! You have seen what happens when unstable elements are let loose in Metropolis... People die, Joh!"

The president slid the report calmly in a desk drawer as he relaxed in his chair.

"People die, Rotwang, we both know that is inevitable."

The man, Rotwang, was visibly stung by this comment. However, he recovered quickly; reminding himself of the reason he was there.

"Through chemical failures in their bodies, yes, people die. Through chemicals destroying their minds, yes, they die! I am talking about something that can be controlled! We can build a more perfect being, Joh, you and I! Death would become irrelevant!"

"I do not understand where this is going. I suggest that you explain yourself at once, otherwise I have other matters to attend to." Fredersen replied bluntly.

"Very well. Do not waste your time on Nibleungen. His experiments have only brought disaster to the city. The funding you lavished upon him will be better spent on my experiment that will guarantee the future!" Rotwang said, his eyes burning with passion as he slammed his robotic hand on Joh's desk. The other hand slowly reached into his coat pocket retrieving folded papers. He handed them to Fredersen, who glanced over what appeared to be blueprints.

Fredersen looked back Rotwang's fist, understanding the man's meaning.

"Very well, you may have Nibleungen's money. Begin work immediately."

# THE END

# SKIES OVER METROPOLIS

In the Fritz Lang film, the world is presented with two contrasting groups: the rich and the slaves. The story showcased both groups and ended with a powerful conclusion. There was little left to explore with these two distinct classes, so I began to search for something in the world that was perhaps unexplored. It was seeing a taxi driver in the film that gave me the idea. Obviously he was not wealthy or powerful, yet he lived above ground. The idea of placing a character in the lower-middle class of Metropolis was one that excited me. There, I thought, was uncharted territory for Metropolis.

When Ron offered me the assignment of writing a Metropolis story, the first thing I had to do was watch the film. I had seen it in film school, but it had been a while. Of course, it has a wonderful story with mesmerizing visuals, but there was something in particular that caught my eye: the airplanes. That lead me to another thought: with all those planes and zeppelins darting about the spires, there must be air traffic controllers keeping them safe. The idea of a man who was typically in a sedentary job becoming a hero appealed to me. It reminded me of another film I greatly admire "The Taking of the Pelham 1,2,3". Also, the juxtaposition of a man who controls one of the tallest towers in the city, yet lives in a dumpy apartment at the bottom of the city, was too good to resist.

To begin with, the central character of this story, Martin Galeen, is a composite of several people. After noticing that most pulp heroes are tall, handsome men in their late 20s, I decided that it would be fun to do a story of a man who did not rely on fighting prowess or brawn. The first person I thought of, and least likely to be an action hero, was an instructor I had in college (I hope he does not recognize himself if he reads this!). I based the physical appearance and demeanor on him. However, I kept thinking of another of my favorite actors, Edward G. Robinson, and tried to channel bits of his persona and style into Martin.

I have always been fascinated by early aircraft, and considering that Metropolis, despite being in the future, used World War I era planes, I had the perfect excuse to write one in. The Crimson Nightmare is an obvious allusion to the flying ace of World War I, the Red Baron. Having recently watched a documentary on aircraft of that era, I took what I learned and applied it to the action scenes of the story. Of course the Artemis 57 is a fictional aircraft, but the basic mechanics of the tri-plane would stay the same. I also wanted a distinctive sound to come over the radio from the pilot. A villainous laugh was far too clichéd to me, I wanted something else. The idea of a raging scream came to me, and putting myself in Martin's place, that would chill me to the bone if I heard it! So then I wondered, why is the pilot screaming?

That answer came from the idea of drug use. It was another aspect of Metropolis that I was curious about: everything was ruled by machines. In high school, I read Aldous Huxley's novel "Brave New World", where the entire planet was ruled by a drug called soma. I wondered: why was there no mention of a drug like that in Metropolis? The solution to that question led to the motivation of my villains (and the reason why Fredersen lets Rotwang create the mechanical woman). In my mind, after the events of this story, Fredersen would have no faith in the choices the Metropolis citizens make, nor in alchemy of any form.

I hope you have enjoyed the story, I am quite proud of this one.

✝✝✝

**ERIK FRANKLIN** - is a writer/actor/filmmaker based in Seattle. Recently graduating with honors from the Art Institute of Seattle in film production, he is the co-President of Franklin-Husser Entertainment LLC. He is working on two upcoming feature films for his company: A dinosaur action film "Revenge of the Lost" and the martial arts comedy "3 Morons Fighting Ninja". You can give the company page a "Like" at: https://www.facebook.com/pages/Franklin-Husser-Entertainment-LLC/290795021042906.

Drawn to pulp fiction through his love of history, literature, and Americana, he is grateful for Airship 27 Productions giving him the opportunity to write his first story. He looks forward to writing more adventures!

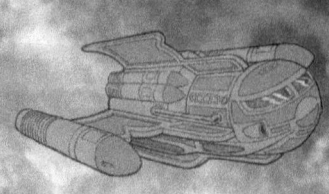

www.ingramcontent.com/pod-product-compliance
Lightning Source LLC
Chambersburg PA
CBHW071239250626
47163CB00001B/249